"Does it hur[...]

Letitia said, as she continued to gently probe Larkin's finger.

"A little." In truth, the only thing he could feel was a pleasant tingling generated by her delicate touch, which he was enjoying immensely. He couldn't remember when he'd felt so pampered, or so aware of a woman's nearness. There was something erotic about her, a dizzying scent that reminded him of sweet incense.

As the thought crossed his mind, an adorable dimple appeared at the corner of her mouth and she emitted a throaty chuckle that gave him goose bumps. "Fortunately, your wounds don't appear to be life threatening."

"True, but it's been so long since a pretty woman held my hand."

Dear Reader:

Romance readers have been enthusiastic about the Silhouette Special Editions for years. And that's not by accident: Special Editions were the first of their kind and continue to feature realistic stories with heightened romantic tension.

The longer stories, sophisticated style, greater sensual detail and variety that made Special Editions popular are the same elements that will make you want to read book after book.

We hope that you enjoy this Special Edition today, and will enjoy many more.

Please write to us:

Jane Nicholls
Silhouette Books
PO Box 236
Thornton Road
Croydon
Surrey
CR9 3RU

The Reformer
DIANA WHITNEY

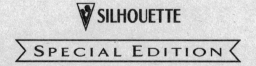

SILHOUETTE

SPECIAL EDITION

*First published in Great Britain 1996
by Silhouette Books, Eton House, 18-24 Paradise Road,
Richmond, Surrey TW9 1SR*

© Diana Hinz 1996

*Silhouette, Silhouette Special Edition and Colophon are
Trade Marks of Harlequin Enterprises II B.V.*

ISBN 0 373 24019 8

23-9608

Made and printed in Great Britain

To Adelle Gilstrap, with much love and appreciation.

DIANA WHITNEY

says she loves 'fat babies and warm puppies, mountain streams and California sunshine, camping, hiking and gold prospecting. Not to mention strong romantic heroes!' She married her own real-life hero twenty years ago. With his encouragement, she left her long-time career as a finance director and pursued the dream that had haunted her since childhood—writing. To Diana, writing is a joy, the ultimate satisfaction. Reading, too, is her passion, from spine-chilling thrillers to sweeping sagas, but nothing can compare to the magic and wonder of romance.

Other Silhouette Books by Diana Whitney

Silhouette Special Edition

Cast a Tall Shadow
Yesterday's Child
One Lost Winter
Child of the Storm
The Secret
*The Adventurer
*The Avenger

The Blackthorn Brotherhood

Silhouette Sensation

Still Married
Midnight Stranger

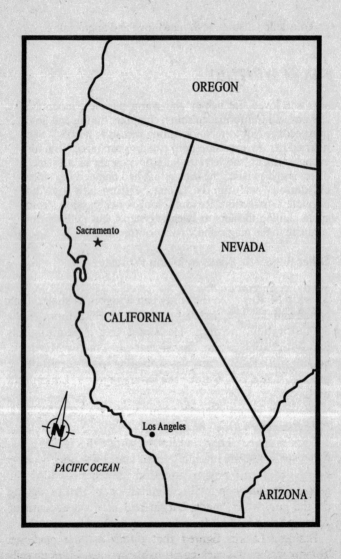

Prologue

Larkin McKay gave the spray can a vigorous shake, then aimed and drew the first sloppy letters on Blackthorn Hall's administration building. He stood back, admiring his handiwork. Beside him, eleven-year-old Tommy Murdock, armed with a similar can, was struggling with his part of the process. "You got to make the letters bigger," Larkin told him.

Blinking, Tommy glanced from Larkin's work to his own. "How come?"

Larkin sighed. They'd all talked about this in the dorm room, only Tommy probably hadn't been listening because he had problems paying attention. Teachers—called the gestapo by detention facility inmates—were always ragging on the guy, which made Larkin real mad on account of Tommy being his best friend.

Besides, Larkin figured that dumb asthma medicine Tommy was always sucking probably mutated his brain cells or something. Since the poor kid couldn't help being kind of slow, Larkin never minded having to tell him something more than once. "We got to make the letters real big so people driving the freeway can read 'em."

"Oh." Pointing the nozzle of his drippy can, Tommy spritzed madly, then gave his ponytailed head a proud toss and stood back, grinning. "How's that?"

Before Larkin could answer, Devon Monroe, who at twelve was the oldest of the four roommates, marched over. "Quit jabbering and get it done."

Apparently Tommy didn't like Devon's tone. He stuck out his skinny chest, which looked deformed because of the stupid inhaler in his shirt pocket, and gave his oldest roommate a slitty-eyed stare. "Hey, just 'cause your old man's rich don't mean you can boss us around."

Devon looked hurt but all he said was, "Old Hogman could show up any minute." He was talking about the chancellor of Blackthorn Hall and subject of the nifty sign they were trying to make so everyone would know *Ogden Marlow is a Nazi.*

At least, that was the plan. Right now, the only thing going on was a spitting contest between Dev and Tommy, who jerked a thumb toward the thin, Mexican-American kid squatting at the edge of the building. "Bobby's keeping watch. He'll tell us if anybody's coming."

Larkin skimmed a quick glance at the group's sentry. At ten, Roberto Arroya was the youngest and the brightest of the four roommates. They all thought it was kind of weird that a kid who'd skipped three grades could end up in reform school. According to Bobby, he'd been "rescued" by welfare busybodies while his mother was on one of her booze binges. For a while, Bobby figured she'd try to get him back. He figured wrong.

So had Larkin. After his own folks got divorced, his mom had married some stuffed-shirt banker with a houseful of rotten kids. Larkin hated his stepfamily almost as much as they'd hated him. That's why he'd run away.

The cops had picked him up a couple of days later, only his mom hadn't wanted him back. Incorrigible, she'd called him. Larkin hadn't known exactly what that meant but it must have been pretty bad because she wouldn't even look at him when she said it. Later, Larkin had gone to court. The judge had given him a really mad look, whacked his gavel and made a long-winded speech about rotten apples spoiling stuff. Larkin had cried and begged his mom not to leave him there, but she'd just walked out of the courtroom with his stepbrother, who'd grinned and flipped Larkin the bird.

Next thing Larkin knew, he was in a smelly bus being hauled off to Blackthorn Hall's processing lockup, which was sort of like a prison in a prison, with dirty cells that were smaller than a closet and a razor-wire fence that reminded Larkin of a movie he'd once seen about Attica.

He'd been all alone and scared out of his mind, until he'd been assigned to bunk with Devon and Bobby and Tommy. Now the four roommates were like musketeers, only better; they were brothers, blood brothers, a real family, even if Tommy had picked a lousy time to start acting like a brat.

Suddenly, Tommy's pale face split in his trademark grin. He wiggled a finger at Devon and squeaked, "Gotcha!"

Devon got a goofy look on his face, then threw up his hands and stalked away, muttering to himself.

Larkin moaned. The prankster of the group never did have a lick of sense when it came to timing. "Geez, Tommy, quit screwin' around. If we get caught, we're gonna be in the Box so long our heads'll be flat."

Giggling hard enough to make himself wheeze, Tommy went back to work in a cloud of blue paint vapor. "Man, did you see Dev's face when I ragged him about his old man?"

Ignoring Larkin's worried stare, he paused to refill his lungs. "Dev's gotta learn to lighten up, you know?"

"Devon looks out for us," Larkin said defensively.

"Yeah, I know."

"You okay? You sound kinda weird."

Ignoring the question, Tommy concentrated on spraying the final word, took a step back and frowned. "That don't look right."

Larkin did a double take, then swore under his breath. "You dork. There's only one *z* in Nazi."

"Oh." He shook the can, then crossed out the extra letter. "There."

"Aw, hell, Tommy, no one's gonna be able to read that—"

An urgent hiss from the corner caught everyone's attention as Bobby leapt up and flattened against the wall. "They're coming!"

In the chaos that followed, paint cans bounced across the grass as the boys tripped over themselves dashing toward a nearby embankment that was shielded by thick shrubbery. Larkin dived in head first, crawling into the heart of the thicket. When he turned around, he saw Devon haul Bobby down inside the concealing foliage, then stare out across the quad. Larkin bellied over, peered above Dev's shoulder and let out a gasp.

Tommy hadn't made it to the embankment. Ogden Marlow and another guy were dragging him away.

Larkin wanted to stop them, only he couldn't move because Devon grabbed hold of his wrist and wouldn't let go. "It's too late," he whispered. "You can't do nothin' now."

Larkin sat back on his haunches, mute with shock. Focusing on a white lump lying between discarded spray paint cans, he knew Devon was right. There wasn't anything he or anybody else could do. That white lump was Tommy's inhaler.

* * *

An hour later, Larkin huddled in the windowless boiler room which had served as the Brotherhood's private meeting place. Pipes rattled in the darkness. A hiss of steam escaped the rusty water heater. It smelled like dirty wet spiders.

He wiped his wet eyes, blew his nose on his shirt and hugged his knees, rocking back and forth while the rough concrete wall scratched at his back. In his mind, he saw Tommy's grinning face, with those dumb, crooked teeth and squatty eyes gleaming with mischief. Tommy always had an angle, some kind of neat idea to make life interesting. Like last week, when he poured a whole quart of liquid soap into the john, or the time he shoved a squashed frog down Butch McCreary's pants.

Come to think of it, that hadn't been such a swift move because McCreary got even by gluing Tommy's ponytail to the back of a chair. Larkin had used the teacher's pinking shears to cut him loose.

Since Tommy's waist-length hair had been his pride and joy, even the loss of a few inches had bummed him to the max. For weeks, Tommy had fretted about exacting revenge. Last night, he'd finally came up with a plan that flat-out guaranteed ol' Butch would go through life with a toilet seat glued to his butt.

But McCreary had lucked out, because that wasn't gonna happen now. It wasn't fair—

A narrow light beam cut through the gloom. "Lark?" Devon called. "You down here?"

Without answering, Larkin scootched into a corner, quivering silently until a burst of light flashed into his face, nearly blinding him. He yanked up an arm to shade his eyes. "Go away!"

Two shadows moved toward him. The smaller one spoke. "Hogman's looking for us," Roberto said. "We can't hide forever."

"I'm not hiding." To emphasize that, Larkin stuck out a brave chin that only quivered a little. "I just wanna be alone, that's all."

Dev aimed the flashlight beam at the floor, away from Larkin's face, then squatted beside him. "The paramedic said it was 'respiratory failure.'" When Devon's voice broke, he rubbed his eyes with the back of his hand. "I tried...honest I did...but there wasn't nothin' I could do."

Larkin shot him a killing look. "Yeah? Well, you didn't try hard enough. You shoulda taken Tommy's medicine to the office right away."

"Hey, that's not fair," Roberto said. "Dev wanted to get us back to the dorm room so we wouldn't get caught, too."

Larkin knew that, but his belly burned with uncontrollable rage. He skewered his youngest roommate with a hard stare. "You were supposed to warn us."

Roberto staggered back as if he'd been shot. "I did, man. I told you they were coming—"

"It was too late!" Leaping to his feet, Larkin balled his fists and screamed at the shattered boy. "You were the sentry! It's your fault, Bobby...your fault—"

Larkin spun against the wall, sobbing, and beat at the concrete until his knuckles bled. He felt hands pulling at his shoulders, yanking him away from the wall. Through a blur of tears, he was vaguely aware that Bobby had shrugged off his own shirt. While Bobby wrapped the shirt around Larkin's torn hands, Devon slipped arm around his shoulders, murmuring words of comfort.

But there could be no comfort. Not now. Not ever. Because Tommy's death hadn't been Bobby's fault, or Devon's either. It was Larkin who'd thought up the idea of painting a protest on the administration building. It was

Larkin who'd pilfered cans of powder blue spray paint from a crew striping handicapped spaces in the parking lot. It was Larkin who'd insisted Tommy be allowed to help, even though everyone knew he couldn't run three feet without having an asthma attack.

It was Larkin McKay who was responsible for Tommy's death and there was no way he could live with the guilt.

Chapter One

"Yo, Dr. McKay! Whatcha want us to do with your balls?"

From the back of the cavernous gymnasium, Larkin looked up from the volunteer schedule he'd been preparing to acknowledge the two youngsters, each of whom was struggling to embrace several basketballs in arms that were a tad too short for the task. "There's a canvas hamper in the equipment room," he called out. "Just toss them in there."

"You got it, Doc."

As the hunching boys shuffled past a neat row of Foosball tables, Larkin pivoted to face the balding man standing beside him. "So, Jack, will we see you Thursday night?"

"If you're sure you won't need me earlier."

"Nope. For once, the volunteer roster is full," Larkin said, hanging the list and clipboard on a wall hook. "Next week doesn't look too good, though. A couple of our most dependable volunteers will be out of town."

"I can take an extra evening, if that would help."

"Yes, it would. Thanks."

Jack Peterson's gaze skittered across the huge arena—once a grocery warehouse—which now housed a variety of teen activities, including two portable basketball hoops, a small video arcade and several billiard tables donated by local business owners grateful for any enterprise that kept neighborhood kids out of their own establishments. "I'm the one who should be saying thanks," Jack said. "If not for you and the youth center, I shudder to think what might have happened to my son."

Larkin laid a reassuring hand on the man's shoulder. "Sammy's a good boy. Thirteen is a tough age for kids, especially around here. He just needs a little extra guidance for a while."

"Yes, well..." Jack cleared his throat, motioning toward the two boys who'd just exited the equipment room. "To tell you the truth, I don't know how you've managed to keep this place under control. It's the only building in three square miles that hasn't been tagged."

"A hard-fought negotiation," Larkin admitted, unable to disguise his pride that the youth center, set in the heart of L.A.'s most volatile gang territory, was a sparkling jewel amid the graffitied walls and garbage-strewn alleys of the inner city. Still, the accomplishment wasn't his alone, so he gave credit where due. "In the end, local honchos finally agreed to mark the center as neutral territory. Anyone is welcome, so long as they're not armed or flying colors."

"It was still a hell of a job, Doc." As the two panting youngsters loped over, Jack slipped an arm around the taller boy. "Ready to go?"

"Uh-huh." Sammy turned to Larkin. "We got the 'quipment room all picked up for you."

The second boy was a pudgy seventh-grader who until recently, had strutted the 'hood dressed like a gang wanna-be. "We swept up and everything. Can we come back tomorrow?"

Larkin ruffled his black hair. "Of course, Joey. I'd be disappointed if you didn't."

Joey grinned.

Jack Peterson edged toward the door with both boys in tow. "I'll see you Thursday, Doc, although it looks like you'll be putting up with these two a bit sooner."

Assuring Jack that he wouldn't have it any other way, Larkin walked the trio toward the street entrance, bid them good-night, and locked the steel security doors behind them.

After Larkin flipped off the overhead fluorescents, a few strategically placed night-lights cast their eerie shadows through the massive room. The window of his private office, shielded by venetian blinds and illuminated from within, dispersed a square of glowing stripes against an otherwise black wall. The beckoning brightness served as a reminder that Larkin's workday wasn't quite over.

After returning to his office, Larkin spent the next thirty minutes completing last minute paperwork, including a grant application, letters of recommendation for some of the center's recent graduates and finally reworking the week's calendar to include two more counseling appointments.

As he penciled in the extra sessions, it occurred to him that there was a cruel irony in successfully counseling troubled families when he'd been unable to maintain a cohesive relationship in his own life.

Even if Larkin had been able to forgive himself the childhood rebellion he blamed for his parents' disastrous divorce, there was no excuse for having failed so miserably at his own marriage. He was a psychologist, dammit, a supposed expert on healing human relationships. Why, then, hadn't he recognized the unhappiness that had driven his own wife to turn her back on six years of marriage? It was a question he'd asked himself a thousand times; he'd yet to come up with an answer.

Dropping the pencil, Larkin leaned back in the chair, rubbing his stiff neck. It had been three years since Bonnie had left him. Three long, lonely years. Although he was no longer in love with his ex-wife, he most certainly loved his two children and missed them desperately.

The ache in his gut was worse at night, when darkness and silence allowed his mind to replay the sound of childish laughter and recall how Justin and Susie had raced into his arms when he came home each evening....

Larkin swiveled around, leapt up and massaged his eyelids hard enough to hurt. Damn, he needed a drink. Larkin wasn't an alcoholic. Sometimes he almost wished he was. Then he'd have an excuse for escapism, not to mention an increased tolerance for the substance he used as a pain-killer for the soul.

He slipped a yearning glance at his desk, wishing he'd tucked a bottle in the drawer to carry him through moments like these. Since he allowed no alcohol on the premises, violating his own edict would be wholly inappropriate, not to mention a breach of the center's conditional use permit. With that in mind Larkin managed to suppress the fierce urge. So far.

But this was an especially bad night. He felt hollow, despite the oxymoron of an empty void sustaining the impossible burden of constant pain. Nothingness was supposed to be numb; Larkin's hurt.

Sighing, he wiped his palms over his face and, as he'd done a million times over the years, silently berated himself for the weakness of his soul. Compared to the tragedies suffered by those who daily sought his help and solace, Larkin's own problems were insignificant. He reminded himself of that and was annoyed by the nonspecific sadness that overcame him this time of the evening.

After eight-plus years of higher education, Larkin was acutely aware of the avoidance behavior that kept him hanging around the center later and later every night. For some unfathomable reason he preferred hunkering in a dark warehouse to enjoying the warmth and comfort of his homey apartment. He didn't know why. There was a nice clean bed at home; a great stereo, where he could enjoy the jazz he favored; a modern kitchen, with all the gadgets required to indulge his passion for gourmet cooking; and last but far from least, several bottles of the mellowest cask-aged whiskey money could buy.

That final thought offered the incentive he needed to flip off the desk lamp, lock his office and head toward the rear door.

The back of the building, lit by a few well-placed security lights, opened onto a paved area of outdoor basketball courts protected by a six-foot chain-link fence bordering the alley where his car was parked.

Once outside, Larkin turned to lock the door and was vaguely aware of an odd sound, like shuffling sneakers. A glance up confirmed that several shadowed figures were hunched at the farthest corner of the building. Frowning, he took a step forward, planning to advise the trespassers that the center was closed for the night.

The moment he moved, however, there was a frantic shout; the figures scattered. As they bolted toward the fence, Larkin's gaze was drawn to the place where they'd been crouching, and to the ugly patch of fresh graffiti marring an otherwise spotless stucco wall. For an instant, he simply stood there, stunned.

The creak of stressed wire brought him out of his stupor. Two of the figures were hanging on the fence like kittens on a window screen; another had cleared the top and dropped to the alley. The fourth, slowed by an awkward limp, had fallen behind the others. Larkin caught him before he reached the fence, grabbing a fistful of sweatshirt and wrestled the struggling youngster to the ground.

"Lemme go! Lemme *go!*" Fists flailing, the boy fought like a wildcat, desperately trying to twist out of Larkin's grasp and nearly succeeding. Despite the impairment that had initially slowed his gait, the kid now displayed surprising strength and a tenacity that under other circumstances might have been admirable. At the moment, however, it was merely annoying.

In the end, Larkin's six-foot-one frame overwhelmed the youngster, enabling him to clamp a hand around the kid's skinny arm and haul him to his feet.

"Stop it!" Larkin growled, dragging the grappling boy back to the defaced wall. "Stop it or I'll throw you over my shoulder and cart you to the police station like a sack of day-old trash."

The boy went rigid. His mouth moved, but no sound came out and a familiar terror clouded his dark eyes. Larkin noticed then that he was very young; eleven, perhaps, certainly no older than twelve. But it wasn't the boy's youth that brought a lump to Larkin's throat. It was the fear in his dark eyes, the same fear that had been in Tommy's eyes as Ogden Marlow dragged him away.

Only this time, it was Larkin's anger generating that fear and his own traitorous hand gripping the arm of a terrified child.

Larkin released him so quickly that the boy stumbled backward, but strangely enough, made no attempt to get away. Instead, he whimpered pitifully and wiped his face with trembling, paint-stained fingers. "I'm sorry, mister, honest. I'll pay... I'll do anything you say, only please—" he swallowed a small sob "—please, don't make me go to j-jail."

It took a moment for Larkin to collect his thoughts. He filled his lungs, exhaled slowly, then spoke in a quiet, non-threatening tone. "What's your name, son?"

"M-Manuel Cervantes."

"What do you go by?"

"Huh?"

"What's your street name?"

"Oh. I dunno…my friends call me Mannie." He sniffed, wiped his nose with his sleeve and angled his wary gaze upward. "Are you gonna call the cops?"

"Do you think I should?"

Mannie shrugged, slid a sideways glance at the newly decorated wall and winced. "I dunno…maybe."

At this point Larkin, too, looked at the wet graffiti and barely suppressed a snort of surprised laughter. Instead of a wall tagged by gang slogans, symbols or territorial markings, the youth center now sported several colorful cartoon characters that were surprisingly well drawn.

To conceal his amusement, Larkin covered his mouth, furrowed his brow and, although he'd already decided not to involve the police, pretended to be considering his options while scrutinizing the apparently talented, obviously misguided and currently disheartened young artist who was now wringing his hands in abject misery.

Beneath the open-front sweat jacket, the boy was wearing a T-shirt emblazoned with vivid, hand-painted cartoon figures, amusing enough, but certainly attire that no gang member would be caught dead in. Larkin considered that confirmation that this youngster wasn't a banger; at least not at the moment, although the trembling youngster was definitely treading dangerous waters, a sea of violence in which too many other kids had already drowned.

But Larkin's gut confirmed that Mannie Cervantes was still salvageable and salvaging kids was what Larkin did. He laid a firm hand on the boy's shoulder. "Let's go have a talk with your folks, son."

Mannie moaned.

Clutching the telephone with both hands, Letitia Cervantes didn't even try to hide her panic. "What difference does it make how long he's been gone? Don't you understand? He was doing homework in his bedroom and now he's...he's just disappeared. He could have been kidnapped!"

A droll voice filtered down the line. "Is there any evidence of foul play...jimmied screen, signs of a struggle, blood—"

"*Blood?* Oh, dear God." Letitia sagged against the sofa as the room started to spin. From the doorway, she heard Mama Rose's horrified gasp and knew without looking that the woman, who was no doubt clutching her rosary beads, had paled three shades at the word *blood.* She wanted to comfort her mother-in-law but, at the moment, was struggling just to control her own terror. "Please...isn't there something you can do?"

The police dispatcher's voice softened. "Don't worry, ma'am. This sort of thing happens all the time. Kids sneak out and parents worry. He'll probably show up in a few hours, but if he's not home by morning, give us a call."

"By *morning?*" Letitia wanted to scream that her son could be dead by then, but the thought was too horrible to put into words, and Rose was wailing, and the dog was yipping, and the dispatcher had already hung up and...and...

And the doorbell was ringing.

Letitia dropped the receiver, which skidded across the floor after bouncing off the noggin of Rose's neurotic Chihuahua. With a pious yelp, the obnoxious animal leapt into Rose's waiting arms while Letitia dashed across the room and ripped open the front door with such force that the walls vibrated.

She clutched her throat, too relieved even to breathe, let alone speak. There was her beloved son with his hands stuffed in his pockets and his gaze riveted on the fashionable sneakers for which his grandmother had spent an entire pension check. He didn't look particularly happy, but he didn't appear to be hurt, either. And he was most definitely alive.

Rose uttered a cry of relief and kissed her rosary, shifting Rasputin in her arms so she could tuck the beads into her skirt pocket.

Letitia herself didn't know whether to laugh or cry or drag Mannie into the house by his ear; so she simply stood there, biting her lip, trying to calm the chaos of her mind.

Finally she pulled her son inside, embracing him in a desperate hug that was not returned. Instead, he went rigid, so she reluctantly released him, took a deep breath and spoke in a firm, maternal voice that belied her fear. "Nana and I have been frantic, Mannie. Where on earth have you been?"

The question was answered, sort of, by a weak shrug followed by even more intense interest in his shoes.

"Mrs. Cervantes?" The strange voice startled her. When her gaze snapped around, she noticed a broad-shouldered man with tousled blond hair and distinguished, wire-rimmed glasses that made him look like a cross between a surfer and an investment banker. She managed a jerky nod, to which the man responded with a warm smile. "I'm Larkin McKay, from the youth center."

"Mr. McKay," she murmured, taking the hand he offered. His touch was warm, surprisingly gentle and oddly comforting. She tilted her head, intrigued by blue eyes so clear one could almost see through them. After a long moment, she retrieved her hand, took a step back and invited him in.

As she closed the door behind him, the full content of Mr. McKay's introduction sunk in. "The youth center over on Whittier?" She turned to her son, who was morosely poking the fringe of a throw rug with his toe. "Is that where you were?"

Puffing his cheeks, Mannie extracted a hand from his pocket, absently raked his mussed hair, and angled a wary glance at Mr. McKay. "Yeah . . . I guess."

"Good Lord, that's nearly five miles away. How did you get there?"

His shoulder twitched in another shrug. "Boomer's brother has a car."

"Boomer?"

"Yeah. You know...ah..." He angled an embarrassed glance toward Mr. McKay, then lowered his voice, running the syllables together to form a barely decipherable name. "WillDoherty."

Letitia blinked in astonishment. She'd known the Dohertys, who lived down the block, for years. William and Mannie had been best friends since preschool and not once in the past eight years had she ever heard her neighbor's son referred to as anything other than William or Will.

But then again, William had undergone a disturbing metamorphosis over the past year, changing from a cheerful and courteous child into a sullen, disrespectful youngster around whom Letitia had grown increasingly uncomfortable. She hadn't exactly forbidden Mannie to associate with William, but had definitely encouraged her son to make other, less petulant friends.

At the moment, Mannie's choice of companion was not at issue; his behavior, however, most certainly was. Letitia's fear for his safety had melted into a peculiar combination of anger and bewilderment that left her feeling drained, and pathetically inadequate. "I don't understand, Mannie. If you wanted to go out, all you had to do was ask. I would have driven you to the youth center. Why did you have to sneak off like that and frighten us to death?"

"I'm sorry, Mom, real sorry. I never meant to scare you or nothing but I didn't, uh, sneak off...I mean, not really." The hand that had been ruffling his hair lowered to cover a nervous cough. Peering over a loosely curled fist, Mannie's gaze skittered past his mother's shoulder and had just settled on his grandmother when a relieved gleam settled in his dark eyes. With a confident smile, he dropped his hand and announced, "I told Nana where I was going."

A claim of extraterrestrial abduction couldn't have been more shocking. One look at Rose's astonished face confirmed that the poor woman was every bit as taken aback as Letitia. "Manuel!" the confused woman sputtered. "Why do you say this?"

Mannie interrupted. "Don't you remember? You were watching 'Wheel of Fortune' and I came in and said I was going to hang for a while and you said okay, so I left... right, Nana?"

His puzzled grandmother tightened her grip on Rasputin, and slowly shook her head. "No, I would not forget such a thing—"

"It's not your fault," Mannie blurted, looking desperate. "I mean, I shoulda known that you don't hear nothing when the 'Wheel' is on, on account of it being your favorite program and all. So just 'cause you don't remember, doesn't mean I didn't tell you. That's right, isn't it? Please, Nana."

Rose blinked at her daughter-in-law, then at Mr. McKay, who was taking in the entire scenario with wise eyes and a reproachful frown. She chewed her lip, then murmured, "Ah, perhaps... I mean, sí, that must be what happened."

Letitia moaned. She knew Mannie had his grandmother wrapped around his finger, but never would have believed him capable of asking her to lie for him. "Mama, you know that's not true."

"No, I do not." Defensive now, Rose dropped the squirming Chihuahua, which promptly bared its teeth and, snarling madly, attacked the telephone receiver that was still lying on the floor. Meanwhile, the older woman continued to plead her case. "Of all people, you know best how I am when my program is on, so if Manuel says he told me, then he told me."

With that, she wrapped loving arms around her grandson, who was nearly limp with relief, and turned to Larkin McKay, her eyes shining with gratitude. "Thank you for returning *mi nieto*," she whispered, while Letitia, reluctant to conduct parental discipline in front of a stranger, remained silent.

"I'm glad I could help," Larkin said, favoring Rose with a warm smile.

As Letitia bent to rescue the telephone from Rasputin's wrath, she noticed a telling look pass between her son and the center's director. It occurred to her that there might be more to the evening's activities than she'd thus far been told. Given the violent atmosphere by which today's kids were surrounded, the possibilities were chilling, but Letitia had never been one to avoid unpleasantries. Over the years, she'd been dealt her share of heartache and had faced it as she faced life itself—head-on.

And Mannie *was* her life; anything that affected him, affected her. No matter how awful the truth, Letitia wouldn't rest until she knew every detail.

After wrestling the curled cord away from the determined dog, Letitia cradled the receiver, straightened, and was trying to gather her thoughts while Mannie stepped away from his grandmother's smothering embrace. Again, he nervously ran his fingers through his hair. This time, an odd orange glint caught her attention. "What's that?"

Mannie's hand froze against his skull. "What's what?"

"Those orange spots on your fingers." She snagged her son's wrist, pulling his hand down for a closer inspection, and noticed a smattering of green as well. "This looks like paint."

When Mannie didn't respond, Larkin McKay did. "It is paint," he said quietly. "Mannie and his friends decided to decorate the back wall of the youth center."

For a moment, Letitia stared dumbly. When the full significance of that statement hit, she staggered back as if she'd been struck. "I don't believe it." She did, of course—the evidence was both colorful and conclusive—but the words had slipped out as a wish rather than a statement of fact. To her horror, however, she found herself hoping her son would dispute it. "Is that true?"

The boy's expression shifted from pained to sheepish to belligerent and finally back to pained. "We were just messing around."

"Messing *around?*" Letitia's mouth was so dry, her tongue stuck to her teeth, forcing her to enunciate each syllable and adding impact to the message. "Pitching pennies is 'messing around.' Playing catch is 'messing around.' Destroying property is not—I repeat *not*—'messing around.' It is vandalism, Mannie, and it is a crime."

Larkin, watching and listening with what he considered to be purely professional interest, noted that Mannie flinched repeatedly during his mother's reprimand and his eyes glimmered with telltale moisture. Apparently the boy hadn't outgrown the need for her approval and was deeply distressed at having disappointed her. Larkin considered that a vindication of his initial instinct that Mannie was basically a good kid following the standard, prepubescent rite of testing limits by driving parents to the brink of insanity.

The boy's mother—who appeared much too young to have a child of Mannie's age—had responded admirably. Although Larkin could see that she was shocked and hurt, she hadn't allowed her feelings to intrude upon required discipline. Her voice was firm, not shrill; her expression was earnest, not twisted by anger; her words were thoughtful, incisive, authoritatively issued.

And she wasn't finished yet.

"I hope you understand the gravity of this situation," she told the miserable boy. "Had Mr. McKay chosen to press charges, you would have been arrested."

Mannie's lip quivered. "I know," he whispered. "I'm real sorry."

"I am not the one to whom you should be apologizing."

The boy took a shaky breath, repeated the apology to Larkin, who accepted with a nod before Mannie angled an expectant glance back at his mother, apparently hoping that the inquisition was over.

Those hopes were soon dashed. "My son will make arrangements to clean up the mess as soon as possible," Letitia told Larkin.

"Huh?" Mannie's eyes were practically bulging. "But Mom—"

"And he will, of course, make the necessary monetary reparations." She slid her son a cool glance, adding, "Out of his allowance."

The poor kid's jaw dropped like a rock. "That's not fair!"

Letitia cowed him with a look. "Actions have consequences, Mannie. Mr. McKay is entitled to have his property returned to its original condition."

"But I wasn't the only one," he insisted. "How 'bout the other guys."

"They aren't my concern, you are. However, if you'd like to give Mr. McKay the names and addresses of those who assisted in this little endeavor, perhaps their parents would encourage them to give you a hand." The suggestion was met by a sullen stare. She sighed. "I didn't think so. In that case, young man, I'm afraid you're on your own."

Rose stepped forward, wiping her palms on the skirt of a print housedress that accentuated her well-formed, if somewhat matronly, figure. "Manuel is right," she told Letitia. "He is only one small boy. What you ask is too much."

Although Larkin was startled that the older woman would openly contradict a parental edict, Letitia seemed less surprised by the interference than resigned to it. "I understand that you're upset, Mama, but I'd prefer to discuss this later."

Rolling her thin lips together, Rose lowered her gaze and, Larkin thought, accepted Letitia's decision. In less than a heartbeat, he realized that initial assumption had been premature. The boy's grandmother defiantly lifted her chin, focusing a flashing black gaze on her daughter-in-law. "The punishment is too harsh, *nuera*. My son would never approve."

Letitia went pale. To her credit, however, her expression never wavered. "Ray was the finest, most honorable man I've ever known. You raised him well, and I respect that. But Mannie is our son, Ray's and mine. My husband expected me to raise him the best way I knew how, and that's exactly what I intend to do."

Larkin's attention was caught by the fact that she'd referred to her husband in the past tense. Whether by death or divorce, it was now evident that Mannie's dad was no longer a viable part of the family unit. That was a shame, because Larkin's experience had proven that fatherless boys were particularly vulnerable to outside influence, especially those for whom no other male role model was available to fill the void.

Mannie, however, was more fortunate than most, having retained at least one strong and obviously capable parent. But a flash of pain in his mother's dark eyes and the telltale quiver at the corner of her mouth indicated that Ms. Cervantes wasn't feeling nearly as confident as her stoic demeanor would suggest.

Still, she squared her shoulders and turned to Mannie, who regarded his mother with sad eyes and a contrite expression. "Have you finished your homework?" she asked.

He slid a questioning glance at his grandmother and was visibly disappointed when she remained silent. Sighing, he answered his mother's question. "Almost."

"Then you'd better get to it."

The boy nodded, swallowed hard, then limped down the hall. After a moment, as Larkin heard the soft click of a closing door, a movement caught his eye. He glanced down and saw the little bug-eyed dog glaring out from beneath the coffee table. Since Larkin was a sucker for anything furry, he automatically bent down to stroke it. As he reached toward the animal's head, it suddenly snarled and sunk a muzzle full of needlelike teeth into his finger.

With a grunt of surprise, Larkin yanked back his hand, vaguely aware that the room had erupted in chaos.

Letitia emitted a horrified gasp and hollered, "Rasputin, no!" to which the creature responded by yipping madly, bouncing a victory lap around the vanquished enemy's feet, then leaping into Rose's waiting arms.

Apologizing profusely, Rose cradled the smug little beast, explaining, "Strangers make him nervous."

"Carpet lint makes him nervous," Letitia muttered, lifting Larkin's hand to inspect the damage, which was limited to a couple of pricks and a minor scratch. "Honestly, Mama, if you don't teach that animal some manners, I'm going to enroll him in obedience class and let a professional trainer do it for you."

Rose couldn't have looked more horrified if her daughter-in-law had threatened to boil her beloved pet in cooking oil. "You wouldn't!"

Under her breath, Letitia muttered, "Try me."

Apparently Rose got the message. Mumbling something about bandages, she rushed off with Rasputin still tucked safely under her arm.

Letitia continued to gently probe Larkin's finger. "Does it hurt?"

"A little." In truth, the only thing he could feel was a pleasant tingling generated by her delicate touch, which he was enjoying immensely. He couldn't remember when he'd felt so pampered, or so aware of a woman's nearness. There was something erotic about her, a dizzying scent that reminded him of sweet incense, and a subtle appeal that went far beyond her obvious beauty. He liked the way she carried herself, with pride and dignity; he even liked her voice. It was soothing, mellow, with the fluidity and the baroque warmth of a well-bowed cello.

As the thought crossed his mind, an adorable dimple appeared at the corner of her mouth and she emitted a throaty chuckle that gave him goose bumps. "Fortunately, Mr. McKay, your wounds don't appear to be life threatening."

He was fascinated by how her eyes, now sparkling with amusement, suddenly lit up her entire face. Of course, he should have been embarrassed to have been caught exaggerating the extent of his injuries simply to prolong the enjoyment of her tender ministrations; oddly enough, he wasn't. "True, but it's been so long since a pretty woman held my hand."

She looked up, startled, but made no other response because her mother-in-law had returned with the bandages.

The woman nervously handed one to Letitia, then laid the box on the coffee table, carefully avoiding so much as a glance at Larkin's injuries. "Is the bandage large enough?"

"I'm not sure," Letitia replied with a smile. "He may need a full cast."

"Madre de Dios," Rosa whispered, obviously shaken. "I didn't realize it was so bad."

"It isn't," Larkin assured her. "Your daughter-in-law was teasing me for being such a crybaby."

"I simply indicated that you needn't rush out and select a grave site." Ignoring her mother-in-law's stunned expression, Letitia wrapped the Band-Aid around Larkin's finger and gave it a pat. "There. Good as new."

Larkin held up his hand, wiggling the bound finger. "Really? That's odd. I could swear there weren't any holes in it when I arrived."

Her quiet laughter warmed his heart. "I really am sorry, Mr. McKay—"

"Larkin, please."

She tilted her head, regarding him for a moment. "That's a unique name."

"I'm told my mother liked birds. Personally, I think she just had a warped sense of humor."

Before she could respond, a flash of tan caught her attention. "Rasputin, no!"

Letitia reached for the bandage box; the dog got there first. Having leapt onto the coffee table, Rasputin triumphantly snagged his prize and dashed away, leaving poor Rose to toss up her hands, utter a request for divine intervention and chase her unruly pet down the hall.

With a pained sigh, Letitia massaged her brow with her fingertip. "As you can see, a nasty temper is not Rasputin's only problem. He's also a thief. Every hidey-hole in the house is stuffed with his treasures."

"A canine kleptomaniac, hmm." Larkin's gaze swept the neat living room, the walls of which were decorated by several lovely paintings including a huge oil portrait of the animal in question. "Have you considered counseling for him?"

"I've considered a lot of things, including wringing his fat little neck. Unfortunately—and I hesitate to admit this—I've grown rather fond of him."

"In that case, have you considered counseling for yourself?"

"You have a point." Smiling, she picked up a pencil and scratch pad from the phone table. "At any rate, I do apologize for the dog's poor behavior, as well as my son's. There's not much I can do about Rasputin. As for Mannie—" She jotted some numbers on the top sheet, then ripped it off and handed it to Larkin. "He'll start the cleanup after school tomorrow. Meanwhile, you can reach me here at the house or fax a list of supplies to my office number."

"I have everything he'll need," Larkin said, although he folded the scrap and tucked it in his pocket. "Since the previous owners were forced to repaint on a routine basis, several gallons of paint came with the building.''

''Considering the graffiti problem in that neighborhood, I'm surprised you didn't use up the paint in the first month.''

He shrugged. ''The building belongs to the kids now. They take pride in it.''

She regarded him with renewed curiosity and, he thought, a healthy dose of suspicion. He didn't blame her. By itself, community pride had provided little incentive to discourage taggers, who were drawn to the most manicured neighborhoods like moths to the proverbial flame. The youth center had been spared only after a series of highly complex and intricate issues were addressed.

Apparently Mannie's lovely young mother suspected as much, but chose not to raise the question. Instead, she opened the front door and smiled. ''We'll see you tomorrow, then.''

''Tomorrow,'' Larkin murmured. And with that word came a sense of excitement and anticipation that he hadn't experienced in years.

Chapter Two

"Man, this is so bogus." Slumped in the passenger seat, Mannie folded his arms like a tight fist, staring down at the torn knees of his oldest and most comfortably worn jeans. "If I get paint on these pants, they're gonna be wrecked."

That concern carried no weight with Letitia, since the jeans in question were little more than a few blue threads stretched between seams. "Life's tough," she murmured, pulling up to the curb and allowing the engine to idle. "But if you're worried, try to be careful and maybe you can get a couple more decades out of them."

Ignoring her son's disgruntled snort, she studied a hand-painted sign above the steel, double door entry which said simply, Eastside Youth Center. Flanking the doors, a pair of large picture windows sparkled as though recently polished. Details beyond the glass were obscured by white venetian blinds, which had been opened just wide enough to capture sunlight and reveal a blur of activity inside the giant structure. What caught her attention at the moment, however, was the building's stucco exterior, which was clean and unblemished.

For a moment, her hopes were buoyed. Perhaps the damage hadn't been as bad as she'd thought. Then Mannie mumbled, "It's 'round back."

Letitia hesitated, then shifted into gear and following her son's directions, pulled into the litter-strewn alley bordering the center's property. As she pulled up beside the chain-link fence, her heart and her hopes sank like a rock. Beyond the asphalt basketball courts which were now clogged with sweaty, laughing youngsters, the entire rear of the building had been defaced by the drippy likenesses of Looney Tunes, Power Rangers and Teenage Mutant Ninja Turtles.

"Oh, Mannie," she moaned. "I can't believe you'd take part in something so...so destructive."

He continued to scrutinize his knees as if expecting them to sprout grass. "We were just having fun, that's all. Besides, it didn't look so bad in the dark."

Swallowing the lump that had suddenly formed in her throat, Letitia pressed the accelerator and drove back to the front of the building. She'd hoped Mannie would be able to complete his chore this afternoon, but now realized that the work would require several afternoons. And Rose had been right to be concerned; it would indeed be a huge job for a single boy, particularly a boy slowed by a congenital hip deformity.

Every mommy-cell in Letitia's body screamed at her to grab a roller and do the work herself; rationally, however, she realized that if her conviction wavered even slightly, her son would recognize that and turn it to his advantage. She knew next to love, the most precious gift any parent could give a child is a strong value system and the self-discipline to live by it.

Besides, Mannie had been physically able to create the problem. Letitia had no choice but to insist that he now accept the consequences, no matter how difficult those consequences might be.

But she didn't have to like it.

When she exited the car and opened the passenger door, Mannie's last hope for reprieve died with the determination etched on his mother's face. Resigned to his fate, he issued a pained sigh and trudged toward the doors as if gallows awaited.

As they entered the spacious building, they were greeted by a teenager wearing a thigh-length T-shirt and baggy cholo pants. "Gotta card?"

"Ah...no, but Mr. McKay is expecting us," Letitia murmured, struck by the sudden din of organized chaos. "Is he available?"

"Doc? Yeah, he's around." The boy twisted his billed cap sideways, glanced over his shoulder and jerked a thumb toward a row of video games lined against the east wall. "Over there, by the arcade."

Following the gesture, Letitia scanned the crowd until she spotted a familiar, tousled blond head towering above a gaggle of youngsters. "I see him. Thank you."

"No big," the boy replied, then melted into a group of similarly attired youths loitering in a nearby corner.

Absently clutching her purse a bit more tightly, Letitia gestured for her recalcitrant son to follow and plotted a direct path toward the arcade.

When less than ten feet away, she saw that the center's director was engaged in serious conversation with an intimidating street tough who, amazingly enough, appeared to hang on Larkin's every word. Not wanting to intrude, she hung back far enough to be discreet, yet found herself close enough to overhear the conversation.

"So the thing is," Larkin was saying, "you've got to put yourself in the other guy's place. Feel what he's feeling, think what he's thinking. Understanding is the key, Matt. If you don't know where someone is coming from, you won't have a clue where he's going."

Initially, Letitia assumed the youth was being counseled on social values and was impressed that someone wearing a nose ring could accept a morality lesson with such interest. Her approving smile lasted about two seconds, just long enough for the reply to burst her idealistic bubble.

"So, like, I'm in the dude's head, getting a bead on if he's gonna box out or crash the boards so I can either alley-oop or pass off, right?"

"You'll pull an extra ten points a game," Larkin assured him.

"Man, that'd be awesome. Thanks, Doc."

Larkin and Nose Ring slapped a high-five, then performed an intricate variety of hand gestures, after which the youth loped away and took his place beneath an indoor basketball hoop at the far end of the building.

Letitia's jaw was still drooping when Larkin turned and spotted her. He lit up like neon. "You made it. Great! Good to see you, Mannie." He gave the boy's hand a hearty shake, then focused on Letitia. It might have been her imagination, but his eyes seemed to glow when he looked at her. "I was hoping you'd come, Ms. Cervantes."

"Please, call me Letitia."

"That's a lovely name. It suits you."

"Thank you." The intensity of his gaze made her palms sweat; she hoped a noncommittal smile wouldn't give her away as she redirected the conversation back to the subject at hand. "Mannie's capable of taking the bus, of course, but the truth is that after all I've heard about this place, I was curious to see it for myself."

"Ah. So we're infamous, are we?" Larkin straightened his glasses, skimming a quick glance around the bustling activity area before his gaze resettled on her and she saw amusement sparkle in his eyes. "Don't believe the ugly rumors. We haven't used thumbscrews in at least a week."

She laughed. "Relax, Mr. McKay...or should I be calling you Dr. McKay?"

"Actually, you should be calling me Larkin, since the formality issue has now been resolved." Smiling, he rocked back on his heels. "So, I assume you've done your homework on the youth center. What have you learned?"

For some reason, Letitia wasn't surprised by his assumption, partially because it was true, and partially because her research had indicated that Larkin McKay was a man who left nothing to chance. "As a matter of fact, I learned that you made it your business to involve the entire community in the center's inception, from the city council to the board of education. Although the youth service programs are supported by civic leaders, churches and synagogues, local police and neighborhood schools, your personal reviews remain somewhat mixed. Most people believe you're a candidate for sainthood, but a few are convinced you're a champion of thuggery who protects thieves and gangsters from the righteous wheels of justice."

"Ouch." He tugged an imaginary dart from his chest. "When you do a background check, you don't mess around. What are you, a private investigator?"

"Nope, just an underpaid accounts payable clerk," she said, then slid him a mischievous grin before adding, "who happens to work at city hall."

He gave a sage nod. "That explains it. Everyone knows that the wheels of government are greased by gossip."

"We prefer to think of it as the study of community conversational patterns."

"With a title that impressive, you should apply for a federal grant."

"Excellent thought," she replied, enjoying both his humor and the amusing repartee that flowed so easily between them. "I'll bring it up at the next staff meeting."

His delighted laugh sent a veritable army of goose bumps marching down her spine. And why not? she thought, feeling strangely giddy. She was a woman, he was a man, and an extremely attractive man at that. A furtive glance at his left hand confirmed that he wore no wedding ring, although in this day and age, that wasn't necessarily evidence of availability. After all, a guy with Larkin McKay's looks, wit and sensitivity certainly would have been snapped up years ago—

Wait a minute. What on earth was she thinking?

In four years of widowhood Letitia's dating experience had been limited to a couple of dinners and a movie, incidents that had, at her insistence, been strictly platonic. To suddenly find herself fantasizing about the attributes and availability of a man she barely knew was sobering, to say the least.

"Is something wrong?" Larkin asked.

"Hmm? Oh. No, not at all," Letitia replied, coughing the tiny untruth out of her throat. Either her dilemma had been reflected in her face or the man was even more astute than she'd realized. In any case, she'd have to exercise more control over her expression and most certainly, over her thoughts. Clasping her hands, she lifted her chin and spoke with measured strength. "It is getting rather late, though, and Mannie has a big job ahead of him."

Larkin studied her with a gaze so astute that he seemed to be reading her mind. Letitia felt her skin heat and prayed her discomfort wasn't evident to the casual observer because there was nothing casual about the way Larkin McKay was looking at her. She could actually feel his gaze penetrating her skin, burrowing deep inside, exploring her most private thoughts and emotions.

Then, just as her tension had become unbearable, he calmly turned to Mannie and spoke as if nothing extraordinary had happened. "Looks like fun, doesn't it?"

"Huh?" The boy blinked and tore his mesmerized gaze from a nearby video game. Seeing that the attention was now on him, he managed an indifferent shrug. "Yeah, I guess so."

"Maybe we can arrange for you to try it out later, after you're done painting."

"I'm never gonna get done," Mannie replied glumly. "It's gonna take forever."

"We'll see." Larkin glanced around and spotted a tall blonde who appeared to be in his midteens.

Two minutes later, armed with instructions to help gather painting supplies, the blonde was towing Mannie toward the maintenance room.

As Letitia watched her miserable son disappear into the crowd, she felt like the biggest traitor since Benedict Arnold. "Maybe I should go with him—"

"He'll be fine," Larkin assured. "Besides, I thought you might like a tour of the facilities. If you have enough time, that is."

For Letitia, "enough time" was a rare luxury. Fortunately, Rose did most of the cooking. Culinary art had never been Letitia's specialty. She did, however, have a carpet to vacuum, a hamper full of dirty laundry and at least two hours of ironing ahead of her, so when she heard herself say, "I have plenty of time," she was certain a playful poltergeist had taken control of her tongue.

Before she could retract the misstatement, Larkin glanced toward the video arcade and motioned to an onlooker who, to Letitia's surprise, turned out to be a fiftyish woman dressed in torn sweats and a baseball cap.

Acknowledging Larkin's signal with a cheery nod, the woman stepped away from the arcade area and turned a watchful eye toward the other activities being conducted throughout the cavernous room.

"That woman, is she one of the counselors?" Letitia asked, feeling ridiculously overdressed in high heels and business attire.

"No, she's a volunteer," Larkin replied, grasping her elbow and guiding her toward a corridor off the main room. "Would you believe she has five kids?"

"Impossible. She looks much too happy."

A knowing smile tugged the corner of his mouth. "Parenting gets easier after a while."

"How long a while?"

"Thirty years or so." He chuckled at her withering stare, then turned to point out a windowed room on the left. "That's one of our rap session rooms, where informal groups gather to talk about things that are important to them. There's always a supervising adult but the kids pretty much run the show."

Through the glass Letitia studied the group of laughing youngsters, most of whom had spurned chairs in favor of colorful throw pillows strewn around the room. Her gaze fell on a man wearing a business suit, who was apparently conducting the session. "Is he a psychologist?"

"No, he's an aeronautical engineer."

"Another volunteer?"

"Absolutely," Larkin said, leading her around another corner in the maze of hallways. "We couldn't survive without them. Of course, we also offer formal counseling sessions with trained psychologists."

"Sounds pricey."

"Fees are based on ability to pay." He stopped at an open door from which a cacophony of young voices was emanating. "This is our Snack Shoppe."

Peering inside, Letitia saw a room lined with vending machines along with a scattered clutch of mismatched tables around which various groups of chattering, whispering and giggling youngsters were clustered. It reminded her of a high school lunchroom, except that its occupants varied in age from junior high school to late adolescence. Considering the heavy traffic and continual use, the room

itself was surprisingly tidy, although myriad trash contain-
ers had been filled to capacity.

"Very impressive," she murmured. "The only thing we
have at city hall is a secondhand couch and an overworked
coffeepot."

"The community has been very generous with its dona-
tions." Leaning over, Larkin whispered, "Actually, the secret is to find a business that has what you want and make
a nuisance of yourself until the owner hands it over to get rid
of you."

Letitia smothered a smile. "Why, Dr. McKay, I'm truly
shocked that a man of your stature would resort to that kind
of harassment."

"I prefer to think of it as successful negotiation. The
center gets something it needs and the business owner gets
a nice tax deduction." His eyes twinkled. "Not to mention
an ironclad promise that I won't be back until next year."

"I suspect that last part is what clinches the deal."

"I suspect you're right." He stepped back, grinning, and
gestured down the hall. "Do you want to continue the
tour?"

At that moment, there was nothing in the world that Letitia wanted more.

"This really is a wonderful place," Letitia said as Larkin
opened his private office door. "You have every right to be
proud of what you've accomplished."

"I wish I could take credit, but the center has been a
community project. It shows what can be done when people put aside differences to work for a common goal."

"The vision was yours," Letitia said, stepping inside the
sparsely furnished office. "Without it, none of this would
exist."

"Anyone can have an idea. Creating a reality, however,
takes hard work."

"You're too modest," she murmured, spotting a pair of photographs lovingly arranged on his desk. There, grinning up from matching five-by-seven frames were school portraits of two beautiful, blond children who looked so much like Larkin that her heart sank to her toes. She slid him a curious glance, which he avoided.

Instead, he opened a file cabinet and began rooting through the drawer. "I have a brochure you might find interesting. It's a shameless sell piece but a local printer donated five thousand copies, so I won't let anybody leave without taking one of the darn things."

As Larkin continued a monologue about application forms and entrance cards, Letitia carefully lifted both photographs to study the smiling little faces. The boy, who looked to be about eight, had his father's round blue eyes and husky build; the little girl, who appeared to be a year or two younger, was a pigtailed version of the boy.

"So with the first rule violation," Larkin was saying, "the blue card is punched and the kid looses certain privileges, like use of the television lounge. The second infraction is total suspension for up to six months—"

"Your children are lovely." Letitia hadn't meant to interrupt him. The words had just rushed out. But when Larkin turned away from the cabinet and saw her holding the familiar frames, a look of incredible sadness crossed his face. She licked her lips and quickly returned the photographs to the desk. "I'm sorry. I didn't mean to intrude."

"You didn't." His smile was, she thought, a bit forced but as he gazed down at the pictures, his eyes warmed. "They are pretty special, aren't they?"

"They're beautiful."

"Thanks." He shut the cabinet and crossed the room clutching a fistful of papers, which he handed to Letitia. "Justin will be nine next summer," he told her. "He loves hockey, hates spelling and lives to torment his sister. Susie just started first grade in September but she's already reading at a fourth grade level. Her mother thinks she's a genius.''

Letitia managed thin smile. ''What do you think?''

''I think Susie's just a quiet little bookworm.'' He smiled fondly and caressed the frame with his fingertip. ''I was just like her at that age. Rowdy kids made me nervous, so I was much happier holed up in my room with the latest masterpiece from Dr. Seuss.''

''That's hard to believe. I could, however, imagine you wheedling milk money out of classmates to support a fund drive for new playground equipment.''

''An understandable misconception, given the fact that I'm about to favor you with my one of my more productive sales pitches.''

''Me?'' Startled, she looked down at the papers he'd given her, then back up again. ''What on earth do I have that you could possibly want?''

He hesitated, sighed and slid her an amused glance. ''I'll refrain from commenting on the obvious, which you see every day in the mirror. What the youth center needs is your time.''

Still reeling from the mirror remark, which under other circumstances she would have considered flirtatious, Letitia found herself stammering. ''Wh-why me?''

''Parental involvement is crucial if Mannie is to receive maximum benefit from the center's programs.''

For a moment, Letitia simply stared, dumbfounded. Then she burst into laughter, surprising both Larkin and herself. ''I'm sorry,'' she said, struggling for control. ''I know you're trying to help, but Mannie is only here now because I didn't give him a choice. Getting him to come back on his own…well, let's just say it would be easier to pull teeth with tweezers.''

''Maybe,'' Larkin said, smiling serenely. ''But if he does choose to come back, can we count on your help?''

A knowing gleam in his eyes gave Letitia pause. Her smile faded into a worried frown. "I wouldn't know what to do. I'm not qualified."

"You have great instincts and you care," Larkin told her. "Those are the best credentials in the world for working with kids."

"I don't know..." She was weakening and he knew it.

"Just think about it, okay? We'll talk later, when I bring Mannie home."

"You don't have to do that."

"I don't mind. Besides, it'll give Mannie and I a chance to get acquainted."

"I see. And with which of your sales pitches do you plan to acquaint him?"

Larkin's sheepish grin did odd things to her heart. "Say, you're pretty sharp. Okay, okay. I promise not to browbeat the boy, but you have to make a promise, too."

"What kind of promise?" she asked, instantly wary.

"That you'll allow Mannie to join the program if that's what he decides to do."

Letitia hesitated, then gave in. "Sure, why not?" Despite a certainty that Mannie would adamantly refuse to set foot in the center again, Larkin's enthusiasm was so contagious that she secretly hoped she was wrong.

Until recently, she hadn't believed her son needed the kind of intense supervision and counseling the center offered. After all, Mannie was never left alone after school, as were many of his peers. Instead, he was greeted by a doting grandmother who filled him with homemade snacks and granted his every wish until Letitia, the killjoy, returned home and asked to see his homework.

For years, the system had worked beautifully. Over the past few months, Letitia had noticed Mannie taking frequent advantage of Mama Rose, who refused to admit that the grandson she adored had become increasingly unruly and disobedient.

Perhaps it was time to try something else.

"So, when is dinner?" Larkin asked, breaking into her thoughts.

"Excuse me?"

"Mannie doesn't seem the type who'd appreciate missing a meal," he explained. "I just wondered what time I should bring him home."

"Whenever it's convenient. It's not fair to make you late for dinner, either."

"My dinner, if one can call it that, is tucked in the freezer, patiently awaiting the fatal moment when I decide to nuke it into oblivion."

"Maybe your wife will surprise you with a pot roast."

Larkin gave her a stunned look. "That really would be a surprise, considering the fact that she lives in Iowa. We've been divorced for three years."

"Oh, I'm sorry," Letitia murmured, her heart leaping like a happy frog. "In that case, perhaps you'd like to join us for dinner. I can't promise pot roast, of course, but—"

"I'd love to."

"You would?"

"Absolutely. The human body can only suffer through a finite number of frozen dinners before it withers and dies. So in a very real sense, you'd actually be saving my life."

"Well, then." She swallowed hard, wondering if she'd really invited a virtual stranger to dinner and if said stranger had truly accepted. "What time?"

"Is eight too late?"

"Eight is fine."

Larkin opened the door for her. "I'll see you then. And Letitia?" When she glanced over her shoulder, he gave her a smile warm enough to fuel a small city. "Thanks again."

"It's my pleasure. Well, I'd better get to the market. I have some shopping to do." With a cheerful wave, Letitia glided gracefully out of the youth center. Then she panicked.

* * *

Around seven-thirty, Larkin made arrangements to have a volunteer lock up at closing time, then wandered out back to check on Mannie's progress. What he saw would have amazed the boy's mother; Larkin, however, was only mildly amused and not the least bit surprised.

Every trace of midnight artistry had been covered by a fresh coat of paint and six youngsters were busily washing paint rollers with a hose. In the midst of the sloppy chore was Mannie Cervantes, laughing with his new pals and bearing no resemblance whatsoever to the bleak-eyed, grim-faced kid who'd death marched to a grisly fate less than three hours ago.

A lanky redhead with a half-shaved scalp spotted Larkin and called out, "Yo G!"—rap slang for "hello," although no one, including the users, were willing to reveal what the *G* stood for. Larkin, however, responded with a raised hand gesture that meant basically the same thing.

The redheaded teenager loped over, grinning. "Everything's good to go, man. Little dude had it going on, but me and the squad fell in to chill it down, y'know?"

Roughly translated, the boy had informed Larkin that the chore was now finished, adding that Mannie had done a good job but he and his friends had pitched in to speed things up.

Larkin gave a nod of approval. "Thanks, Mick. I knew I could count on you."

"No blow, bro'." Mick glanced over his shoulder and spoke to a teenager with shoulders the size of Montana. "Hey, homes, I'm foldin'. Wanna bounce?"

"Yeah." After tossing a damp roller into the pile, the youth wiped his face with a paisley bandanna, cast a wistful glance at the freshly painted wall and turned to Mannie. "Those were fly 'toons, man."

Blustered by the unexpected compliment, Mannie stammered, "Y-you mean you liked 'em?"

The youth shrugged. "Yeah, why not?"

"Gee, thanks. I mean, uh, peace up, homes." Mannie held up an awkward hand, which the husky youngster high-fived before joining his pals and disappearing into the building.

Flushed with excitement, Mannie rushed over to Larkin as fast as his bum leg would carry him. "Wow...that was so awesome."

Larkin laughed. "May I assume, then, that you found the afternoon somewhat enjoyable?"

"It was great! Mick and Snooker and Big'un and the other guys were so cool. They even said I could hang with them."

"They're good kids," Larkin agreed. "I'm glad you all hit it off."

"Yeah, I like Mick. He's a...a..." After a moment's concentration, Mannie brightened. "He's a real humming duck."

Not wanting to shake the boy's blossoming confidence, Larkin managed to conceal a snort of surprised laughter with a cough. "I'm not sure Mick would appreciate being called an ugly woman who smells bad," he told the crest-fallen boy. "Don't worry. Any new language takes prac-tice. In a few weeks, you'll be driving your mother crazy because she won't understand a word you say."

Now that was incentive. "Do you really think so?" Mannie asked, his eyes huge.

"I guarantee it." Larkin laid a hand on the boy's shoul-der. "We'd better get going. Your mom is going to have dinner on the table at eight sharp and I promised we'd be there on time."

"We?" Mannie jerked to a stop. "Mom didn't ask you to eat with us, did she?"

"As a matter of fact, she did." Larkin frowned, realiz-ing that Mannie might resent the intrusion. "Is that a prob-lem?"

Covering his eyes, the boy shook his shaggy head and moaned. "This is Wednesday."

"Does that make a difference?"

"Nana plays bingo on Wednesday."

The significance of that statement escaped Larkin, and he said so.

Mannie heaved a long-suffering sigh. "When Nana plays bingo, Mom hasta' cook."

"Ah." Larkin was beginning to get the message. "I take it cooking isn't your mother's finest talent?"

"Mostly she does okay with hamburgers and stuff, but if she tries to get fancy on account of having company and all—" Suddenly the boy's eyes widened as if he'd been struck by a horrible thought. "Mom didn't say nothing about goin' shopping, did she?"

"Well . . . actually, she did."

Mannie slid Larkin a woeful look. "Man, we're in big trouble."

Chapter Three

"I hope you're hungry. I made enough for a small army."

As Letitia retrieved a shallow casserole from the oven, an indefinable aroma wafted through the kitchen. At the table, Larkin exchanged a wary glance with the boy seated beside him. "It, ah, smells wonderful."

Mannie rolled his eyes. "It smells, all right— Ouch!"

Letitia set the hot dish on the stove, yanking off her oven mitt as she glanced happily over her shoulder. "What did you say, sweetie?"

"Nothin'," Mannie muttered, rubbing the sore spot where Larkin's elbow had connected with his ribs. "I didn't say nothin'."

Rasputin, lurking by the stove in hopes of catching a tasty tidbit, sniffed the air, whined, and skulked out of the room.

Larkin was beginning to wonder if Mannie's assessment of his mother's culinary skills had been accurate. Absently fingering a bowl of sweetener packets, he cleared his throat and managed to sound unconcerned. "Is there something I can help you with?"

"Not a thing," came the cheery reply. "We can dig in as soon as the rice is done." A hiss of steam puffed from a saucepan. Lifting the lid, she angled a triumphant smile over her shoulder. "Gentlemen, dinner is served."

Mannie heaved a sigh of regret.

"I tried something different," Letitia said, spooning the colorful pilaf into a serving bowl. "Since we're having fish as a main course—" The spoon hovered over the pan as she gave Larkin a worried glance. "You do like fish, don't you?"

He assured her that he did.

Looking massively relieved, she returned to her chore. "Anyway, it occurred to me that rice cooked in water would be, well, boring. I wanted to use fish stock, but all the market had was canned chicken broth, so I improvised."

At the final word, Mannie emitted a low moan which irritated Larkin and made him feel oddly protective. "Creativity is the mark of a good chef," he announced, fixing his reluctant table companion with a defiant stare. "Besides, chicken broth is frequently used as a substitute for fish stock."

"Oh, I didn't use chicken broth," Letitia said as she placed a reeking bowl of rice on the table. "I bought canned clams and drained the juice."

Avoiding Mannie's smug grin, Larkin fought a gag reflex until his eyes watered. "That was very, ah, clever."

Letitia's cheeks pinked at the praise. "I hope you like it."

Neither Larkin nor Mannie could manage a response. Instead, they watched with a combination of hope and trepidation as she retrieved the main course, which had been cooling atop the stove.

Letitia set the casserole on the table with a worried frown and a caveat. "It didn't turn out exactly like the picture, but

I followed the directions to the letter, so it should taste okay."

Larkin thought she mumbled, "I hope," under her breath, although his complete attention was focused on the casserole's contents—withered pink chunks floating in curdled milk. He was, of course, much too courteous to inquire as to the source of those unidentifiable chunks.

Mannie, however, had no such inhibition. He leaned over the table, staring into the bowl with an incredulous expression. "What is *that?*"

"Scalloped salmon." Letitia slid into her chair, looking a little nervous. "It's supposed to be a European delicacy."

The boy reared away from the dish as if expecting something to emerge and attack. "It looks like roadkill."

Larkin would have thrown the boy a warning look except he couldn't take his own eyes off the casserole. And he had to admit, something in there *did* appear to be moving.

Whatever it was landed on his plate as Letitia ladled him a gigantic portion, then repeated the favor for her son, who had paled three shades and appeared ready to pass out. After dishing up the smelly rice, she delicately spread her napkin in her lap, and gave them a tense smile. "Well, *bon appétit.*"

Larkin took a deep breath and gingerly poked his fork into the pilaf. If one ignored the aroma, it didn't really look too bad so he took a small bite. Unfortunately, it tasted exactly like it smelled.

A furtive glance across the table revealed that Letitia, too, had started with the rice. Her eyes widened in shock; her jaw froze; her lips twisted. With a strained grimace, she managed to swallow and reached casually for her water glass, a glaring contrast to Larkin's panicked grab and gulp technique.

She sipped lightly, then replaced the glass and stared down at her plate. "Perhaps clam juice wasn't such a good idea after all."

Larkin opened his mouth to dispute that, but realized that even if he could think of something soothing to say, his tongue had gone into shock, rendering him momentarily mute.

Fortunately, the doorbell chose that moment to ring. Mannie leaned his chair back on two legs, lifted the curtain and peered out the kitchen window. "It's the paper boy."

"It must be collection day." Letitia laid her napkin on the table and rose graciously. "I'll just be a moment."

Larkin hoisted his fork and smiled. The moment she disappeared into the living room, he and Mannie exchanged a telling look, then grabbed their plates and nearly knocked each other over trying to reach the sink.

Five minutes later, Letitia returned to find two empty plates and a matching pair of relieved expressions. Mannie leaned back, patting his stomach. "Man, I'm stuffed."

"I couldn't eat another bite," Larkin agreed, unable to meet her stunned gaze.

She stood there for a moment, hands clasped, eyes wide. Then she sighed and reached for the telephone. "What kind?"

"The usual," Mannie said, tossing a crumpled napkin on the table. Then he hopped up and ambled into the living room while his mother ordered pizza.

"Last piece, Raspy," Mannie said, dangling a pepperoni round in front of the dog's pointed little snout. "Chow down."

Having already eaten the equivalent of two doggy-size slices, Rasputin gave the meat a halfhearted sniff, emitted a squeaky burp and toddled over to his tiny, beanbag bed. Mannie shrugged, popping the rejected pepperoni in his own mouth. He mumbled, "Got homework," between chews, then headed to his bedroom.

From her post at the kitchen sink, Letitia didn't look up from the satisfying chore of jamming the final morsels of scalloped salmon and rice into the garbage disposal. She flipped the switch, muttering, "Rest in peace," as the disposal whirred away every trace of her latest disaster.

Behind her, Larkin dumped the pile of paper plates and empty pizza box into the trash. He eyed the stuffed container. "Is there somewhere I can empty this?"

"Hmm? Oh, Mannie will take it out in the morning. That's one of his chores."

"Well, I certainly wouldn't want to intrude on his chores."

She smiled, feeling foolish. Despite the man's good humor, she knew perfectly well that the entire evening had been a disaster. "Are you still hungry? I have cookies or something—"

"No, thanks. I'm fine."

Letitia doubted that. The poor guy had wolfed down half a pizza and she suspected that only good manners kept him from claiming even more. She'd never seen anyone with such an appetite. Too bad she hadn't managed to provide a meal worth eating.

Sniffing the rancid air, she then grabbed a can of air freshener to give the kitchen its third spritz of the evening. The scent of fishy potpourri wasn't wonderful, but it was somewhat better than the alternative. From the corner of her eye, she caught Larkin struggling to suppress a smile. "Go ahead and say it," she said with a sigh. "I can take an enormous amount of ridicule."

"Effort should never be ridiculed."

"I nearly poisoned you. Surely, you have one or two comments about that."

He slid easily back into his chair. "Actually, I'm flattered that you went to so much trouble in the first place."

Letitia looked up from the coffee she was pouring. "I was trying to impress you."

"Oh, you did." He accepted the steaming mug with a grateful smile. "In more ways than one."

"I'll bet." Joining him at the table, she emptied two packs of sweetener into her own coffee. "Next time, I'll stick to one of my tried-and-true specialties."

"Which are?"

"Meat that can be fried and any side dish that comes in a box. I'm the queen of packaged macaroni and cheese."

He chuckled. "I like macaroni and cheese."

"So do we, fortunately." She concentrated on toying with her coffee mug because every time she looked up, those Newman blue eyes were gazing right at her, sending her poor heart into convulsive palpitation. "Anyway, I prefer to devote my energy to things that I'm good at."

"Such as?"

She didn't have to look up to know that he was grinning at her. "Well, let's see. I love knitting, crochet and embroidery, but I hate mending, and absolutely refuse to darn socks. If something needs a button, I'll consider it but anything with a serious hole gets tossed out."

"Sounds reasonable. What else?"

"I like crossword puzzles, but won't play Scrabble—"

He stiffened. "I love Scrabble."

"Then you and Rose should hit it off. She's the house champ. I, on the other hand, panic at the sight of a Q tile, but I'm pretty good with routine house maintenance like minor carpentry and plumbing. Electrical stuff I leave to the pros, but gas engines and I get along fine. If your carburetor ever clogs up, give me a call."

He hiked a brow. "Do you do transmissions?"

"Sorry."

"Pity." He heaved an exaggerated sigh and sipped his coffee.

Feeling comfortable now, Letitia scrutinized the attractive man seated across from her and was surprised to realize how much she liked him. Larkin McKay was friendly and warm, with a quirky sense of humor that she found particularly appealing. He was, she decided, an excellent role model for her son. "So, besides being gastronomically stoic, what other outstanding traits do you have?"

A snort of tickled laughter sent a spritz of coffee dribbling down his chin. He set the mug down, dabbing the moisture with the back of his hand. "I'm not sure I have any outstanding traits."

"Now, Dr. McKay, don't be modest."

"In thirty-one years of living, I've been accused of many things. Modesty has never been one of them. Now you've used that word twice in one day, which can only mean that your judgment is much too generous."

"Perhaps I simply recognize something that others have overlooked." Tilting her head, she fixed him with a deliberate gaze that made him squirm, which seemed fair enough considering how often he'd done the same to her. Somehow, she took no pleasure from reversing the situation and was oddly perturbed at herself for having unnerved him. She glanced away, as much to give herself space as to alleviate his discomfort. "So, do you like sports?"

He replied quickly, sounding relieved by the change in subject. "I like basketball."

"Really?" She chanced a quick glance and saw that he did seem more relaxed. "Mannie's a football freak. He used to play all the time, until his friends grew old enough to take the game seriously."

"His disability became an issue?"

She shrugged, trying to suppress her anger at the memory of how they'd taunted him off the team. "As little boys, they didn't care that Mannie couldn't run as fast or kick as hard. As big boys, they did."

Larkin pursed his lips as if considering a question he was reluctant to ask.

Assuming he was curious about her son's physical problem, Letitia volunteered the information. "Mannie was born with a hip malformation," she explained. "He's had several surgeries over the years, each of which has helped immensely, but what he really needs is a hip replacement and that's best left until he stops growing.''

An empathetic sadness softened Larkin's gaze. He spoke gently, with deep feeling. ''It must have been difficult for him, being ostracized by kids who had once been friends and coming to terms with the fact that he was different.''

Letitia simply nodded.

Larkin was silent for a moment, staring off into space as if lost in his own little world. After a moment, he spoke, but his gaze was still locked somewhere in the past. ''All kids want to belong,'' he said softly. ''That's a normal part of growing up, but for physically challenged children, the quest to fit in can become a desperate obsession. They deny their limitations by pushing themselves, engaging in activities they know are dangerous but they're so eager for acceptance by their peers, that magical, all-consuming prize, that they're willing to risk everything, even their lives, to achieve it.''

There was a whisper of experience in his voice and an exquisite loneliness in his eyes that touched Letitia to the core. ''You sound like a man who has been there.''

''Hmm?'' He blinked, as if surprised by her presence, then managed a slow, sad smile. ''No, not me. A friend, someone I knew a long time ago. Mannie reminds me of him.''

Struck by the poignancy in his eyes, Letitia wanted to know more about this oblique, long-ago friend but sensed that the subject was one Larkin wasn't prepared to explore. As his mind had wandered into the past, the humorous sparkle had drained from his eyes, replaced by a sorrow so deep, so moving that Letitia had been shaken to her toes.

Apparently Larkin recognized her discomfort. He shifted in his chair, forced a thin smile and said, ''Hey, weren't we talking about hobbies?''

''Yes, I believe we were.'' Letitia reluctantly returned her focus to the original topic. ''All right then, what other sports do you like? Besides basketball, of course.''

He feigned shock. "There *are* no other sports besides basketball."

"So that's it—work and basketball? How dull."

"I beg your pardon, but I'll have you know that I'm a fascinating person who leads a rich and varied life."

Smiling, she leaned forward and called his bluff. "Consisting of?"

"Well . . ." He paused to wipe a grease spot off the laminated table top. "Did I mention Scrabble?"

"Uh-huh."

"And basketball?"

"Several times." She shook her head, tsking. "Basketball and Scrabble. Well, I'm certainly impressed."

"Wait a minute. I'm thinking." Closing his eyes, he touched his index fingers to his temples and emitted a godawful monotone hum that reminded her of an off-key Gregorian chant. After a moment, he stopped humming and looked at her. "I'm pretty good at Donkey Kong."

"Is that one of those video games at the youth center?" When he indicated that it was, she responded with an indifferent wave. "That's work, and work doesn't count."

"Oh." He squeezed his eyelids shut, tighter this time.

"You're not going to hum, are you?"

One eye opened. "I was thinking about it."

"Must you?"

"Yes, I must."

She flicked her wrist. "Carry on, then."

He did, deliberately embellishing his hum with a *waa-waa* sound that tickled her immensely. Just as her amused chuckle broke free, Larkin sighed, dropped his hands to the table and spoke with exaggerated gravity. "That's it, then. The only other hobby I have—and you're not going to like this—is the practice of, ahem, the culinary arts."

She stared in astonishment. "Cooking?"

He nodded. "I'm quite good at it."

She sat like a stone before tossing her hands in frustration. "Oh, well, that really tears it. Tonight's disaster would have been bad enough with a normal person—"

"What do you mean, normal?"

"—but I have to humiliate myself in front of a closet gourmet. What else could possibly go wrong?"

"Actually, I've been out of the gourmet closet for some time—"

"I don't believe this." She fixed him with a squinty-eyed stare. "Are you telling me you can actually prepare an edible coq au vin?"

"Of course, although I use coq au vin as a base for more complex creations, sort of like a wine-based chicken roux—"

"Enough!" Pushing away from the table, she blurted, "This is all Rose's fault."

Taken aback, Larkin could do little more than ask the obvious question. "What is Rose's fault?"

"My lack of epicurean skills," Letitia explained, primly brushing the bodice of her silky blouse. "After all, if Rose hadn't been such a wonderful cook, we might have divided household chores differently and I would have been forced to expand my kitchen repertoire. So you see, I can't possibly be held accountable for what happened tonight."

Chuckling, Larkin draped a lazy arm over the back of the chair. "Oddly enough, that makes sense. Scary, isn't it?"

No longer able to maintain her fake indignation, Letitia leaned back and laughed. "Had you going, didn't I?"

"Does that mean that you don't blame your poor mother-in-law for the clam juice?"

"Of course I blame her. You don't think I'm going to take responsibility for something that stupid, do you?"

"I certainly wouldn't."

"Well then, there you have it."

Larkin leaned back, smiling, with a gleam in his eye that could have been interpreted as admiration. "One of the things that surprised me most about your family was the love and mutual respect you share."

"Why would that surprise you?"

"When several generations share a home, there's frequently a great deal of friction. It's commendable that you and Rose have negotiated an agreement that works for everyone."

"Rose is a jewel," Letitia murmured. "She was my rock when Ray died. She's been my best friend ever since. I don't know what Mannie and I would do without her."

Larkin sipped his coffee, seeming lost in thought. After a moment, he broke the comfortable silence that had settled between them. "How long has your husband been gone?"

"Over four years." Propping her elbows on the table, she lifted her coffee mug as if to shield painful memories. "One day he was a robust, healthy 28-year-old. The next, he was in a hospital bed, dying." The mug trembled in her hands. She set it firmly on the table. "Something burst inside his heart. The doctors think he might have suffered a childhood injury that weakened one of the aortic valves."

"I'm sorry," Larkin said. "That must have been a horrible shock."

"Rose and Mannie were devastated."

He leaned forward, regarding her thoughtfully. "What about you, Letitia, what were you feeling?"

"Nothing," she replied softly. "I died with him."

For several long seconds, a melancholy hush shrouded the room. After hours of animated conversation, there was suddenly nothing to say. Letitia felt all weepy inside, as she always did when thoughts turned to her husband's tragic loss, but this time she was aggravated at herself.

Across the table, Larkin was watching her quietly, sending invisible waves of sympathy that seemed strangely tangible. His silent understanding was more healing than a dictionary of spoken words. She was grateful, deeply grate-

ful, but also determined not to inflict a maudlin theme into
what had been an otherwise enjoyable evening.

Forcing a bright smile, she hopped up from her chair.
"Are you sure you don't want some dessert? If you don't
like cookies, I think there's a box of instant pudding in the
pantry."

"No, thanks." Larkin stood. "It's getting late. I should
be going." The news was unduly disappointing, considering the hour. Letitia was buoyed when he added, "I've had
a lovely evening. I hope you'll allow me to return the favor."

"You bet."

Their gazes held for a moment before Larkin looked
away, pushing his chair up to the table with a scrape that
rousted the sleeping dog. Rasputin yawned, hopped out of
bed and followed the humans into the living room.

Larkin paused by the coffee table, angling a smug glance
at their tiny canine shadow. He pulled a polished whistle out
of his pocket, winked at Letitia, then carefully laid the shiny
object on the exact spot where Rose had placed the bandage box last night.

Bewildered, Letitia started to question the odd behavior
but Larkin touched a finger to his lips, silencing her. He
nodded toward the kitchen door, where Rasputin was lurking with bright little eyes. "So, all you have to do is sign
Mannie's blue card and make sure he brings it whenever he
comes to the center."

"All right." She cast a furtive glance over her shoulder in
time to see a fat ball of hair belly across the carpet and slink
behind the couch. "I still can't figure out how you talked
Mannie into joining."

"He made a lot of friends today." Larkin, too, was
watching the crafty animal weave his way toward the coffee
table. "They had more to do with his decision than I did."

"It's amazing," Letitia murmured, her gaze riveted on the whistle. "Who'd have thought that kids would have given up play time to help a boy they'd never even met before."

"Youngsters can be very generous." He'd barely finished speaking when Rasputin suddenly leapt out from behind the couch, claimed the shiny prize and scurried down the hall. Larkin laughed. "There. Now the little duffer won't feel left out."

Letitia shook her head. "You're encouraging him to be a thief."

"He was always a thief. I'm just controlling the loot." He took Letitia's hand as if to shake it, but simply held it instead. "So, I'll see you Friday at the center?"

A frisson of doubt skittered down her spine. The concept of supervising dozens of exuberant youngsters was daunting, particularly when she was beginning to doubt her ability to control her own son. But Larkin's enthusiasm was contagious and she heard herself say, "I'll be there."

Then, with a pleased smile and a whispered, "Good night," he was gone.

Letitia was alone with her memories. And her doubts.

Larkin twisted the key and stepped into darkness. He hated darkness in a room or in a mind. As he fumbled for the switch, his fingers shook a little. They always did, until he flipped the smooth plastic lever and every lamp in the apartment glowed with reassurance.

Then he felt better.

Discomfort with darkness—he was loath to call it fear— had been a constant companion since his time at Blackthorn Hall. Rationally, he realized it was a normal reaction to the trauma of having been incarcerated in a four-by-four concrete vault known as the Box. After confessing and taking responsibility for the "Nazi" vandalism, Larkin thought he'd spent two days there, but it might have been three. There was no way to be certain. Time didn't exist without sunlight and stars, and he'd been too numbed by grief to care. He had, in fact, welcomed the cruel punishment. It had been no less than he'd deserved.

If not for Larkin, Tommy would have lived to chase his dreams, to grow and prosper, to experience love. If not for Larkin, the Brotherhood would still be complete.

As always, guilt turned his gaze toward the breakfast bar, where he focused on the ever present bottle of bourbon and sparkling shot glass which stood at the ready. Habit directed him toward the bourbon, a bracing ritual for the nightmares to come, nightmares that were inevitable except for those times when sleep eluded him completely.

But tonight as he reached for the bottle, an unexpected image appeared in his mind, an amusing recollection of Letitia's first taste of clammy rice.

Larkin smiled then chuckled aloud, recalling her expression of shock and chagrin. Lord, she'd been adorable. He had to admit that under a most trying circumstance, she'd managed to handle herself with admirable restraint. Most people would have been mortified to the bone by such a blatant social faux pas; she, however, had used humor to turn an extremely uncomfortable situation into an experience that was amusing and, eventually, enjoyable.

The evening was, in fact, one of the most delightful he'd spent in years. He'd actually been comfortable, physically and psychologically. When they'd all been seated around the table, laughing and arguing over the last piece of pizza, Larkin had felt more emotionally complete, more comfortably at home than he could ever remember. Even in his own house, surrounded by his wife and the children he adored, Larkin couldn't remember feeling so totally at ease.

Which was certainly a sobering thought.

Why was it, he wondered, that he hadn't ever realized how much tension had permeated his marriage? Perhaps because he'd never known anything else. All he recalled of early childhood were snippets of bitter parents locked in a constant state of feud. After their divorce, his mother moved him into a strange house, where he was ignored by a coldly arrogant stepfather and tormented by hostile stepsiblings who considered him an unwelcome interloper.

It didn't take a genius to ascertain that Larkin had spent much of his life obsessed with creating what he'd so desperately craved as a child—a happy, secure family life. That had been his number one priority when he'd married his college sweetheart and they'd happily started a family of their own.

Then things had gone terribly wrong. To this day, Larkin didn't understand why; he did, however, realize that since he felt responsible for his parents' divorce and subsequent problems with his stepfamily, he'd probably been responsible for the collapse of his own marriage as well. Which was, of course, the reason he'd made the perfectly rational decision to avoid future emotional entanglements like the proverbial plague. It was a decision he'd neither recanted nor regretted until last night, when he'd first laid eyes on Letitia Cervantes.

He could still smell the exotic fragrance of her hair, still see the mischievous sparkle in her dark, bedroom eyes. She was a rare beauty, but beyond physical perfection, she possessed traits of more eminent value—a loving heart and a generous soul. She was without doubt a most extraordinary woman—

The telephone rang, jarring him from his pleasant mental sojourn. Annoyed, he strode to the living room, snatched up the receiver and snapped a less than gracious, "Hello."

"So the wandering headshrinker has finally returned. I was beginning to think you'd given up on your apartment and decided to roll out a sleeping bag on your office floor."

"The thought has crossed my mind," Larkin replied, instantly cheered. "Until then, my real friends use the answering machine."

"Hell," Devon snorted. "You don't have any real friends."

"Then I guess I'll stick with you and Bobby." Shifting the phone, Larkin flopped on the sofa and kicked off his loafers. "So, what's happening?"

"Not much. Oh, by the way, Jessica wanted me to thank you for the Christmas gift."

Larkin laughed out loud. "So, you didn't have one already?"

"No, oddly enough, yours was the only bronze-plated hockey puck we received."

"Good. Two would be ostentatious." Larkin sat up long enough to rearrange a throw pillow behind his neck. "I figured you could keep it in your trophy case, next to the Pulitzer," he added, referring to the prestigious award Devon earned during his years as a war correspondent. Now, as a celebrated journalist for the *Los Angeles Times,* he was well on his way to a second nomination. "I figured that if you're ever tempted to believe your own bio, the hockey puck will remind you of what your friends think."

A hearty chuckle filtered over the line. "In that case, I'm surprised you didn't bronze an anatomical replica."

"I tried, but the sculptor refused. He said it was too lewd."

"Ah. Well, it's the thought that counts. And while we're on the subject of lewdness, what are we going to do about a bachelor bash for Bobby?"

"How about the usual?"

"I doubt he'd appreciate being blindfolded, stripped to his skivvies and tied to a palm tree."

"Neither did you, but that didn't stop us."

"True, but it's winter now and Erica would skin us alive if her beloved spent their honeymoon cuddled up with a box of tissue, sipping cough medicine instead of champagne." A background voice caught Devon's attention. "Okay, sugar. Drive carefully. Love you."

"I love you, too," Larkin cooed.

"Cute, birdman. Jessie has to go into the office for a few hours. She said to say, 'hi.'" There was a shuffling sound, as if Devon was shifting the telephone. "Anyway, I figured we'd better plan something a little more low-key. Bobby's name has been on the front page long enough."

Although disappointed, Larkin had to agree. To the world, their little Bobby was known as Roberto Arroya, the Elliott Ness of federal prosecutors, who was faster than a speeding racketeer and able to leap crooked politicians with a single bound. "Okay, so we'll come up with something else. There's plenty of time."

"I don't know, man. The wedding's only a few weeks away. Which reminds me, you should order your tux."

Larkin groaned. "Tell you what, why don't you just tie *me* to the freaking palm tree?"

"Quit your complaining. You always start out with a snivel and a moan, then end up with females tripping over each other to get your attention."

"It's a curse," Larkin agreed. "I was thinking this time I might, umm, bring somebody…just to keep the love-struck stampede under control."

After a stunned silence, Devon's incredulous voice vibrated through the receiver. "You mean, an actual date?"

"Well, I don't know if you could call it that—"

"Good Lord, man, it's about time. Who is this amazing goddess and why in hell haven't I heard about her?"

"Oh, for crying out loud." Larkin pinched the bridge of his nose, wishing to high heaven that he'd kept his mouth shut. Both Devon and Roberto had been prodding him to start dating again but despite the fact that it had been three long years since the divorce, Larkin hadn't been ready. He still wasn't.

He was, however, ready for friendship with a person of genuine affinity. The fact that this person happened to be of the female persuasion was pure happenstance. "She's the mother of one of the center's kids," he told Devon. "Just a very nice lady who works hard to support her family. I thought she might enjoy a day off and a little fun, that's all."

"Yeah, right."

Rankled by Devon's smug tone, Larkin switched back to a safer topic. "Anyway, I'll give some thought to Bobby's bash and see what I can come up with. Oops...got another call."

"What call? I didn't hear any click—"

"There it goes again." Larkin tapped the hook button to simulate a clicking sound. "Gotta go."

"Wait a minute—"

Smothering a guilty twinge, Larkin smoothly cradled the receiver. He'd call Devon at the office tomorrow and make amends. Who knows, maybe by then one of them would come up with an alternative to the prewedding prank that had been a Brotherhood tradition since his own marriage nine years earlier.

At the moment, however, fatigue settled over him like a warm blanket. Forgetting the untouched whiskey on the counter, Larkin wiggled his stocking-clad toes, tossed a forearm over his eyes, and drifted off to sleep.

That night, his mind didn't relive Tommy's death. That night, he dreamed of a dark-eyed woman. And that night, for the first time in years, Larkin slept without fear.

Chapter Four

Perched in the window seat of the living room's bay window, Letitia watched Larkin send a smooth, spiral pass down the cul-de-sac toward Mannie. The boy stuttered sideways before reaching up to snag the football in midair. Larkin grinned, gave a thumbs-up signal, then loped down the street. After a congratulatory backslap, he demonstrated how to arc the caught ball into a secure body tuck.

Or at least that's what Letitia thought he was doing, since everything she knew about football could be stuffed in a thimble with room left over. On the subject of her son, however, she was an expert; it didn't take a mother's love to recognize the joy sparkling in Mannie's young eyes. He was clearly having the time of his life.

"The kitchen is clean," Rose announced from the doorway. "Mr. McKay's cooking utensils are in a bag on the table."

Letitia glanced over her shoulder. "You didn't have to do that, Mama."

"Someone had to," she replied, methodically wiping her hands on a tea towel. "Such a mess. One would think the pope had come to breakfast."

"It was brunch, not breakfast, and I told you I'd clean up the kitchen." Swinging her foot to the floor, Letitia shifted to face her inexplicably annoyed mother-in-law. "When I mentioned to Larkin that you always prepared a big meal after church, he thought you'd enjoy having someone else cook for a change. He thought...we both thought it would be a nice treat for you."

Rose stared at her hands for a moment, then tossed the towel over her shoulder. "The food was strange. Why does he cook eggs in pudding bowls?"

"They were baked eggs, Mama, and he used custard cups so each egg would cook in its own seasoning. Besides, they looked pretty that way, don't you think?"

She shrugged. "They looked like eggs in pudding bowls."

"Mama—"

"But if you want your eggs in a bowl, I will cook them that way. You don't have to bring strangers in to do it."

Letitia stood, stunned. "Larkin's hardly a stranger."

"A man I do not know is a stranger," she insisted, then lifted her chin. "I thought you liked scrambled eggs, *nuera,* that's why I fix them so often. If you want something else, tell me. I can make spinach souffle or potato pancakes that look like lace doilies, and if biscuits taste better in the shape of little submarines, I can do that, too."

"Of course you can. You're a magnificent cook." Sighing, Letitia massaged her forehead. "I'm sorry, Mama, I never meant to hurt your feelings. When I asked Larkin to—"

"*You* asked?"

Letitia looked up. "He wanted to take us out for brunch, but since you don't usually care for restaurant food, I thought you'd enjoy this more. Besides, I was, well, curious. He claimed to be such a gourmet and after I'd made a darned fool of myself trying to show off last week, I guess I thought he might have been exaggerating and, uh—'' She coughed lightly, then managed a sheepish smile.

Rose's frown melted into a knowing nod. ''You were hoping to call his bluff, hmm?''

''Something like that. Unfortunately, he's every bit as good as he said, so when it comes to humiliating epicurean blunders, my Scalloped Salmon Surprise is still at the top of the list.'' Letitia glanced through the window, assuring herself that Larkin was still out front before adding, ''The truth is, Mama, I really do prefer my eggs scrambled. Please don't tell him, though. He worked so hard.''

Finally, the woman's lips loosened into a maternal smile. ''I won't tell.'' Just then, a raucous cheer from the yard drew both women's attention. Rose crossed the room, peering over Letitia's shoulder. ''What is happening out there?''

''Football is happening.'' Grinning, Letitia stepped aside and slid an arm around Rose, drawing her closer to the window. ''Look at Mannie's face, Mama. How long has it been since you've seen him so happy?''

As Rose watched the frolicking males, a wistful expression crossed her face. ''Is that his father's football?''

''Yes.'' Letitia's reply was tempered by caution, along with the realization that Rose must be remembering years gone by, when Ray had taught his young son to hold the same football. At that time, the ball had been much too large for the boy's tiny hands, but his father had been undaunted. Despite Mannie's small size and restrictive disability, Ray, who'd made the varsity team in his sophomore year, had been determined to pass his own love of the game on to his son. And he'd succeeded.

A lump formed in Letitia's throat. Mannie missed his father so very, very much.

Rose suddenly straightened and stepped away from the window. ''It's cold outside. Manuel should be wearing his jacket.''

Before Letitia could respond, the woman crossed the living room and disappeared into the kitchen. In a moment, the back door opened signaling that Rose had gone into the backyard, probably to tend her garden.

Sighing, Letitia slumped down on the window seat, cursing her own insensitivity. She should have realized her mother-in-law would be unnerved by the sight of another man playing with her grandson. Although Letitia certainly wasn't going to discourage Larkin McKay or anyone else willing to indulge Mannie's desperate need for the attention and companionship of an adult male, Rose's feelings had to be taken into consideration. How that could be done without infringing on Mannie's right to play ball in his own front yard, now that was a dilemma.

But since said dilemma couldn't be solved in the next five minutes, Letitia slipped on a sweater and went outside to join the fun.

Waving from the sidewalk, she caught Larkin's eye. He straightened and waved back, grinning. He was still looking at her when the football bounced off his chest. Staggering backward, he rubbed his breastbone, looking surprised, then embarrassed.

Frustrated, Mannie jammed his hands on his hips. "Aw, man, that was a dying quail. How could you miss it?"

"Guess I got sidetracked." As Larkin scooped up the ball, he angled a furtive glance toward the sidewalk. She was still there, so fresh and beautiful that she took his breath away. He'd have liked to pretend his lungs had been deflated by the errant football rather than her beauty, but the sassy gleam in her eyes revealed that she hadn't been fooled.

Larkin still had the ball tucked under his arm when Mannie, following his gaze, turned to look over his shoulder and saw his mother standing there. "Hey, Mom! Watch this."

Signaling for a high pass, Mannie hunched forward, legs spread, balancing his weight on the balls of his feet.

Larkin backpedaled, rotating the ball between his hands until the lace was properly aligned beneath his fingers. "Ready?"

"Gimme a bomb, okay?"

"You got it." Larkin reared back and threw a smooth spiral that arched above the telephone wires, then dived down to burrow straight into Mannie's waiting arms.

"Aw'right!" Mannie hollered, spiking the ball into the pavement and wiggling his butt in an awkward victory dance that made his mother laugh out loud.

Larkin jogged back toward the house. "Good one, tiger."

Mannie stopped dancing as Larkin passed him and headed to the sidewalk. "Are you quitting?"

"Just taking a break," he called back, "Keep the ball warm."

The boy issued a bored sigh and began tossing the ball in the air.

"That was very impressive," Letitia said. "Apparently basketball isn't your only sport after all."

"It's the only one I'm good at, therefore it's the only one that counts."

"I don't know, that looked like a pretty fair throw to me."

"It was adequate." Larkin wiped his forehead with his sleeve and hoped he didn't look as sweaty as he felt. "Mannie's got a good eye, though. He's a talented kid."

"Yes, he is." A cool breeze ruffled her hair. She shook a shiny strand out of her face, turning her head and raking her fingers underneath the shoulder-length mass of wooly dark curls. "Rose was right. Mannie really should be wearing a jacket."

"That's mommy talk," Larkin teased, hoping she hadn't noticed the gooseflesh on his own bare arms. "No macho eleven-year-old would be caught dead in outerwear unless the temperature dips below freezing."

Letitia shivered, crossing the open bodice of her cardigan. "I think it just did."

If Larkin had been sixteen, he would have taken that as a cue to put his arm around her. Then she'd lay her head on his shoulder, where one thing would lead to another and—

He blinked. What on earth was he thinking? This woman, this admittedly lovely woman, had offered him kindness and friendship, and here he was, a grown man suddenly aquiver with adolescent hormones, daydreaming about stealing a kiss. Right here on the sidewalk. In front of her house.

In front of her son.

There was no doubt about it. Larkin McKay, champion of the psychologically challenged, had himself gone stark, raving mad. Celibate insanity, that's what it was. Too many lonely nights; too many cold showers.

A warm hand glided along his arm. "Larkin?"

"Hmm?"

"Are you all right?"

His gaze was riveted on the slender fingers embracing his biceps. "Sure. Never better. Why?"

To his chagrin, she retrieved her hand and tucked it under her sweater. "I don't know. You suddenly looked a little odd."

"I was, ah, thinking."

She brightened. "Oh? About what?"

"About, uh..." *About how that gorgeous hair would look spread out on a pillow.* "Uh...about..."

"You're getting all sweaty. Are you sure you're okay?"

"Fine," he mumbled, praying that the most sensitive part of his anatomy wouldn't react to the erotic images flashing through his mind. He coughed into his hand, peered over his fist and focused on Mannie, who was impatiently passing the football from one hand to the other. His gaze slipped from the boy's bored expression to the T-shirt he wore, another version of the hand-painted attire he'd worn the first night Larkin had seen him.

Since then Larkin had learned that the boy's grand-mother had stenciled much of his wardrobe with rock band logos and vivid replicas of favorite cartoon heroes. "I understand that Rose is quite an artist."

Understandably startled by the abrupt change of subject, Letitia followed his gaze to her son's vivid shirt. "Well, yes, as a matter of fact, she is. She painted the watercolor landscapes in the living room. And the oil portrait of Rasputin, of course."

Now that was news. "I didn't realize she was that good."

"Oh, yes. A couple of Santa Monica galleries carry her work when it's available, although she doesn't paint nearly as much as she used to."

"Why not?"

"I don't know. Rose lost a lot of her sparkle when Ray died. Things that once gave her great joy don't seem to hold her interest anymore."

Larkin rubbed his chin. "Maybe we can do something about that."

Tilting her head, Letitia fixed him with a narrowed gaze. "I'm beginning to recognize that look in your eye. What are you up to, McKay?"

"Who, me? Why, nothing, nothing at all."

Obviously unconvinced, she placed her hands on her hips and tapped an impatient rhythm with her toe.

Larkin shrugged. "Some kids at the center have commented that they'd like to have shirts like Mannie's, that's all. A few have even mentioned that it might be fun to spruce up the activity room with a mural. Nothing fancy, of course, just some, ah, cartoons and the like."

She stared at him as if he'd lost his mind. "You want Rose to make shirts for everyone at the teen center?"

"Of course not," he replied with great indignation. "I would never take that kind of advantage of anyone, let alone a sweet woman like your mother-in-law."

Somewhat mollified, Letitia concentrated on folding the cuff of her sweater. "Well . . . good."

Pushing his advantage, Larkin laid a hand on his chest, feigning distress. "I'm hurt, Letitia, hurt and dismayed that you actually think I'd ask poor Rose to take on such a monumental project all by herself."

"I'm sorry, really, I honestly didn't—" Letitia's eyes widened, then narrowed into slits. "What do you mean, 'by herself'?"

"The kids will do most of the work."

She backed away, warning him with a look. "Don't even think about it."

"But the center needs an art director. Rose is perfect for the job."

"Rose doesn't want a job and she doesn't need one. My salary is more than enough to take care of the family."

"Good, because I can't afford to pay anything."

"Another 'volunteer' position?"

He spread his hands and grinned.

"Rose would never agree." Folding her arms, she hiked her chin and set her mouth in a stubborn line that he found particularly appealing. "Besides, I don't want Mannie coming home to an empty house."

A flick of his wrist dismissed the argument. "Hours are flexible. We'll work something out."

"Larkin—"

"Where is Rose, anyway?"

"In the backyard. Listen, Larkin, she won't do it. Other than church, grocery shopping and bingo, Mama rarely goes out of the house—" Letitia bit off the final word as a dented sedan screeched into the cul-de-sac, raced up the street and squealed to a stop in front of Mannie, who ambled over to talk to a boy leaning out the rear passenger window.

Letitia was instantly tense. "That's Will Doherty. He and Mannie used to be friends."

Larkin recognized the boy as one of Mannie's coconspirators in the graffiti incident. Unfortunately, he also recognized the older youth who was slumped in the front passenger seat. At least two other kids were in the back seat with Will. "Do you know the rest of those kids?"

"Will's brother, Jason, is driving. I don't recognize the others." She glanced up at him, apparently alerted by his grim expression. "Do you know them?"

"I know that one." He nodded toward the teenager, who was wearing sunglasses and a gang bandanna tied beneath a billed cap. "He's Todd Minger, street name JoDog, a bad-news boy in every sense of the word."

"Does he go to the center?"

"He used to, until I caught him with a .38 and a pocket full of crack cocaine."

Letitia went white. "Good Lord, what did you do?"

"Tore up his blue card and kicked him to the curb." Larkin slid his hands into his pockets, staring at the youth who could have, but for the grace of God, been a mirror image of himself at that age.

"You must have been furious," she murmured.

"I was disappointed. The youth center could have offered a new beginning for Todd. Instead, it was just another stop on a one-way trip to nowhere."

"A new beginning?" Confused, she glanced toward the boy, who was barely sixteen years old, and looked it.

"A year ago, Todd stole a car and was sentenced to six months in a juvenile detention facility. I managed to get him an early release, but it was conditional on regular counseling sessions and daily involvement in the youth center's activities. When Todd broke the center's rules, he also violated his probation and was sent back to finish his time."

The story shook Letitia to her soles. "Are you telling me that my son is talking to a convicted felon? Oh, Lord." She raised her hand and stepped forward, but before she could call Mannie away, Larkin stopped her.

"Don't say anything to him now," he said quietly. "If you embarrass him in front of his peers, he'll have to overcome the humiliation by proving himself on their turf. Trust me, you don't want that."

"But—"

"Shh. Look." Larkin nodded toward the group, where Mannie had just stepped away from the car. "Your son will make the right decision. Let him do it on his own."

Letitia stood stiff as a broomstick, wringing her hands and chewing her lower lip. After what seemed a small eternity, the car sped away. Still clutching his football, Mannie headed toward the sidewalk. "Are we gonna' play or what?"

"In a few minutes, sport." A sideways glance at Letitia confirmed that she was nearly weak with relief. "Meanwhile, why don't you toss a few with your mom?"

Letitia's eyes widened. "I've never thrown a football in my life."

"Then it's about time you learned," he said cheerfully.

Mannie couldn't have looked more horrified if Larkin had suggested sacrificing small animals at midnight. "Football's for guys," he finally sputtered.

That was, of course, absolutely the worst thing he could say. Even Larkin winced as Letitia pulled herself up to her full, five-foot-three-inch height and skewed her son with a withering stare. "Excuse me? I must have misheard, because surely you weren't implying that I'm incapable of flinging an oddly shaped hunk of inflated rubber from Point A to Point B." She leaned over until their noses were an inch apart. "That wasn't what you meant, was it?"

Wisely, Mannie agreed that it wasn't what he'd meant at all.

Two minutes later, Letitia was fishing the football out from under a car and if her black scowl was any clue, plotting a cruel revenge. Since it seemed a judicious time to make himself scarce, Larkin slipped quietly into the backyard to meet with his new art director.

Weekends at the youth center were an exercise in organized mayhem. Letitia sidled through a corridor jammed with shouting youngsters, most of whom spoke a slurred rap slang that was completely unintelligible to the untrained ear. Thus far, Letitia herself had gotten by with the use of rap literate translators or, if necessary, a suitably blank stare which required the reluctant youth to revert—temporarily—to a more universally understood form of speech.

At the moment, however, her mission was one of observation rather than communication. A new class was listed on the activity roster posted on the gymnasium bulletin board, one Letitia had to see to believe.

But even as she peered through the window of the appointed room, she wondered if her eyes were deceiving her. There was Mama Rose, bustling between rows of students, each of whom was fastidiously stenciling a T-shirt. "Will wonders never cease?" she murmured, eyeing the row of painted patterns lining the walls. "How on earth does he do it?"

"Huh?"

Whirling, Letitia stared into the inquisitive face of a gum-snapping girl with a waterfall of skinny braids sprouting from her scalp. "Oh...sorry. I was, uh, talking to myself."

The teenager raised a penciled brow. "Whatever turns you on, girlfriend." With that, she yanked the door open and joined her shirt-painting peers.

Undaunted, Letitia sneaked another peek through the window. When Larkin had suggested commandeering Rose's artistic talents, it had taken all of Letitia's self-control to keep from laughing in his face. Not in her wildest dreams had she believed that anyone on this earthly plane could convince her stubborn mother-in-law to face dozens of brush-wielding teenagers. Somehow, Larkin McKay had done the impossible.

Granted, the youth center's esteemed director was reputed to be a gifted negotiator who, if one believed the rumors, could talk snowballs out of a cactus. But this was even more incredible. For Larkin to garner this kind of commitment from a woman who resented, possibly even disliked him was nothing short of miraculous. Whatever the amazing man possessed should be bottled and donated to the warring nations of the world. Maybe the United Nations could use it to spike the water.

Meanwhile, it occurred to Letitia that if she was spotted lurking by the window, Rose would probably drag her inside and put her to work. Since she had other plans—hopes, really—for the afternoon, she ducked away and headed toward the gymnasium.

The gym was crammed to the rafters. On the south end of the huge arena, a basketball game was in full swing; at the arcade, the buzz and boom of video games was punctuated by raucous shouts and groans of frustration; groups segregated by gender exchanged hopeful looks and flirtatious jibes; pinballs whirred; whistles blew; bells rang. Normal chaos. All was well.

Winding her way toward the front of the building, she scanned the surging crowd, looking for Larkin. As a last resort, she checked his office. The venetian blinds were drawn, but the door was open so she peeked inside. He was there, on the telephone, with his back to the door. Letitia stepped back, waiting, and heard a twinge of agitation in his voice.

"I'll see you soon, pumpkin... I know. I miss you, too. Hmm? Okay, let me talk to your brother. I love you."

The chair squeaked and Letitia heard rustling, as if he'd shifted position. She peeked in and saw that the receiver was now clamped between his chin and shoulder, and he was flipping pages in one of those daily desk calendars. "Justin? Hi, son. How's it going?"

Letitia ducked away from the doorway, scolding herself for remaining close enough to hear his conversation. Eavesdropping was rude, uncivilized and unacceptable. It also provided a rare opportunity to observe Larkin's relationship with his own children, so in this instance her conscience was overwhelmed by curiosity.

"Everyone has chores," Larkin was saying. "I'm sure John wouldn't expect you to do more than your share...hmm?...well, what does your mother say?" After a lengthy pause, Larkin's voice became tense. "Of course she still loves you, Justin. We both love you very, very much. When you come out here for spring break, we'll talk about why you feel that way.... What? No, that's not all right. I'm not blaming you.... Justin?" Another pause. More rustling. When he spoke again, it was with deliberate calm. "Relax, sport, everything's going to work out. Let me talk to your mother, okay? I miss you, too, son."

Letitia leaned against the wall. She knew little about Larkin's family, except that his ex-wife had remarried and moved to a farm in Iowa—or was it Ohio? No matter. Either place was a long way from California, and from the father who quite obviously adored them. It was so sad. The tender way Larkin spoke to his children, the tremulous inflection of his voice revealed his deep love and how profoundly he'd been affected by their loss.

In a moment, the conversation resumed. "Bonnie? What's going on?" Larkin's tone, although even and without rancor, conveyed none of the tenderness he'd displayed with his children. "Justin says your husband expects him to do everything short of plowing the fields.... Yes, I know it's a farm.... Yes, I know farm kids have chores, but Justin and Susie need time to adjust. This is all new for them." The chair squeaked again. A strained silence fell over the room.

Letitia took a chance and peeked into the office. What she saw nearly broke her heart. There was Larkin, slumped forward with his elbows propped on his knees, looking for all the world like a man on the brink of emotional meltdown. He'd turned slightly, allowing her a glance at a profile that revealed such inner anguish that it took all her strength not to burst into his office and gather him in her arms.

He pinched the bridge of his nose and sighed. "I know it's difficult for you, too. All right.... Yes, I really do understand. But what about spring break? We'd agreed that the kids would spend it with me—" He suddenly straightened. "What has hockey got to do with it?" Another long pause. "Of course I want Justin to do things he enjoys, but he'd only miss one game and he wants to come out here...." He shook his head, heaving a pained sigh. "I don't know. After taking a week off to fly out there for Christmas—"

Larkin listened for a moment, then swiveled around and angrily swiped a notepad off his desk. "No, dammit, I'm not blaming you because Susie got strep throat right before Christmas. I'm not blaming you for anything, but we have to work together on this. I think the kids feel like they have to choose between us and it's tearing them up inside. We can't let that happen."

He was rubbing the back of his neck when he twisted his head and saw Letitia. For a moment, he simply stared at her, stunned. Then he blinked, lifted one finger to signal she should wait, then ducked his head to end the conversation. "Listen, Bonnie, I've got to go. We'll talk about this later.... What? Of course you're doing the best you can. We'll work things out. Okay.... Bye."

Larkin stood with a wisp of a smile. "I didn't expect to see you today."

Since she'd made a big fat hairy deal out of being unable to volunteer on Saturdays, his surprise wasn't unexpected. "I finished my errands early," she told him. "And since I was in the neighborhood, I thought I'd drop by and kill two birds with one stone.''

He lifted a golden brow. ''Which birds, with what stone?''

''Merely a figure of speech. I have the highest regard for our feathered brethren.'' Shifting her shoulder bag gave a moment to gather her thoughts. ''The truth is that I couldn't believe anyone, even you, could have talked Rose into teaching kids to paint T-shirts. I had to see for myself.''

''And?''

Letitia shrugged. ''And she's in Room 16, painting T-shirts. How'd you do that?''

''I made the suggestion. She took it.''

''That's a crock. Rose has never taken a suggestion she didn't come up with on her own.''

''In that case, maybe you've answered your own question.''

''Must you always be so esoteric?''

''Hazards of the profession, I suppose, yet an undeniable part of my charm.'' An amused twinkle faded into a wariness that betrayed his next question. ''So, how long have you been waiting?''

''A few minutes.''

He nodded toward the phone. ''You heard?''

Denial seemed pointless. ''Yes.''

She'd hoped that he'd elaborate on what she'd overhead. Instead, he stared silently at the desktop as if fascinated by his own strumming fingers. After a long moment, Letitia opted for a gentle prod. ''Would you like to talk about it?''

He glanced up, startled. ''Hey, I'm the resident psychologist around here. That's my line.''

''Then use it, Doctor.''

The smile started at the corner of his mouth and stretched upward, tugging reluctant lips along for the ride. ''All right. Would you like to talk about what you heard?''

"As a matter of fact, I would. Over lunch?" For a moment, she feared he'd refuse. She had, after all, invaded a very personal, obviously painful part of his life and she wasn't the least bit misled by the flippant humor with which he'd tried to deflect her attention. Right now, Larkin McKay needed to have a friend; Letitia needed to be one.

Chapter Five

It was a puffy-cloud day, slightly cool, with the brilliant blue sky that was a rarity in the L.A. basin—even in January. Munching hot dogs from a local convenience store, Letitia and Larkin strolled the sidewalk a few blocks from the youth center. So far their conversation had been pleasant enough, benign discussions of weather, center activities and how thrilled Mannie had been to pull a B-minus on that math test he'd been sweating. Easy conversation. Simple subjects. Uncomplicated avoidance of the emotional turmoil bubbling beneath the surface calm.

Remarkable, Letitia thought. Beside her, Larkin sauntered loosely, chatting about this and that, quick to smile, quick to laugh, portraying a man who, to the casual observer, appeared rested, relaxed and supremely happy. His eyes betrayed him. Behind the carefree smile was a troubled man, a worried man. A man in pain.

Over the past two weeks she'd learned a great deal about Larkin McKay, perhaps even more than he'd be comfortable having her know. She understood, for example, that he was empathetic, innately kind, generous and extraordinarily sensitive to the feelings of others. He was exceptionally astute at recognizing and broaching barriers people erected to conceal their true feelings, but he hid his own behind a shield of witty quips and wisecracks. Sort of a "let me help you but keep your distance" attitude that drew people in with one hand and pushed them away with the other.

Letitia instinctively understood his reasoning. A person capable of such deep emotion was also deeply vulnerable. She'd seen that vulnerability in his eyes, as he'd spoken with his children. And about them. So he protected himself by tucking his own emotions into a murky corner of his soul; the man who always had time for others had none for himself.

That was sad.

"Do you want the rest of that?" Larkin asked, eyeing her half-eaten hot dog.

"No, not really." She handed it over and watched it disappear in two man-size bites. He crumpled the wrapper with the others in his fist and set his sights on the small bag of potato chips she was opening. "Forget it," she told him without looking up. "I'm not crazy about hot dogs, but I'd kill for these."

"They're fattening. Six of those chips will make your hips look like the Titanic."

"Oh, really?" She smiled sweetly, popped a chip in her mouth and crunched it down. "Umm-m-m." She slid her tongue along her lips, deliberately licking off every grain of salt. "Yummy."

Larkin jammed his hands, and the weenie wrappers, in the pocket pouch of his sweat jacket. "You're a cruel woman."

"Indeed I am, and one more remark about my hips will turn you into a seriously injured man."

"Have we touched upon a sore subject here?"

"Not as sore as you'll be if you don't drop it." She bit into a crisp chip, savoring it with exaggerated moans of pleasure. A sideways glance confirmed that Larkin, too, was licking his lips. His blue eyes were wide, pleading. She held the bag closer to her body, pretending to ignore him.

Until he began to mew like a starved kitten.

Uttering a sharp oath, she shoved the bag into his chest. "You are pathetic. Three and a half hot dogs, two bags of your own chips and a soda, and you're still begging for food. Do you have a tapeworm or something?"

"Just a healthy appetite." He shook a handful of chips into his palm then returned the bag. "See, *I* know how to share."

Letitia peered at the microscopic crumbs clinging to the cellophane lining. "You're a real peach."

"Thanks." As they passed a trash container, Larkin retrieved the weenie wrappers, wadding them between his palms as he executed a jerky fake to his left. "The fans are on their feet," he announced to his startled companion. "It's a tough shot…the championship is at stake…can he make it?" He leapt up, deposited the crumpled wad with a graceful, overhead lob, then jogged backward with his fists in the air. "And the crowd goes wild!"

Letitia simply stared.

He fell into step beside her, grinning. "So, how about a movie tonight?"

The toe of her sneaker caught in an invisible crack. She stumbled, righted herself before Larkin could steady her, and stared straight head. "Are you talking about renting a video or going to a bona fide theater with popcorn on the floor and gum under the seats?"

"I was thinking theater."

"Are Rose and Mannie invited?"

He coughed lightly. "Well, I suppose they could be, but I had a less crowded scenario in mind."

"So, this would be like an actual date?"

"Is that a problem for you?"

"No, of course not." She swallowed hard. "The truth is that I haven't been on a real date in quite a while."

"How long is 'quite a while?'"

"Well, let's see. Ray and I were married the day after my high school graduation and we'd already dated for two semesters, so I figure it's been about—" she made a production of doing math on her fingers "—thirteen years."

"You're joking." He stopped abruptly. Letitia kept walking. After a moment, he caught up again. "Do you mean that in the four years since your...ah, since you've been alone, you've never had a legitimate date?"

She slid him a wary look. "Nor an illegitimate one, for that matter. Why, does that qualify as a chapter in your abnormal psychology text?"

He gave a grim nod. "I'm afraid this is more serious than I thought. You will, of course, need intensive personal counseling."

"Ah. In that case, I'm sure you'd be happy to give me a referral."

"Actually, I thought I'd handle the case myself. Do you doubt my qualifications?"

"No, only your motives." The chuckle she'd been fighting finally slid out. "Does this therapy of yours involve returning to your place to study etchings?"

"Sorry, I don't have any etchings."

"Pity."

"But if you want to see some, I can always grab a nail and scratch the heck out of the walls."

The teasing remark was meant to amuse her; for some odd reason, it did just the opposite. Every muscle in her body tensed. Letitia panicked inside, not because of what Larkin had said but because of the intimacy she'd suddenly envisioned. The thought of being alone with him in the privacy of his home, breathing his air, sharing his personal space was...was...

Exhilarating.

Not offensive. Not impertinent. Not even frightening. The mere fact that she, a demure widow with an eleven-year-old son could actually be excited—yes, even aroused—by the erotic images floating through her mind was completely unacceptable, a scandalous betrayal of her husband's memory. Rose would be horrified.

"Have I upset you?" Larkin asked.

"No, of course not." True enough, since she'd done such a fine job of upsetting herself.

As they walked in silence, Larkin ducked under the drooping branch of a determined acacia that had thrust roots into the neglected city parkway and somehow survived. He slipped Letitia an occasional glance, to which she responded by studying the weblike cracks spidering through the worn concrete.

When she felt him turn away, she looked up and caught a glimpse of sadness in his eyes that bored straight into her heart. It was the same expression he'd worn when he'd hung up the telephone after speaking to his children. "You miss them terribly, don't you?"

Oddly enough, he knew exactly what she was talking about. "Yes. Sometimes late at night, when the apartment is so still I want to scream just to hear a human voice, the whisper of their laughter breaks the silence. I know it's in my mind, yet it seems so real, as if they're playing in the next room."

Letitia, too, remembered nights she'd lain awake discussing the day's events with her deceased husband. And swearing that she'd received an audible response. "What do you do when that happens?"

"I pretend they're really there. Then the next morning, I flop on my office couch, recite the normal progression of the grief process, and send myself a bill." He reached up to flick away the scrawny limb of another arboreal survivor, then kicked a pebble and jammed his hands back into his jacket.

"That must sound pretty sappy. After all, you've suffered the permanent loss of a loved one, whereas my kids are alive and happy and only a plane ride away."

"Loss is loss. It hurts, and there's nothing sappy about that." She regarded him curiously. "Are they really? Happy, that is."

"Most of the time I think they are. At least, I hope so. But children—astute parental manipulators that they are— have a thousand clever ways to turn situations to their own advantage. As their father, my job is to separate exaggerated hype from genuine fear, then do my level best to eliminate both."

"Under the best of circumstance, that's never easy, but being so far away, well, I honestly don't know how you do it."

He shrugged. "Bonnie and I try to support each other."

The mention of his ex-wife's name produced a strange ache in Letitia's chest. She heard herself blurt, "Do you still love her?" Before Larkin, who was visibly startled, could respond, she groaned and covered her eyes. "I can't believe I asked that."

"I'm a little surprised myself."

She dropped her hand and stared straight ahead. "Salt deprivation withers the brain," she mumbled. "If you hadn't eaten my potato chips, I would have made an intelligent and reasonably germane comment, such as, 'It's admirable that you both could put differences aside for the sake of your children.'"

From the corner of her eye, she saw the flash of his amused grin. "I said that we *try* to support each other. We don't always succeed. If we got along all that well, we'd still be married."

Which brought up another juicy question this time, however, Letitia would have bitten off her tongue before posing it.

Fortunately she didn't have to. Larkin responded as if reading her mind. "Actually, that's a bit misleading. The truth is that Bonnie and I got along quite well. We never fought, rarely argued and never seemed to disagree on anything of importance. I was content and comfortable, which is why the divorce came as such a shock. To me, anyway. Apparently Bonnie had been unhappy for years. In retrospect, I realize the warning signs were there but I'd been too busy probing other people's psyches to heed them."

Larkin fell silent as a low-rider packed with teenagers cruised by with its stereo booming. The reverberating beat faded slowly as the car moved on down the block. "Bonnie and I met in college," he said when the noise had dissipated. "Right from the start, we had a lot in common. Both of us were psych majors with full scholarships. Both of us loved kids and couldn't wait to start our own families. Since we were best friends, who did nearly everything as a team, it seemed natural that we do that together, too."

"So you were both fairly young when you married?"

"Yes, but as it turned out, that worked to our advantage. Youth breeds stamina, and stamina is what we needed to hold down jobs, have babies and work on advanced degrees all at the same time. I was still working on my masters' when Justin was born. By the time Susie came along, I'd earned a Ph.D. and hung out a shingle in a ritzy West L.A. high-rise. That, it seems, was the beginning of the end, although I didn't realize it at the time."

"Your wife wasn't happy about you opening your own practice?"

"My practice wasn't the problem. The location was. Bonnie never really liked L.A. She was from the Midwest and had always expected to return after she'd completed her education. When we got married, I assumed that expectation had been relinquished. I later learned that it had only been delayed."

Letitia was beginning to get the gist of the problem. Starting a new practice took money, time and commitment; it certainly wasn't a venture one would initiate on a short-term basis. "Hadn't the two of you talked about where you'd settle down to raise your children?"

He considered that slowly, almost methodically, rolling his lips and setting his jaw as if mentally calculating complex mathematical theory. "We each talked," he finally said. "Neither of us listened."

That didn't make sense and she said so.

He cupped a hand behind his neck, absently massaging it as he spoke. "For years I discussed specializing in setting up a practice that catered to the rich and troubled. Their money couldn't buy happiness, but it could certainly pay the fees of a trained professional to help deal with their problems."

Letitia said nothing but her reproachful frown spoke volumes.

Larkin smiled. "Disillusioned?"

"I'm a little surprised," she admitted. "You don't seem the type to... ah, well—"

"Choose patients based on ability to pay?" When she issued a reluctant nod, his smile widened, although his eyes remained pensive. "My values have been seriously overhauled the past couple of years. At that time, my family was my first priority. I wanted to give them things I never had. Besides, the way I figured it, I was well trained, highly educated and entitled to commensurate compensation. Why shouldn't I be able to buy my kids new coats without having to eat soup for a month?"

Since the question was clearly rhetorical, Letitia didn't bother to respond. Instead she concentrated not only on Larkin's words, but his subtle body language—a stiffening of his shoulders, the tiny muscle twitch below his jaw, a discernible tightness at the corners of his mouth.

"I always included Bonnie," Larkin said. "We looked at office rental brochures together, talked to banks about loan costs, sketched out capital equipment budgets and discussed tax benefits. She never objected so I assumed we were in agreement. Thinking back, I realize that expressing concern about city schools and extolling the virtues of raising kids in a rural environment was, in fact, a thinly veiled protest. But I wasn't so dense that I didn't realize she was homesick, so I magnanimously suggested she and the kids go back to Iowa for a nice, long visit. Naturally, I didn't think it would last three years.''

"She never came back?"

"Nope. That first summer she rekindled the flame with her high school sweetheart."

"Was that John?" she asked, recalling the name from the phone conversation she'd overheard.

"Yes, John Haggarty. Apparently he'd just inherited the family farm, which is only a mile or so from her parents' place. Anyway, he and Bonnie got back together and the next thing I know, some guy in a Smokey the Bear hat is serving me with divorce papers."

"But what about the children? Surely, she didn't have a right to move those children out of California without your permission."

"She'd established legal residency for herself and the children before filing. I could have fought her in court—and probably won—but when I flew back there, the kids were so happy. They loved life on the farm. Bonnie had been right.'' Larkin paused, blinking rapidly and aiming a light cough into his fist. He swallowed hard. "We agreed on joint custody and liberal visitation. Besides having the kids spend eight weeks each summer with me, along with a week at Christmas and Easter, we've also agreed that I'll be able to see them any time I can fly out for a weekend, which I try to do at least three or four times a year."

Letitia folded her arms against a sudden chill. "That must be so difficult for you," she whispered. "I can't imagine..."

The words evaporated like so much steam. There was nothing to say, nothing that could ease the heartache reflected in his sad eyes. If he'd sued for full custody and won, two very young children would have been wrenched from their mother's arms and from the lifestyle they'd chosen. War would have broken out between the embattled parents, a war in which there could be no winners, and the kids would be the biggest losers of all.

Finally, Letitia touched his arm. "If it's any comfort, I believe you did the right thing."

"It is a comfort." His grateful smile warmed her heart. "Thank you for understanding."

Letitia did more than merely understand Larkin's pain; a part of her actually felt it. Mannie was the center of her life. Losing Ray had been devastating but if, God forbid, she and her son were ever separated, she honestly didn't think she'd have the strength to go on. It seemed terribly unfair that a man who'd brought so many families together should be denied a relationship with his own children.

She was so lost in thought that for a moment, she barely noticed that they'd stopped walking. When she glanced around to get her bearings they were standing by her car, which was parked in front of the youth center.

Larkin, shifting from one foot to the other, aimed a nervous nod toward the building. "I should get back to work."

"Me, too. Back to my errands, that is."

"Thanks for stopping by." His smile was slightly pained. After a hesitant moment, he spun on his heel and strode to the door.

As he reached for the handle, Letitia heard herself call out, "Is seven too early?"

He looked up, bewildered. Then his eyes began to glow softly. "Seven is perfect. I'll pick you up."

"Great," she said, proud that her voice sounded cheery and firm. With a nod and a smile he disappeared into the building. Letitia managed to enter her car and drive off, but she didn't have a clue where she was going. Her head was swimming, her stomach nearing revolt.

A date, an honest-to-goodness date. What had she been thinking? She'd been out of circulation so long, she didn't even know the rules of this new, liberated society. Did etiquette still require men to open doors? She didn't want him to think she was too stupid to twist a knob; then again, it would be far worse to stand there like a grinning fool and let a door slam into her nose.

And what were the rules about money? Should she offer to pay her own way, or would that insult him? Maybe he'd be insulted if she didn't. Oh, Lord. Which insult would be less grievous, making him look stingy or making herself look stingy?

And what if he wanted to kiss her good-night?

Even worse, what if he didn't?

The more she fretted, the more frightened she became, yet there was no turning back. Whether tonight ended up as a lovely evening or a terrible mistake, she couldn't shake the feeling that life as she'd known it would be never be quite the same.

The bathroom was still steamy from his shower, but the mirror was clear enough for Larkin to see flaws he hadn't noticed in years, along with a few new ones. Had his nose always been crooked? And why were his eyebrows all tweaked? Either he'd slept on his forehead or a pair of sick blond caterpillars had crawled above his eyelids and died. He grabbed a tube of hair gel and glued the damned things flat. The effect was rather obvious and less than flattering.

Muttering to himself, Larkin snatched up a washcloth, scrubbed off the gel, then smoothed the damp brows into place and hoped for the best. He leaned closer to the mirror, frowning. Was that a pimple on his chin? He poked at the tiny red spot. Oh, God. It was. After ten years of clear-skinned bliss, this had to be some kind of sadistic joke. But it was no joke. The lousy pimple was glowing like a road flare.

Horrified, he yanked open the medicine chest, searching the sparse contents for something, anything, that could make the damn thing disappear in the next hour and a half. All he found was alcohol, so he dabbed some on his chin. It made him smell like a hospital.

Maybe Letitia wouldn't notice.

Then again, maybe she would. Maybe she'd say something like, "Why do you smell like a hospital?", so Larkin would have to answer, "Because I put alcohol on my pimple," and she'd say, "You mean that giant crimson bulge in the middle of your chin?" and he'd say, "Yeah, that's the one," and she'd say, "Eeewwww, it's disgusting," and he, of course, would have to kill himself.

Feeling sick, he grabbed for the washcloth.

Thirty seconds later, his glowing chin smelled like soap and his attention had been redirected to the damp mop of hair stretched back over his scalp. Normally he simply ran a comb through his hair and let it do what it wanted. Now, however, it was just, well, lying there looking flat and decidedly unappealing. He wished he had Roberto's hair, which was thick and lush, with a hint of curl that seemed to drive women wild. Of course, Bobby probably spent hours with a blow-dryer to get that sexy fullness—

At that point, Larkin realized that he, too, owned a blow-dryer, although he couldn't remember the last time he'd used it. But desperate times called for desperate measures. He still couldn't believe Letitia had agreed to go out with him. She was probably sitting at home right now, staring at the telephone and trying to think up an excuse to back out. Not that he'd blame her, particularly since he'd been brutally frank in revealing the true extent of his own flawed nature. He'd expected her to run away, screaming; but she hadn't. At least, not yet. Of course, she hadn't seen his pimple, either. Maybe more stylish hair would take her mind off his chin. And his tweaked eyebrows.

Larkin dug through the linen closet and found the dryer behind a stack of *Psychology Today* magazines that he'd been meaning to read. Back to the mirror, where he gave his forlorn reflection a final, critical glance, then flipped the switch and blasted his flat, wet hair into a bushy mane that made him look like a blond Liberace.

Swearing a blue streak, he dropped the dryer on the vanity and got back into the shower.

Forty-five minutes and three wardrobe changes later, Larkin was fretting over whether to wear an exotic men's cologne, which might clash with his outdoorsy deodorant, or stick with his usual spicy after-shave, which could give a mistaken impression that he hadn't considered the evening important enough for cologne.

He finally chose the cologne.

Then he looked at his watch, polished his glasses and with a final shaky breath, headed out the door.

Drab.

That was the only description Letitia could muster about the reflection staring back from the mirror. Blah brown eyes. A woolly frizz of unmanageable hair. Skin pallid with pure, unadulterated fear. If she didn't do something fast, Larkin would take one look at her and run screaming into the night.

Fortunately, modern science and chemistry had combined to offer at least a partial solution to her dilemma. What didn't come naturally could always be painted on; or in desperate cases such as her own, slathered with a trowel.

She dumped the contents of her cosmetic bag onto the vanity and frantically sorted through a cache of multihued shadows and blushers. She needed color, lots of color. A shocking pink blush caught her eye, along with a vivid teal lid color. She grabbed a fat sable brush and went to work.

Five minutes later, a garish clown stared out from the mirror. Moaning, Letitia scrubbed off the mess and started over. This time, she settled on a frugal application of muted rose cheek color and a luxurious plum shadow. She frowned into the mirror. Better, she decided. Not wonderful, but a definite improvement.

Her focus shifted to her hair which, thanks to the overly zealous application of a steam hair-setting system, now sprang from her scalp in an unruly mass of electrified spirals. She'd only used the steam curlers once in the past five years; now she remembered why.

Since it was too late to start over, Letitia tugged a handful of frantic curls away from her face and fastened the mess atop her head with a pretty, mother-of-pearl comb. She decided that the result was passable, at least from the front.

Rushing from the bathroom to her bedroom, she narrowly avoided tripping over Rasputin, who was napping in her doorway, then hurried to the full-length mirror on her closet door. She scanned the finished product from the ground up—neat beige pumps with midsize heels; a simple brown skirt to set off the creamy angora sweater knitted two summers ago, then wrapped in tissue to await a special occasion; and from her ears, a dangle of hammered gold loops that were casual, yet elegant. She dabbed her favorite scent behind each ear, then glanced at her bare wrist and realized she'd left her watch in the bathroom.

She spun around, stepped over the yawning dog, and found the watch on the vanity, where she'd left it. As she struggled with the miniature clasp, a task complicated by nervous fingers, she suddenly lost her grip and the watch plopped onto the pile throw rug.

Frustrated and feeling harried, she paused for a long sigh before bending to retrieve the item. That hesitation provided a window of opportunity for the crafty canine lurking in the hall. Rasputin shot into the bathroom, snagged the watch and scurried away in a blur of flashing teeth and churning legs.

"No!"

The protest was useless and Letitia knew it. She chased the animal down the hall, through the kitchen and finally into the laundry room, where the malleable Chihuahua squeezed into a ridiculously small space and disappeared behind the washing machine. He popped out a moment later, tail wagging, eyes bright, mouth empty.

She glared at him. "You are such a brat."

Rasputin just sat there looking immensely pleased with himself as Letitia formed a wire coat hanger into a hooked retrieval tool. She hoisted her skirt, climbed onto the washer and peered through the tangle of hoses and wires behind the machine.

A glint caught her eye. Lowering the hanger, she probed Rasputin's newest hidey-hole and during the next few minutes fished out a purple sweat sock, a tiny earphone for Mannie's pocket radio, a gold hoop earring Letitia thought she'd lost at the mall, Larkin's shiny silver whistle and finally, her wristwatch.

Since the whistle legitimately belonged to Rasputin, Letitia dropped it back behind the machine. After fastening the watch around her wrist, she carried the other items into the living room where Rose was reading a magazine and Mannie was engrossed in watching a game show on T.V. She tossed the earphone in her son's lap.

He spared it a glance, then refocused on the blaring television. Rose, however, gave Letitia her full attention. The woman's reproachful gaze swept her daughter-in-law like a cold wind. "The skirt is too short."

"It's longer than most, Mama. At least it reaches my knees."

"In winter, a lady's knees should be covered." Rose laid her magazine aside and studied Letitia's sweater. "Is that new?"

"Not exactly. I made it a couple of years ago."

The woman nodded. "Did you intend the neckline to be so revealing?"

Startled, Letitia glanced down and saw the same thing she'd seen in the mirror, a modest scallop-edged scoop just below her collarbone. "What's wrong with it?"

Rose clucked softly. "At least you're not going to church."

Doubt swelled into panic. Since her mother-in-law hadn't uttered a critical phrase in twelve years, Letitia took the woman's comment seriously. Rose didn't have an unkind bone in her body. If she said Letitia was inappropriately dressed, then Letitia believed it. "Maybe I should change."

Mannie glanced up. "You look hot, Mom."

Letitia cringed. That was, of course, the effect she'd been hoping to achieve, but she hadn't expected her eleven-year-old son to notice, let alone comment on the result.

The doorbell rang. Letitia froze.

"I'll get it!" Mannie sprinted across the room before Letitia could draw a breath. He yanked open the door. "Hi! I mean, Yo-G!"

"Right back at you," Larkin said, stepping inside. He exchanged a complex series of hand gestures with the excited boy, greeted Rose politely—she acknowledged him with a nod—then he glanced up and saw Letitia. A strange expression crossed his face. "Hi," he whispered.

Concealing the sweat sock and earring behind her back, she managed a nervous smile. "Hi."

"You look lovely."

A reproachful grunt filtered from Rose's chair. Letitia ignored it. "Thanks. You look nice, too."

"Thanks."

They stood there, smiling like fools, until Mannie broke the awkward silence. "What're y'gonna see?"

"Hmm?" Larkin blinked. "Oh. Well. I, ah..."

He looked frantically at Letitia, who took comfort from the realization that he, too, was nervous. So nervous, in fact, that she suspected he hadn't even looked at the newspaper movie listings. "What do you recommend?" she asked her son.

Larkin looked relieved and grateful as Mannie rattled off several titles and, to his mother's surprise, knew where each one was playing. "If you like blood and guts," the boy was saying, "there's a real neat monster movie at the Plaza."

"I think we'll pass on that." Letitia angled a glance at Larkin. "Unless you like horror movies, that is."

"Not particularly. What kind of films do you prefer?"

"I don't know. Romantic comedies, I guess, or a good whodunnit."

"I'm sure we can find something in that category."

"I'm sure we can." Anxious to leave, Letitia sidled toward the hall. "I'll, ah, just get my purse."

"Take your time." Larkin said, then slipped his hands in his slacks pockets and turned to Rose. "By the way, the kids are raving about your art class."

The woman issued a reply, which Letitia didn't hear because she was already halfway down the hall. Once inside her bedroom, she tossed the sock and earring on her bed, closed the door and struggled to regain her composure.

After a moment, she went to the mirror, studied her reflection and honestly couldn't understand why Rose had been so critical. Certainly, the sweater wasn't baggy, but it wasn't tight, either, and the neckline was more modest than some of her business blouses. The skirt was slim without being clingy and she'd frequently worn the beige pumps to church without so much as a skewed glance from her mother-in-law.

In fact, Letitia thought her attire was quite proper. Since changing clothes at this point would require bothersome explanation, she simply grabbed her purse and returned to the living room where Rose and Larkin were engaged in pleasant conversation.

The discussion ended when Rose glanced up and saw that Letitia was wearing the same outfit.

"I'm ready," Letitia announced, avoiding her mother-in-law's gaze.

Larkin bid Mannie and Rose good-night, then patted Rasputin's head and laid a braided plastic key ring on the coffee table. The dog fairly quivered with excitement. A moment later, when Larkin opened the front door, the key ring was gone.

The date had officially begun.

Chapter Six

Letitia shoved her angora sleeves up to her elbows, ducked under the open hood and leaned across the lap blanket Larkin had draped across the fender to protect her clothes. She aimed a flashlight beam on the exposed carburetor. "Okay, try turning it over."

The engine emitted a long, dragging whine. Focusing her attention on the fuel injectors, she called out, "Are you pumping the accelerator?"

Larkin stuck his head out the driver's window. "Yeah."

She sighed. "Turn it off." When the engine shuddered to a stop, she replaced the air filter and was tightening the wing nut as Larkin exited the car. She set the flashlight down and stepped back, wiping her hands on a rag. "The injectors aren't spraying."

He raked his hair, muttered a soft oath and glared into the engine compartment. "Fuel pump?"

"That'd be my guess."

"Damn."

"Hey, it could be worse," she said brightly. "At least you don't need a new transmission. I'm sure that shift hesitation can be fixed with a minor gear adjustment."

"Wonderful." His glum gaze landed on the grease rag in her hands. "I wanted this to be a memorable evening, but this wasn't exactly what I had in mind. I'm sorry."

She tossed the rag aside and gave his arm a sympathetic pat. "There's nothing to be sorry about. This certainly isn't your fault, although I have to admit to a moment of suspicion when the car started to lose power."

The comment startled him. "Suspicion?"

"Of course. I thought, 'Oh, no! Not the old running-out-of-gas routine.' But the fuel gage was at full and I heard that weird little buzz coming from the tank, and besides, the look on your face—" She shook her head, chuckling. "Brando himself couldn't muster that kind of horror on cue."

He managed a smile. "Of course I was horrified. If—and I'm not admitting to anything here—but *if* I had a devious scheme in mind, I sure as hell wouldn't have implemented it on—" he squinted up at a dimly lit street sign "—the corner of 155th and Celia in front of an all-night Stop 'N Go."

"Oh? And where would you have implemented a devious scheme? If you had one, that is."

"Gee, I don't know," he said with a sly gleam. "Maybe a secluded pull-off a half mile west of Topanga Canyon and Mulholland Drive."

"Hmm, that's pretty specific for a man without a plan. Any movie theaters around there?"

"Not a one, but the view is magnificent."

The chuckle she'd been fighting finally slipped out. "Sounds lovely, but I suspect it's rather a long walk from here."

"Everywhere is a long walk from here." After glancing around the dark neighborhood, Larkin's gaze settled on a phone booth in front of the convenience store. "I'd better call for a tow."

Letitia's smile faded as the reality of their situation sank in. She knew Larkin had a legitimate problem to deal with. If they left the car here and took a cab to the show, his vehicle would be stripped before they reached the theater. On the other hand, it would take at least an hour, maybe more, to have the car hauled to a secure garage lot, where it would languish until the shop opened in the morning.

There was no doubt in her mind that their date had just come to an abrupt and unceremonious end. The sting of disappointment was surprisingly sharp.

Larkin shrugged out of his wool blazer and draped the garment around Letitia's shoulders. "Wait in the car," he said, escorting her around to the open passenger door. "I'll be back in a few minutes."

She slid into the seat without comment, but did manage a smile of encouragement before shutting the car door. Larkin winked through the window, then loped across the street.

From her vantage point, Letitia could see the phone booth in the convenience store parking lot. Actually, it wasn't a booth at all, just an open pay phone set into a narrow plastic shield that offered neither privacy nor protection from the elements.

As she watched him dig change out of his pocket, then sort through his wallet to extract what appeared to be a variety of credit cards, her heart sank. Replacing a fuel pump wasn't cheap and unless Larkin belonged to an auto club with emergency road service, towing fees would cost a pretty penny, too. And then there would be cab fares and car rentals while his own vehicle was being repaired. All in all, a high price to pay for a date that had officially lasted less than twenty minutes.

Of course, Letitia had no detailed knowledge of Larkin's financial situation, but there were subtle clues that he wasn't a wealthy man, including hints offered by the blazer he'd wrapped around her shoulders. The jacket was clean, of course, and freshly pressed, but a telltale thinning around the cuffs indicated many years of use. Besides the fact that most of his clothing appeared to be comfortably worn and his leather-look vinyl watchband was dangerously cracked, a man with money to burn certainly wouldn't be driving a ten-year-old sedan with an odometer pushing six digits.

Letitia fretted about Larkin's poor car, wondering if there was something she could do to help. If, for instance, they did the work themselves, they could save the labor costs that would doubtless add up to a serious chunk of change. Unfortunately, she'd never installed a fuel pump, but Larkin seemed to have at least a basic knowledge of combustion engines so perhaps between the two of them and a do-it-yourself manual—

A tap on the window startled her. Larkin was peering through the glass. She rolled down the window. "Is something wrong?"

"No. The tow truck will be here in half an hour or so, but I have a couple more calls to make and, well..." He gave her a sheepish half smile. "I, uh, ran out of change."

"Ah. Well, worry not. I have plenty." Rooting through her pocketbook, which was on the seat beside her, she pulled out a bulging change purse. "For candy bar vending machines," she explained, handing it to him. "You know the old saying—'A day without chocolate isn't worth getting up for.'"

He hefted the fat little purse in his palm. "You realize, of course, that chocoholism is symptomatic of deeply rooted childhood trauma linked to a neurotic fear of the Easter Bunny."

"Really? Hmm. Maybe that's why I'm so fond of rabbit stew."

He straightened, tsking. "This is worse than I thought. Call for an appointment. I'll squeeze you in."

"You're too kind."

"I know. It's a curse."

Before Letitia could do more than issue a snort of amusement, Larkin was already jogging back to the phone booth, so she snuggled down in the seat, swallowed up by his huge jacket. The garment exuded Larkin's warmth, as well as his scent. She breathed deeply, taking his essence into her lungs, allowing this exotic part of him to permeate every fiber of her body. Closing her eyes, she imagined how delicious it would feel to be cocooned in flesh-and-blood arms instead of empty sleeves.

The image was erotic, yet strangely soothing. There was a strength about Larkin McKay, a remarkable resilience that made her feel as if there were no crisis he couldn't control, no disaster he couldn't resolve. She felt safe with him, physically and emotionally protected.

The truth was that she absolutely loved being with him. When they were together, the world somehow seemed brighter. Jokes were funnier; colors more vivid; even the air around them smelled fresher, more vibrant. In the short weeks since they'd met, Larkin had become a very special, very important part of her life.

Letitia sat up, stunned and unnerved, not so much by the fact that she enjoyed Larkin's company, but by the revelation that his presence had become powerful enough to actually alter her life. Each morning she woke up thinking about him. Throughout her busy day, she'd find herself daydreaming about a funny remark he'd made or a particular kindness he'd shown.

Sometimes the sudden image of some silliness they'd shared would pop into her head and she'd find herself laughing out loud at the most inappropriate moments. Her boss had been eyeing her strangely; even her co-workers had begun to whisper. Through it all, Letitia simply glided through the office with a cheery grin and a heart full of happiness.

There was no denying it. Letitia was smitten. Big time.

* * *

Larkin wasn't sure how he got through the next hour. He remembered making the phone calls and purchasing two cups of coffee from the convenience store. He remembered Letitia's starlight smile when he'd handed her one of the steaming cups, because his heart had started to pound so hard he'd thought he was having some kind of attack. He even remembered pulling a deck of cards from the glove box and issuing a gin rummy challenge, which was probably the stupidest thing any adult male in recorded history had ever done on a first date.

Letitia, who was too well-bred to shove the deck in his ear, had pretended to be thrilled by the opportunity to play cards on the front seat of the same car she'd partially dismantled. After all, doesn't every woman dream of sticking her head in an engine because her date, who can't afford dependable transportation, barely knows the difference between a camshaft and a driveshaft?

As for her elegant, cream-colored sweater . . . well, she'd probably been wondering if angora was washable. Now she'd have a chance to find out.

So far, the entire evening had been such a series of disastrous fiascos that Letitia would probably swear off dating for another thirteen years.

But the night wasn't over yet. There was one last chance to make amends. As the lights of the tow truck bore down on his crippled car, Larkin was determined to take it.

With its front tires hoisted off the pavement, Larkin's poor car dangled from the giant winch like a prize marlin. The truck driver handed a clipboard and pen to Larkin, who scrutinized the attached form, glanced down the street, scrawled something on the form, glanced down the street, handed the clipboard back and glanced down the street again.

Letitia, watching from the curb, dutifully followed each gaze and saw nothing more interesting than a neighborhood dog sniffing the base of a street lamp.

Back at the truck, Larkin and the driver were engaged in quiet conversation. Business cards were exchanged. There was more discussion, abruptly suspended as headlights appeared down the street. Larkin anxiously studied the approaching vehicle, only to look away, disappointed, as a nondescript passenger car cruised by.

Letitia shifted inside Larkin's cavernous blazer, more restless than bored. She assumed that Larkin was waiting for a cab. He'd probably phoned for one after calling for the tow truck. She also assumed, since Larkin had politely dismissed all suggestions of alternate activities, that said taxi would be used to deposit her back on her own front porch, thus ending their evening.

So far, she'd managed to conceal her disappointment. None of this was Larkin's fault, of course, nor was it hers. It was just one of those things; best laid plans, and all that rot. But if Larkin ever asked her out again—and at this point, that seemed to be one heck of a big 'if'—Letitia vowed to carry a fan belt, a set of plugs and a spare fuel pump in her purse.

A revving engine distracted her. The tow truck was leaving.

As the sick car was dragged away, Larkin stood there with the melancholy expression of one watching an ambulance cart off a critically injured friend. He heaved a sigh, scratched his head, then stuffed his hands in his slacks pockets and trudged toward the curb where Letitia was waiting.

"Where's it going?" she asked.

"A place over on the east side. It's only a few miles from here." He managed a quick smile before his attention was again riveted at the far end of the dark, deserted street.

"I imagine you're anxious to follow and make sure it's properly secured."

"Hmm?" He dragged his gaze back to Letitia. "No, everything will be fine. My car has spent so much time at that garage, it exchanges Christmas cards with the owner. I think they're in love," he added, discreetly checking his watch.

Letitia was just about to suggest calling Rose to pick them up when another pair of headlights appeared in the distance.

Larkin tensed. "I hope that's our ride." He stepped off the curb, leaned out and raised an arm. A yellow turn signal began blinking. "Aha!" With a triumphant grin, Larkin returned to slip a gallant arm around Letitia's shoulders as a gleaming white stretch limousine pulled up to the curb.

With an effusive sweep of his hand, Larkin executed a generous, medieval-style bow. "M'lady's carriage has arrived."

While Letitia stood there dumbstruck, a uniformed chauffeur emerged. "Hey, Doc," he called out, grinning. "Sorry I'm late. It took a little time to...ah, well, you know." That oblique statement was punctuated by a knowing wink.

Larkin responded with an even broader grin. "No problem, Dan. It's good to see you."

Letitia, alerted by a draft on her tongue, managed to close her mouth as the two men chatted briefly. She studied Dan Walker, whom Larkin had introduced as the owner of the limo service, then suddenly snapped her fingers when she remembered where she'd seen him before. "You volunteer at the youth center, right?"

Dan beamed. "Just about everyone with kids ends up at the center, sooner or later. I've got five myself, so for me it was sooner."

"Dan's been with us since the beginning," Larkin explained. "He's donated hundreds of dollars of limo time for fund-raisers and last summer, when a Disneyland trip for underprivileged children was threatened by a bus strike, he lined up every car in his fleet and gave those kids a ride they'll never forget."

Ducking his head in embarrassment, Dan walked around to the passenger side, shrugging off the praise. "Everyone's got to contribute." The chauffeur clicked his polished heels, tipped his hat and opened the rear door to expose the limo's expansive, elegant interior.

"It's so beautiful," she whispered.

Larkin took her hand to steady her as she stepped onto the plush crimson carpet. The passenger compartment looked like a small living room, complete with a crushed velvet sofa, matching bucket chairs, a tiny refrigerator and compact oak cabinets. Letitia hesitated, then sank onto the luxurious sofa at the back of the cabin. Illumination was provided by soft sconces and romantic twinkle lights scattered over the ceiling. A glass partition separated the driver's seat from the passenger compartment. There was a small, round speaker embedded in the glass, presumably for communication between the two areas, and a rich red privacy curtain, now open, which could be drawn for total seclusion.

She was so awed by her impressive surroundings that it took a moment to realize that Larkin was still outside. Scooting forward, she peered through the open door and saw him engaged in whispered conversation with Dan. He appeared to be asking questions, to which his friend consistently replied with a nod and a smug grin. Larkin, looking massively relieved, slapped Dan's shoulder, then dug into his pocket and pulled out his wallet. Dan stepped back, waving his hand in refusal. Larkin extracted several bills, slid his wallet back into his hip pocket, then pressed the money into the limo driver's hand and folded the man's fingers forward.

Before Dan could issue another protest, Larkin ducked inside the limo. Letitia slid over to make room while the chagrined driver hovered in the doorway with a fistful of disputed currency. Larkin smiled at him. "So are you going to put this baby in gear, or what?"

Sighing, Dan stuffed the bills in his pocket and shut the limo door.

A few minutes later, the limo was cruising up the west-bound freeway on-ramp. Larkin stretched his long legs out, crossing his ankles, and slipped one arm along the back of the sofa. "Have you ever had a limo ride?" he asked.

"Once, for my high school prom. But it certainly wasn't as fancy as this one."

"This is the VIP model. It has everything but a Jacuzzi hot tub. Are you impressed?"

"Oh, yes."

"Good."

"But you didn't have to do this. We could have taken a taxi to...to..." She glanced out the tinted windows. "Where are we going, anyway?"

"You'll see," he said, his eyes dancing.

Frankly, Letitia didn't care where they were going. The passing freeway signs proved that he wasn't taking her home, which relieved and delighted her. She sighed, happy and contented. "This is lovely," she murmured. "Much better than a cab."

"After all I've put you through, you're entitled to first-class treatment. Since Air Force One was tied up tonight, this was the best I could do on short notice."

Letitia snuggled deeper into the sumptuous cushions. She had no doubt that Larkin McKay could do just about anything he put his mind to, and that included hitching a ride on the presidential jet.

Just then he blurted, "Is it making you hot?"

She sat up, startled.

Larkin wiped his forehead. "I mean, the jacket," he mumbled, nodding at the wool blazer that was still wrapped around her shoulders.

"Oh. Maybe a little." Although the limo's interior was quite toasty, she was nonetheless reluctant to relinquish the jacket and the sense of intimacy it gave her. But she also realized that a sweaty woman wasn't the world's most appealing companion, so she finally shrugged the garment off.

Larkin tossed it on one of the empty chairs. "I, uh..." He cleared his throat, leaned back and shifted restlessly. "I'm really sorry about tonight."

"There's nothing to be sorry about." After an encouraging pat on his knee, she quickly withdrew her hand, laying it demurely in her own lap. "Besides, I'm having a wonderful time."

"Are you?"

"Absolutely. I feel like a queen."

"In my eyes, you are a queen," he said softly.

Something in his voice made her look up. It was a mistake. She was instantly mesmerized by his intense gaze. Her heart leapt; her pulse raced. She couldn't have looked away if she'd wanted to.

But she didn't want to. His scent enveloped her; his warmth drew her in; his aura reached out, embracing her with silent strength. She felt nurtured, cherished. Loved.

Loved.

The word slid so easily through her mind, it scared her half to death. She looked abruptly away, staring out the window as if entranced by the blur of passing scenery, although they could have been speeding through a blizzard, for all she knew. The only image she saw was the one in her mind, an instant replay of Larkin's eyes glowing with dark sensuality, and the nuance of his parted lips, moving ever so slowly toward hers.

Had she not turned away in panic, he would have kissed her. Instead, she'd felt him stiffen and withdraw. She regretted that, deeply.

Retreat had been an instinctive reaction, considering how long it had been since she'd felt this close to a man. Even more shocking had been the subtle signals sent by her own body indicating that it, at least, was willing, perhaps even eager to consider a more intimate union. The thought made her hands sweat. Ray had been the only man with whom she'd shared that ultimate intimacy. Their sex life had been wonderful, sometimes tender, sometimes playful, always intense and satisfying. Since his death, Letitia had been comfortably celibate, missing the emotional closeness they'd shared more than the physical act itself.

After so many years, the first fluttering of arousal seemed strangely foreign. She was troubled, wondering if Ray would consider her feelings as a betrayal of his memory. She doubted it. Her husband had been a generous man; he'd have wanted her to be happy. There was no reason for Letitia to feel guilty. But she did.

Beside her, Larkin fidgeted. The sofa dipped as he shifted positions. "Would you like me to take you home?"

She shot a stunned glance over her shoulder. "No, of course not. Why?"

"You suddenly seemed uncomfortable. I thought this might not have been such a good idea after all."

"It's a wonderful idea." She sighed and leaned back in the seat. "Now you know why I haven't been out in so long. I'm a lousy date."

He took her hand, cradling it between his palms. "That's okay," he murmured, stroking her palm with his thumb. "You're a damned good mechanic."

She laughed. "Hey, I think this is where you're supposed to protest that I'm a wonderful date and you just adore my company."

"You are and I do."

"Hmm. That didn't resonate with the conviction I was hoping for."

He stared down at her hand for a moment, apparently unaware that each caress of his thumb sent tiny shivers down her spine. "If I told you what I'm really feeling, it would scare you to death."

She should have been surprised by his insight, but wasn't. Larkin had a gift for reading her thoughts, intuiting needs that she didn't even know she had. When they'd first met, his acute perception had shocked, even disturbed her. Now she found it comforting. Smiling, she gazed outside again and this time, actually noticed that they'd left the freeway and were winding through a rugged canyon.

Again, Larkin interpreted every nuance of her expression. "We'll be there soon."

"Dare I ask, where?"

"Not yet."

"Well, then, may I inquire as to what you have in store once we arrive at this as yet undisclosed location?"

After due consideration, Larkin leaned over and opened one of the oak cabinets to reveal a fairly good-size television, along with a video rental store bag, bulging with VCR tapes. "I promised you a movie, didn't I?"

Letitia knew her mouth was open again. This time, she didn't bother to close it as Larkin sat cross-legged on the floor, sorting through the bag. "I know these aren't exactly first-run, but the guy at the video store said he'd pick out the newest releases. Hopefully, there's something in here you haven't seen yet."

He pulled out a tape, read the title and synopsis out loud, then passed it on to her and dug back into the bag. One by one, Larkin handed her a dozen videos, each either a romantic comedy or a mystery.

By the time the bag was empty, Letitia was surrounded by fat plastic boxes and Larkin was grinning madly. "I thought I'd pass on the gum under the seats, but if you want atmosphere—'' He used his index fingers to beat a drum roll on the side of another cabinet, then he flung it open to reveal a massive tub of buttery popcorn and enough chocolate bars to stock a vending machine. ''Ta-da!''

All Letitia could say was, ''Where's the soda pop?''

''In the fridge,'' he replied without missing a beat. ''And just to add some class to our makeshift theater...''

As he opened the tiny refrigerator, her sputter of surprise dissolved into delighted laughter. There, beside an impressive array of chilled soda cans, was a magnum of champagne and two fluted goblets.

Letitia wiped her eyes. ''No wonder you spent so much time in that silly phone booth.''

Retrieving the champagne bottle, Larkin dispensed with the foil seal and began twisting the wire cork stay. ''It's the least I could do. Besides having your clothes cleaned, of course. By the way, I'll pick them up tomorrow afternoon, okay?''

''That really isn't necessar—'' She jumped as the cork popped.

''A friend of mine is a dry cleaner. Guarantees his work, twenty-four-hour turnaround so I can have your things back by Monday evening.'' As he talked, he filled the champagne glasses with bubbling liquid. ''Is that soon enough?'' he asked, offering her one of the glasses.

She slipped her fingers around the crystal stem. ''Monday is fine,'' she murmured, realizing that further protest was futile. ''Thank you.''

He sat beside her, holding up his glass as if preparing to propose a toast. As his gaze slipped past her shoulder, he suddenly smiled. At that moment, the limo cruised to a stop. ''We're here.''

Letitia looked out the window and gasped. Below them, Los Angeles had been transformed from an asphalt city to a magnificent festival of light, vibrant, glistening, pulsing with life. ''It's breathtaking.''

"I hoped you might enjoy it." Larkin raised his glass. "To popcorn and movies, to cities after dark, and to the beautiful woman who has made these things, and this night, so very special."

Letitia's heart quivered with emotion. There was so much she wanted to say, but there was this giant lump in her throat and her eyes were all misty. In the end, her muteness didn't matter. Their glasses clinked softly. They shared a knowing smile.

Larkin reached for the remote.

For the rest of the evening, they sipped champagne, munched warm popcorn, enjoyed a double feature of spine-tingling intrigue and there, parked on a secluded pull-off a quarter mile from Topanga Canyon and Mulholland Drive, Letitia Cervantes fell in love for the second time in her life.

It was 2:00 a.m. before the white limo cruised into the cul-de-sac. Dan, having spent the evening napping in the front seat, emerged, rested and refreshed, to open the door for his glowing clients, both of whom seemed to float rather than walk up the winding path to the brightly lit porch.

Every nerve in Larkin's body was alive with sensation. He not only felt the warmth of Letitia's hand in his, he was acutely aware of each slender finger nestled against his palm, and the smooth curve of every polished nail. Her skin was soft, incredibly so, like the velvet petals of a fragile flower with a fragrance twice as sweet. Even now that glorious fragrance wafted around him like loving fingers, stroking him, arousing him, caressing the very core of his being. He was dizzied by her scent, bewitched by her charm, enchanted by her beauty. Sometime during this magical night, an inert part of his soul had awakened, pulsing with a vibrancy he'd never known. He was alive again. And he was unbelievably happy.

They were on the porch now, but he couldn't bring himself to release her hand. Not yet, not while moonbeams danced in her eyes and her midnight hair glimmered with starlight.

Letitia looked up with a shy smile, expectant, he thought, with a touch of apprehension. "I had a lovely evening."

"So did I."

They were facing each other, their fingers still tightly entwined. She didn't seem ready for that final good-night. Neither was Larkin.

But suddenly he couldn't think of anything to say. More precisely, he couldn't say anything he was thinking. Certainly he couldn't tell her that his heart was pounding like a love-struck adolescent's. Nor could he confess that he was so overwhelmed by her nearness that he sometimes forgot to breathe.

His aching lungs reminded him that this was one of those times. The air slid out all at once. Then he inhaled deeply too deeply, with a rasping breath that to his own sensitive ears reverberated like a gasp of pure terror.

She pretended not to notice. "It's late. I guess you must be pretty tired."

He'd never been more awake in his life. "Not really."

"Oh." Her gaze focused in the middle of his chest. "Neither am I."

Larkin stood there as if his feet were rooted to the porch. His mind was spinning, his body awash with sensation. All night he'd been fighting the urge to sweep her into his arms and kiss her senseless. He'd resisted only because he hadn't wanted to rush or frighten her. Over and over, he'd reminded himself that she was vulnerable, inexperienced.

As if he wasn't.

Oh, he'd had plenty of dates since the divorce. Nice women, attractive women, women with pleasing personalities and enjoyable humor. And each time, Larkin spent the entire evening wishing he'd been somewhere else. Anywhere else. But not alone. Never alone.

That was the problem. He'd used those lovely people as a crutch against loneliness, and he'd hated himself for it.

But with Letitia, it was different. He hadn't wanted to be anywhere else, with anyone else. Hours had disappeared in the blink of an eye; still, he was loath to relinquish these final fleeting seconds and continued to clutch her delicate hand in his own clammy mitt while struggling for something—anything—that would prolong this glorious moment.

It was hopeless. The indomitable Larkin McKay, he of the glib tongue and invincible wit, a man whose gift of gab could transform a tightfisted Scrooge into a bleeding-heart philanthropist, who could counsel hard-core enemies into lifelong friends, suddenly couldn't have spit out a coherent sentence to save his soul.

Letitia heaved a sigh. "I should go in." But she made no move to do so.

Larkin slid his right thumb up her angora sleeve, shivering as the silky wisps brushed his palm. "Yes," he murmured. "I suppose you should."

God, he wanted to kiss her. Did he dare—?

In a flash, she hoisted up on tiptoes, touched the back of his neck with her free hand and brushed her lips across his cheek. "Thank you," she whispered, her eyes huge. "For the most wonderful evening of my life." She would have withdrawn then, had Larkin not caught her waist and pulled her closer.

He hesitated, judging her willingness through the pliancy of her body. When she melted against him, lifting her parted lips, something inside his chest cracked. He brushed his mouth against hers in a kiss both tender and exquisitely erotic. She tasted sweet, moist. A frisson of excitement skittered down his spine; heated blood raced through his veins; a liquid warmth exploded somewhere deep in his belly.

After a small eternity that was much too brief, she turned gently away and laid her cheek against his chest. Larkin held her, stroking her thick hair, waiting—as perhaps she was— for his knees to stop trembling. He kissed the top of her head, and as he turned his face to rest his cheek against the silken nest of curls, a movement at the window caught his attention.

There, barely visible behind the porch lamp reflecting in the glass, Larkin saw Rose Cervantes peering through the parted drapes. Their gazes met, held for a split second, then the drapes flowed together and Rose was gone. But not before Larkin had recognized the pain in her eyes. And the fear.

Chapter Seven

Mama Rose was rolling biscuits when Larkin peered through the kitchen door. She glanced up briefly, then returned to her work without so much as a flicker of expression. "Is football practice over?"

"It's starting to rain."

She set the rolling pin aside, wiped her hands on her apron and reached for a water glass to use as a biscuit cutter. "Where is Letitia?"

"Over at the neighbor's. Clogged drain." Larkin sauntered to the kitchen table. "I offered to help, but she seemed to think I'd just get in the way."

As he sat down, Rose's shoulders tensed, a clear indication that she fervently wished he'd get out of her kitchen but was too polite to say so. Instead, she punched biscuit rounds out of the flat dough so forcefully that he wondered if the glass rim had scored the cutting board. "Letitia is a very capable woman," she said.

"Who doesn't need a man underfoot, hmm?"

Rose glanced over her shoulder, hiking a black brow. "Men have their uses."

Larkin chuckled. "I guess I asked for that, but I think I'll pass on the question of exactly what those uses might be."

The woman returned to her chore, but not before Larkin saw the amused twinkle in her eye. He leaned back, watching her work. "You're pretty good at that," he said.

She twisted the glass into the dough as if squashing an insect. "My biscuits don't look like little submarines, but they taste good."

Puffing his cheeks, Larkin blew out a breath and concentrated on scratching a mar in the laminated tabletop. He didn't need his Ph.D. to figure out that Rose was still steamed about the brunch he'd prepared a couple of weeks ago. That had been yet another miscalculation on his part. He'd hoped she'd enjoy being pampered and served. Unfortunately, she'd eyed his fancy baked eggs with something akin to disgust and had pointedly requested a steak knife for the crispy potatoes that were the pride of his culinary repertoire.

Obviously, his plan to use their mutual interest in cooking as an icebreaker was another loser. It was time to improvise. "By the way, the owner of that clothing store on Pico has agreed to donate three dozen T-shirts for your project."

"Three dozen!" The glass froze in midair. Rose spun around, eyes glowing. "*¿Es verdad?*"

"Cross my heart." Larkin traced an *X* on his chest and grinned. "All I had to do was show him a sample of your work and ask him if he thought such magnificent art belonged on old, torn up shirts just because so many kids couldn't afford to buy new ones."

"I can't believe it. Three dozen." Rose bit her lip, turning away to set the glass on the counter. As she wiped her hands on her apron, her shoulders quivered and when she faced Larkin again, her eyes were shimmering with a rush of grateful tears. "The children will be so happy. Thank you."

Touched, Larkin shifted in the chair and gave an awkward shrug. "You need it, I scrounge it. That's the deal."

Rose considered that. "We need paint, too."

"I'm working on it."

"Particularly red. The children are very fond of red."

"Lots of red. Got it."

"And brushes? There aren't enough to go around."

"Okay, brushes, too. Anything else?"

She smiled, her eyes twinkling. "Not at the moment."

He wiped his brow. "You drive a hard bargain, Mrs. Cervantes . . . or may I call you Rose?"

"You may call me Mrs. Cervantes."

"Ah. Yes, of course." Sighing, he slumped in the chair as the woman returned her attention to moving doughy rounds onto a baking sheet. Larkin sat there, lost in thought, only vaguely aware of a sudden *thump* emanating from the living room. He paid no attention to the noise, or to Mannie's shouts of frustration. Rose was going to be a hard sell. She was a bright woman, able to intuit intent and size up a situation with amazing accuracy. Larkin had misjudged her more than once. Obviously, she had seen through his lame attempts to skirt the real issue and had been offended by his lack of candor.

So he lifted his elbow to the table, propped his chin on his hand and drove straight to the heart of the matter. "It must be difficult for you to see Letitia with a man other than your son."

The subtle sharpening of her shoulder blades was the only indication that she'd heard him.

At that inopportune moment, a tan blur caught Larkin's attention as Rasputin scurried into the kitchen with a blue sweat band dangling from his mouth.

Mannie loomed in the doorway, shouting. "Drop it, you little rat-faced thief!"

Rasputin tossed Larkin an "isn't this fun?" look before churning his stubby legs and dashing into the laundry room with his furious young master right behind him.

Larkin winced at a reverberating metal *boom,* which sounded suspiciously like an eleven-year-old climbing over the washing machine.

"Let go!" Mannie hollered.

The demand was followed by a throaty growl.

"You're such a brat..."

Grr.

"Geez, Raspy, you're gonna tear it..."

Grr.

There was another loud *clunk,* following by a swishing noise, more canine protests, more human muttering and finally, a shout of triumph. Mannie emerged with his hard-earned, if slightly soggy prize, then stalked through the kitchen without so much as a glance at either his grandmother or Larkin and disappeared into the living room. In a moment, the television blared.

Rasputin poked his head through the open laundry room door. Apparently satisfied that the coast was clear, he pranced out with a crafty gleam in his eye and slipped into the hallway on a new mission of mischief.

At the sink, Rose was washing the chicken she'd retrieved from the refrigerator while Larkin had been distracted. She worked quietly, without looking up or responding to his previous statement. Obviously, the subject Larkin had tried to broach was one she didn't wish to discuss.

Despite an ability to exercise admirable control over her emotions, there was no doubt that Rose Cervantes was deeply troubled about Larkin's relationship with her daughter-in-law. Larkin understood, even empathized with those concerns, but feared that allowing Rose's resentment to fester in silence would create a strain that could eventually affect the entire family. In his experience, the only way to deal with fear was to face it, head-on.

Other people's fear, that is. Never his own.

"You resent me, don't you?"

Rose ripped a paper towel off a nearby roll and patted moisture off the freshly washed chicken. "You are a fine man, Dr. McKay. I have no right to resent you."

"If someone invaded my home, disrupted my routine and ingratiated himself with my family, I'd resent him." He waited for a response. When she gave none, he leaned back, regarding her. "I don't blame you for viewing me as an intruder."

"You are not an intruder. You have been invited."

"But not by you."

Rose gave the chicken a stinging whack and plopped it in a roasting pan. "This is Letitia's home, and Manuel's. They have a right to share it with their friends."

"It's your presence that makes this a home," he said softly. "Perhaps that's why I feel drawn here, to experience for myself what it's like to be part of a real family."

She hiked a thick brow, regarding him with eyes that tried, but couldn't quite manage, to conceal her compassion. "Letitia told me how much you miss your children. I'm sorry."

"Thank you."

"Still, there must be others to comfort you . . . your parents, or your brothers and sisters?"

An odd pain moved through his chest. He waited until it dissipated. "No."

She frowned. "Your parents have passed on?"

"No. That is, I don't think so." He glanced away from her horrified expression. "The truth is that I've been estranged from my family for some time."

Rose stared at him as if he'd committed heresy. "How is this possible? Your parents gave you life. How can you reject them?"

"Actually, it was the other way around. Not that I blame them," he added quickly. "I was never a little angel, but when my parents divorced, I became a real hellion. After a couple of weekend visits, my father had had enough of me. He moved away and I never heard from him again. A few months later, my mother remarried and my life went downhill fast." Larkin flinched at the bitter edge on his voice. He hadn't meant to expose so much of himself and hoped Rose hadn't noticed.

She had. Her dark eyes softened. "You did not get along with your mother's new husband?"

"No, but in all fairness, I didn't make much of an effort to get along. The fact is that I wasn't a particularly pleasant child. I despised my stepfather, I despised his children and in a way, I probably even despised my mother for having disrupted my life without my permission." He managed a thin smile. "So you see, I really can understand how you feel."

"You were a child," she insisted, reaching into the fridge for a handful of fresh herbs. "It's not the same."

"Close enough." He watched her stack the bunched herbs on the cutting board. "What's that?"

"Hmm?" Rose followed his gaze to the herbs she was about to chop. "Oh, just basil and thyme."

Intrigued, Larkin stood for a better look. "I've never seen basil with leaves like that."

"I grow it myself," she said proudly. "It's a variety my mama always kept in her garden. The flavor is much bolder than the spindly supermarket kind." She plucked a fat leaf from the bunch and offered it to him. "Try it."

He nipped off the leaf tip. "Wow. Pungent."

Rose smiled. "You like it?"

"It's terrific." He chewed slowly, savoring a renewed burst flavor. "This would make pesto sing like Pavarotti."

Obviously pleased by the praise, Rose returned her attention to chopping the remaining herbs. "Would you like me to pot you a cutting?"

"If it wouldn't be too much trouble." By this time, Larkin had moved to the counter and was peering over the woman's shoulder. "Herb stuffing?" he asked.

"No." She scooped the chopped herbs into a bowl of softened butter. "Your mother must have been upset by such discord between her son and her husband."

"Yes, I suppose she was, although at the time, I wasn't inclined to consider her point of view."

"What happened?"

"I ran away. The herb butter is for the biscuits, right?"

"No." She reached for a garlic press. "Running away was a childish thing to do."

"Well, I *was* a child."

"Your mother must have been frantic. I hope she tanned your bottom when you got home."

"I never got home. Say, how much garlic are you going to put in there, anyway?"

"Never?" Rose laid the press aside, her chin puckered with anger. "How could you have been so cruel to your own mother?"

Startled, Larkin looked into the woman's furious eyes and debated whether he should tell her why he'd never gone home. When her hand twitched toward her chopping knife, he blurted, "She wouldn't take me back."

Rose gaped in disbelief. "That can't be true."

He managed what he hoped was a nonchalant shrug. "Like I said, I'd become a royal pain in the butt. I deliberately forced my mother to choose between me and her husband. She chose him."

"But you were just a boy! Where did you go?"

His jaw tightened. "Foster care, eventually."

Rose looked away, shaking her head and mumbling in Spanish. After a moment, she snatched up a wooden spoon, creaming the herbs and garlic into the softened butter. When she turned the wooden spoon around, using the handle to gently lift the skin from the breast meat, Larkin was totally confused. "What in the world are you doing to that poor chicken?"

She slipped him a secretive smile. "Put on an apron, *gringo*. Maybe you'll learn something."

"The grass is wet," Rose grumbled. "It's cold."

Letitia tucked her hands in her jacket pocket, flipping her head sideways so the wind would blow her hair out of her face. "You didn't have to come, Mama. But I'm glad you did."

"The dishes are done. The floor has been mopped. Even Manuel's things have been picked up and put away. Why should I sit in a clean house with nothing to do?" Rose hoisted her empty canvas tote, slipping the handles over her shoulder. She blew into her hands to warm them. "It's silly to eat a big meal, then run around the park like squirrels to work off the food. Why eat in the first place?"

"Larkin says exercise is good for the constitution. Besides, he and Mannie spent most of the afternoon cooped up because of the rain. I think they were going stir-crazy." To prove her point, Letitia gestured toward the two males, one large and one small, racing toward the park pond.

Larkin would win, of course. Mannie's legs were shorter, his hip deformity made for an awkward gait and he was further disadvantaged by the agitated Chihuahua zigzagging in his wake and nipping at his heels. Still, the boy was holding his own. More importantly, Mannie was having a whale of a good time, laughing and sweating and literally glowing with excitement.

Seeing her son so happy made Letitia's heart swell. She watched eagerly, relishing each minute detail of Mannie's exuberance. When he and Larkin disappeared over the brow of a hill, she glanced at her mother-in-law. "Actually, Larkin only dropped by to pick up some clothes he was going to take to the dry cleaners. It was nice of you to invite him for dinner."

Rose shrugged. "He helped cook it. He might as well help eat it."

Letitia studied the woman's expressionless face, hoping for a clue as to what had happened this afternoon. Something certainly had, because Letitia had returned from unclogging a neighbor's drain to find Larkin and Rose garbed in matching lace-trimmed aprons, hunkered over a baking dish, spooning what appeared to be green butter under the skin of a raw chicken. It had been without a doubt one of the most bizarre sights Letitia had ever witnessed. "You seem to be warming up to Larkin," she said.

"One must be cold to warm up. I was never cold."

"Not at the youth center. You and Larkin seem to get along splendidly there, but you have to admit, Mama, that whenever he's been at the house you've been a bit, well, cool."

"Have I?" A wet leaf landed on the sleeve of Rose's coat. She flicked it away. "I'm an old woman. I have no need to impress a man simply because he happens to land on my porch."

Letitia jolted to a stop. "Are you saying that I do?"

"I said what I said. Nothing more."

Since Rose continued to traipse up the hill, Letitia put her own feet back in gear and hurried to catch up. She fell into step beside the older woman just as she crested the hill and the distant pond came into view. "I'm not a flirt, Mama, and I certainly don't throw myself at men. You know that. It hurts to have you imply otherwise."

Rose tucked her hands in her coat, staring down at the pond to avoid her daughter-in-law's gaze. "You are a good woman, *nuera,* with a pure and trusting heart. Such hearts are fragile, easily shattered by even the best of intentions.''

The obscure warning sent a tingle of trepidation down Letitia's spine. She had the distinct impression that Rose knew something, something vital, but before she could ask for details, her attention was diverted by a din of frantic quacking at the base of the hill. A certain yipping Chihuahua was running circles around a flock of ducks, trying to herd them back into the pond.

Beside her, Rose chuckled. ''Rasputin thinks he's a sheepdog, but he confuses feathers for wool.''

Since the dog in question had recently pilfered and irreparably chewed her favorite mother-of-pearl hair comb, Letitia wasn't feeling as charitable. ''He's probably planning to steal one and drag it home to his hidey-hole.''

''Don't be unkind.'' Rose fixed an adoring gaze on the scurrying animal. ''You know my sweet little *perro* is gentle as a baby.''

''A baby polar bear,'' Letitia muttered, still peeved at the neurotic mutt. ''Look, he's scaring those poor ducks half to death.''

''He's playing, that's all.''

''Well, the ducks aren't having much fun.'' Shading her eyes, Letitia called out to her son. ''Mannie, pick up the dog and carry him until we get past the pond.''

Mannie issued an acknowledging nod and loped through the quacking herd. He'd just bent to retrieve Rasputin when the dog suddenly spotted a new challenge—a huge goose emerging from the pond, stepping on Rasputin's self-proclaimed turf without so much as a thank-you-kindly. The dog quivered at the indignity, then dived between Mannie's legs and rushed the startled goose, barking a frenzied protest. The goose went on alert, arching its slender neck, raising its wings and emitting a blood-chilling hiss that did little to dissuade a determined dog on a mission of honor.

Rose gasped in alarm.

"Oh, my God," Letitia murmured, then sprinted down the hill hoping to head off the confrontation. A five-pound Chihuahua stood no chance against a forty-pound goose with an attitude and a bill strong enough to crack every bone in the delicate little dog's body.

Mannie and Larkin had also recognized the danger, and were bolting from different directions in a desperate attempt to intercept Rasputin before he reached his potentially deadly foe.

The dog was too fast for them. In less than a heartbeat, he'd skidded to a stop in front of the hissing goose. A split second later, the goose had clamped onto Rasputin's neck, hoisted the yelping dog off the ground and was shaking him so violently that Letitia feared the poor little animal must already be dead.

She screamed. Rose screamed. Mannie screamed.

Then Larkin reached out in midstride to grab the goose's neck. The huge bird dropped the dog and whirled on Larkin, who scooped up the limp Chihuahua with one hand and tried to fend off the attacking goose with the other. Rasputin, very much alive and yelping frantically, clawed his way to Larkin's shoulder and leapt onto his head. Since Larkin needed both hands to reach up and retrieve the panicked animal, he tried to push the goose away with his foot.

The goose responded by clamping onto his kneecap. Larkin bellowed. As he tried to swat the creature away, Rasputin slid down over Larkin's face and bounced off his chest. He caught the canine fumble in midair just as the irritated goose reared up, wings spread, and bit his other knee. Yelping a phrase usually not heard in mixed company, Larkin spun around, clutching Rasputin like a football.

"Handoff!" Mannie hollered, rushing forward.

Larkin faked left, then passed the terrified dog under his arm as Mannie dashed by. The boy tucked Rasputin against his chest and charged away from the pond.

The furious goose followed, only to find itself confronted by an even more furious woman wielding a canvas tote. Rose reared back and whacked her bag against the fat, feathered breast. "Shoo!" The goose waddled back a few steps, cocking its head. Rose stamped her foot. "*Shoo!*"

Whether alerted by the indomitable fury of a protective pet lover or the lingering scent of a plucked cousin seasoned with herbs, the goose instantly retreated and waddled serenely back to the pond.

Letitia ran to Mannie, panting. "Is...he all right?" A pair of bulging brown eyes peered over the boy's forearm. "Oh, Raspy," she moaned, snatching the quivering animal out of her son's grasp. "You scared us to death."

Rasputin whined and licked her chin.

Letitia's heart melted. She gave the dog's warm little body a hug before handing him to her relieved mother-in-law, who kissed her beloved pet's head, then tucked him safely into her tote.

Larkin limped over, still muttering under his breath.

"Ah, our hero," Letitia said, smiling.

He gave her a slitty-eyed stare. "You mock a wounded man?"

"Not at all. In fact, I'm truly impressed at your valor in fending off that ferocious feathered beast."

"The damned thing bit my knee."

"I know. I'm sorry. Does it hurt terribly?"

"Yes," he said, sulking adorably. "For two cents, I'd turn that nasty animal into next Sunday's dinner."

Letitia glanced over her shoulder. "Mama, do you have two cents?"

Rose straightened, hoisting the tote-turned-doggy-bed. "There will be no goose cooked in my kitchen."

"Why not?" Larkin asked. "Think of it as a fat chicken."

"It's not a chicken, it's a goose, and it's much too pretty to cook."

"I wouldn't consider any animal with a pair of yellow Vise-Grip clamps sticking out of its face as pretty," he complained, reaching down to massage his bruised knee.

Letitia laughed. "You're just angry because the goose won."

"I rescued the dog, didn't I?"

"Yes, you did. I'm very proud of you."

He brightened. "Are you really?"

"Of course I am. You and Mannie were both very brave."

Mannie, who'd jogged over in time to hear his mother's compliment, grinned happily. "So, does that mean we each get an extra piece of pie?"

"I don't know if you were *that* brave."

Larkin, taking exception, drew himself up to his full six-foot-plus height. "Oh, really? Well, let's see *your* bruises, hmm?"

Letitia sighed. "Point taken. But just one slice."

"Aw'right!" Mannie spun and dashed away, hollering over his shoulder to Larkin. "First one home gets the biggest piece!"

Larkin limped a couple of steps forward. "That's not fair. I can hardly walk."

Leaning over, Letitia whispered, "Guess what? There's only one slice left."

Larkin gave her a horrified look, then spun around and sprinted away as if his shorts were on fire.

Chuckling, Letitia swept a windblown strand of hair out of her eyes and watched the pie-hungry man shoot across the park, not slowed in the slightest by his goose-bruised knees. "I swear, Mama, that guy can consume more food in a single meal than most people could put away in a week."

"A healthy appetite is good," Rose replied, trudging forward with her tote, now heavier by five doggy pounds, hanging from her crooked arm. "Makes a man strong."

Letitia fell into step beside her mother-in-law. "Yes, well it makes a woman fat. That doesn't seem fair, does it?"

"Life isn't fair, Letitia. You should know that by now."

There was no sadness in Rose's voice, yet her rational, matter-of-fact tone made the comment even more sobering. The woman's oblique warning, made only a few minutes ago, still bothered and bewildered Letitia. *Such hearts are fragile,* Rose had said. *Easily shattered by even the best of intentions.*

Letitia couldn't fathom what that ominous prediction could possibly have to do with her, or why Rose had uttered those words with such a sense of foreboding. If she simply posed the question, Letitia knew that she'd receive an honest reply. Rose Cervantes was a forthright person, frequently candid to the point of being blunt. But beyond the curiosity was a very real apprehension. For the first time since her husband's death, Letitia was truly happy; she didn't want that happiness tainted by anything. Even the truth.

So Letitia ducked her head as she walked, and studied the pattern of raindrops clinging to the moist grass carpet. It was colder now, with a bone-chilling dampness that cut through her clothes like a frozen blade. A gray pall shrouded the land. The sun was setting, and its residual warmth would soon dissipate into icy darkness. Another storm was coming. She could smell rain in the air.

Beside her, Rose suddenly spoke. "You like him, don't you?"

Letitia stiffened. "Larkin? Of course I like him. He's been very good for Mannie."

"Has he been good for you, too?"

A stinging warmth spread up her throat. "I enjoy his company, if that's what you mean."

Thankfully, Rose made no comment about her defensive tone, saying only, "He is a personable young man."

"Yes." Letitia tossed her hair back, facing into the wind. She slanted a glance at her mother-in-law and, recognizing the woman's pursed lips and thoughtful expression, realized that the conversation wasn't over.

She did not, however, anticipate Rose's next comment. "You are in love with him."

A small gasp rose from Letitia's throat, hanging in the thick air. She couldn't deny it, yet wasn't ready to confirm it, at least not out loud, and certainly not to the mother of the man she had loved for most of her life.

After a moment, Letitia found her voice and used it cautiously. "Why would you say such a thing, Mama?"

Rose didn't reply immediately. Instead, she gazed out at the darkening sky with an indiscernible expression. When Rasputin poked his head out of the tote, she absently stroked the animal without breaking her visual link with the sky. "Your eyes shine for him," she said finally. "The way they once did for my son. I see the light in your face, *nuera*. I see your heart in your smile."

Flooded by a rush of emotion, Letitia didn't trust her voice—and didn't know what to say anyway—so she remained silent.

"I'm not so old that I don't understand love," Rose whispered. "And I'm not so cruel as to begrudge your happiness. Raymond would not want you to live your life alone, nor would he want his son to go fatherless."

"Then why—" Her voice broke. She cleared her throat and tried again. "Then why does this sound like a warning?"

"Because it is a warning. You are like my own flesh, and I love you more than my next breath. Your pain is my pain."

"I'm not in pain, Mama."

"You will be, child." A startling shimmer of tears gathered in her dark eyes. "Dr. McKay is a good man, a man of great compassion who has saved none for himself. A wounded heart can't be freely given, *nuera*, nor can it accept the love it is offered."

The hairs on Letitia's nape lifted. "Are you saying that he still loves his ex-wife?"

"He may. He may not. I don't know." Sighing, Rose whispered a command to Rasputin, who promptly disappeared inside the tote, presumably to lie down. They walked in silence for a moment, then the woman quietly conveyed the conversation she and Larkin had had earlier in the afternoon when he'd revealed part of his troubled childhood.

"Oh, God," Letitia whispered, when Rose had finished speaking. "To have been rejected by both of his parents and raised by strangers...? I can't imagine anything more horrible. No wonder his own divorce was so devastating. It must have been like reliving the past and seeing his worst fears replayed in the eyes of his own children."

"A terrible tragedy," Rose murmured. "But there is something worse, much worse."

A deadly pressure settled on Letitia's chest, making it difficult to breathe. "What could possibly be worse?"

The woman stared into the distance, shaking her head. "I don't know. He wouldn't speak of it."

The paradoxical statement took Letitia by surprise. "Wait a minute. How can you know what you haven't been told?"

A sad smile creased her handsome face. "In the same way I know that you love him. I feel it, in here." She pressed her palm against her bosom. "There is an emptiness in his spirit, a pain that doesn't heal."

"Then I'll help him," Letitia insisted. "Larkin has spent his life helping others. Whatever private torment he is suffering, I won't let him go through it alone."

"He must. His demons are his own." Rose suddenly turned and grasped Letitia's hands. "Don't you understand, *nuera?* There is no room for you in his heart, because it's filled with too much pain. I'm sorry for him. I ache for him. But I love you, Letitia, and I don't want you to be hurt."

She stood there, frozen, then swallowed hard and peeled her fingers from the woman's convulsive grip. "I won't be hurt," she whispered, patting her mother-in-law's trembling hand.

Their eyes met, a silent exchange of questions and answers and something even deeper. There was a shuddering sigh from one, or perhaps both, then Rose turned away and walked wearily to the edge of the park. After a moment, Letitia followed.

The sky was nearly black now. Another storm was coming. She could smell rain in the air.

Chapter Eight

As usual, the corridor was packed with noisy youngsters, although Letitia now weaved through the crowd with considerable expertise. She was comfortable at the youth center, familiar with the routine of organized chaos of which she had become an integral part. She'd even picked up enough slang for basic communication with most of the kids. Rap-speak was still confusing—she had difficulty remembering that "bad" meant "good" and being called a "freak" was a compliment—but all in all, she usually managed to get the gist of most conversations.

As she passed the open door of Room 16, she paused to wave at Rose, whose class had proven so popular that she'd added two extra sessions to her already generous volunteer schedule. Ordinarily, that would have meant two more dinners for Letitia to prepare, a situation that wouldn't have pleased poor Mannie. Larkin, however, had come to the rescue, spending nearly every free evening at the Cervantes home and routinely cooking on those nights when Rose wasn't available.

Rose, bless her, had not only accepted Larkin's encroachment on her kitchen, she'd actually encouraged it. A few days earlier, when Larkin had referred to her as "Mrs. Cervantes," Mama had slid him a thoughtful look and informed him that he could now call her "Rose." Larkin had seemed exceptionally pleased.

At first, Letitia had been leery about her mother-in-law's change of heart, particularly after the dire warning she'd issued during that fateful walk in the park two weeks ago.

Since then, however, Rose had made no further mention of her concerns. Although Letitia knew her mother-in-law's trademark intuition was usually accurate to the point of clairvoyance, she'd convinced herself that for once Rose's ominous prediction had missed the mark entirely.

During the past weeks, Letitia and Larkin's relationship had blossomed into a full-fledged romance; he'd filled her heart with happiness and her life with new purpose. They'd spent hours talking, sharing hopes and dreams for a future that seemed to Letitia as inexorably intertwined as was their present. Barely an hour went by without one of them phoning the other, just to chat about what had happened since they'd last spoken.

Every morning Letitia awoke bursting with the anticipation of seeing him again. Every night she drifted to sleep with her lips still tingling from his kiss.

Rose had been right about one thing; Letitia was deeply, irrevocably in love.

She flattened against the wall as a new wave of giggling kids crushed into the jammed corridor, then sidled out into the gymnasium, where the mass of humanity was spread into manageable portions. Sighing, she glanced across the huge room toward Larkin's office. He was there, hunched over his desk. She smiled, her heart singing, as it always did at the sight of him.

With her gaze still riveted across the room, she glided past the video arcade and was almost to Larkin's office door when she heard her son's voice. She stopped, glancing around until she spotted Mannie standing by the water fountain, engaged in awkward conversation with a giggling girl. A group of boys were clustered a few feet away, watching and whispering. When Mannie looked toward his friends, one of the boys gave a thumbs-up signal. At the same time, the girl glanced at her own cadre of encouragement, a group of preadolescent females bunched into a separate cheering section apart from but within deliberate viewing proximity of the boys.

Mannie and the girl, a pretty little blonde with huge blue eyes, continued to gawk at their feet, their friends and occasionally, slant a furtive glance at each other.

Letitia swallowed hard. She always knew that eventually her son would recognize and appreciate the charms of the opposite sex; she just hadn't thought it would happen so soon. He was only eleven, for goodness' sake, a mere child.

A mere child who was openly ogling a sweatered female chest that but for two vague little bumps was as flat as an ironing board.

Obviously, it was time for the dreaded facts of life discussion. Letitia felt sick. The only parental guidance she'd had about such things had been at her own wedding reception when her mother had whispered, "He'll want to do things tonight. Let him." Then Mother had slipped into the crowd, leaving Letitia to stew about just what kind of horrible things her new husband could possibly want to do.

Of course, she'd been massively relieved to discover that he'd only wanted sex. She knew all about that, thanks to explicit diagrams sketched on the high school's bathroom wall.

Letitia would, of course, like her own son to have a more formal explanation. She just didn't want to be the one who had to give it. She glanced through the open door of Larkin's office and smiled. Not only was he a male, he was a psychologist to boot. Surely he'd been trained in discussing sexual matters with young people.

She slipped into the office, closing the door behind her. "Hi, handsome."

Dropping his pencil, Larkin looked up with a melting grin. "Hi yourself, gorgeous."

Without taking her eyes off him, Letitia reached over and pulled the cord, closing the venetian blinds. "So, what really important stuff have you been up to today? Besides waiting for me, that is."

He stood, reached her with two steps and swept her into his arms. "Nothing is more important than waiting for you, unless it's actually being with you."

She lifted her lips. "You're with me now."

"There is a God," he whispered, then took her lips in a slow, sweet kiss.

His mouth was so warm, so loving. She melted against him, sliding her hands around his back, thrilled by the rippling strength of his muscles beneath her palms. For these brief moments, time was suspended. There were no deadlines, no government checks to issue, no dinners to prepare; they were alone on earth, oblivious to the crush of young humanity seething just beyond the closed door.

When her lips parted, inviting a more intimate touch, he accepted so eagerly that her knees turned to fluid and blood pulsed through her veins like molten lava.

As always, the kiss ended much too soon. Letitia stepped back, smiling and shaken. "Whoa. You sure know how to get a person's attention."

"I could say the same about you." Larkin tenderly brushed her cheek with his knuckle. "I'll miss you tonight."

Letitia sighed. "I'll miss you, too. Do you really have to go? I mean, from what I've heard about bachelor parties, everyone will probably be too blitzed to notice if you're not there.''

"They'll notice," Larkin said, chuckling. "There's only going to be four of us."

"Does that include the exotic dancer that bursts out of the cake?''

"No dancer, no cake. Sorry.''

"How about stag films?''

"Now why would we want to sit around staring at a bunch of grazing elk?''

She gave his arm a playful slap. "So far, this doesn't sound like much of a party.''

"No, I don't suppose it does," he said, suddenly pensive. "Just an evening of reminiscence and a toast to the demise of another Brotherhood bachelor.''

"Brotherhood? Is that some kind of college fraternity?''

"Hmm?'' Blinking, Larkin pulled his gaze from somewhere in the past. "Oh, no. It's just a holdover from when we were kids.''

"Like a secret society?''

He shrugged, looking strangely sad. "In a manner of speaking, I guess it was.''

Letitia regarded him for a moment, wondering about the distant look in his eyes, an expression that always appeared when conversation brushed on a past he seemed reticent to discuss. "So the man who's getting married on Saturday is a member of this Brotherhood?''

Larkin didn't answer directly. Instead, he managed what Letitia thought to be a rather thin smile, took a couple of steps backward and sat on the edge of his desk. "Have you decided what to wear to the wedding?''

Crossing her ankles, Letitia leaned against the closed door and folded her arms, very much aware that her question had been soundly ignored, although uncertain as to why. Whenever Larkin had spoken of Roberto Arroya—whom he called Bobby—it had always been with pride that his friend had attained a position of prestige and power as a federal prosecutor.

Unfortunately, Letitia hadn't met Roberto since his volunteer hours at the center hadn't yet coincided with her own. She had, however, been introduced to Devon Monroe, a journalist for the *L.A. Times* whose byline graced some of the paper's juiciest investigative pieces.

A few days ago she'd stumbled into Larkin's office and found the two men huddled in whispered conversation. The first thing that struck her was the easy banter between the two men and the intuitive, almost secretive closeness they shared. Later, when she and Larkin had been alone, she'd asked about that. Larkin had said only that they'd met as children and been friends for a long, long time. Then he'd abruptly changed the subject.

Just like he'd done now.

There was so much Letitia knew about Larkin McKay, and so much more she wanted to know. Every time the topic strayed too far from the here and now, his eyes glazed with sadness and he smoothly guided the conversation toward something entirely different. One of these days, Letitia would try to guide it back again.

But not today. Today, she'd respect his wishes and swallow her questions. "Actually, I know exactly what I'm going to wear to the wedding. I bought a new dress that's going to knock your socks off."

He emitted a low whistle. "Sounds dangerous."

Considering what she'd paid for the darn thing, she certainly hoped so. "I'll be meeting some of your friends for the first time. I want to look nice so you'll be proud of me."

Reaching out, he pulled her into his arms. "I'm always proud of you," he whispered, nuzzling her neck. "And you'd look nice wearing a gunnysack."

Intimately cradled between his thighs, Letitia shivered as Larkin's tongue touched the pulsing vein at her throat. "Since you're going to be the best man, I don't think stenciled burlap would be the best complement to a powder gray tux.''

"Hmm. You could be right.'' Lifting his head, he touched a fingertip to the moist trail his mouth had left on her skin. "But no matter what you wear, you're going to be the most beautiful woman there.''

"I doubt the bride would be pleased to hear that.''

Larkin smiled. "You'll like Erica. She's one of the truest, most down-to-earth people I've ever known.''

"I'm looking forward to meeting all your friends.'' Letitia followed his gaze to the wall clock. "What time do you have to leave?''

"Soon.'' His hands dropped to his knees, releasing her. "Are you and Mannie going home now?''

Reluctantly, she stepped away. "I am, but Mannie will probably catch a ride with Rose later. Since he's out there making goo-goo eyes at a winsome blonde, I suspect he'll want to stay around for a while.''

Larkin smiled, running his fingers through Letitia's thick, dark curls. "I've always preferred brunettes myself, but to each his own, I suppose.''

"I suppose,'' Letitia mumbled. She cleared her throat, struggling to broach the subject of asking Larkin to consider having a man-to-boy talk with her son. "It's just that he seems, well, awfully young to be . . . ah . . . you know.''

Hiking a brow, Larkin eyed her with undisguised amusement. "Are you trying to tell me that Mannie and his young lady are engaged in an act of 'you know' right in the middle of the gymnasium? Hmm. Our sponsors will be most perturbed.''

She gave him a withering look. "That's not funny.''

"No?'' He flinched at her narrowed stare. "No, I guess it isn't.''

Unable to maintain her forced indignation, she tossed up her arms and laughed. "All right, maybe I am being a little overprotective, but that's what mothers do. The truth is, I suddenly realized that my sweet little boy is almost as tall as I am. Mannie is well on his way to becoming a hormone-pickled adolescent and I haven't a clue what to do about it."

Larkin, bless him, managed not to laugh, despite the unmistakable twinkle in his eyes. "Unless I missed a crucial chapter in my college biology text, I'm not sure there's anything you can do. Hormones happen. Without them, the poor kid would spend his entire life with a hairy head and bald chest, not to mention a permanent spot singing soprano in the church choir. You wouldn't want that, would you?"

"Actually, yes." She absently rubbed her arms and studied a worn trail in the carpet leading from the doorway to Larkin's desk. "The bottom line in this dilemma is that I simply don't know how to discuss sexual matters with a boy."

"Ah, I see. Would you like me to have a talk with him?"

Her shoulders sagged in relief. "I'd be grateful for the rest of my life."

"Not nearly long enough, but it will have to do." He stood, grasped her shoulders and planted a kiss on her forehead. "I'll send you a coded message when the deed is done."

"What's the code?"

"Let's see, how about 'the eagle has landed'?"

"I think that one's been used."

Following Letitia to the door, Larkin opened it for her. "Grateful people shouldn't be picky."

"You're right. 'The eagle' it is." She hesitated. "Will you call me tonight after the party?"

"I was hoping you'd ask. It might be late, though."

"I don't care." Letitia still hovered in the doorway, reluctant to leave. "By the way, who's the fourth man?"

Larkin's smile faded. "Excuse me?"

"You said there'd be four of you at the party tonight, but I don't recall you mentioning anyone other than Roberto and Devon, so I just wondered who else would be there."

A small muscle twitched at the base of his jaw. "No one else."

There was that look again, that clouded expression of warning that the conversation had once again veered into forbidden territory. Only this time, as Larkin fixed his gaze over her head, Letitia realized that she'd inadvertently stumbled upon an important clue; she just couldn't quite figure out what it was. "Perhaps I misheard," she said finally.

When Larkin again focused on her, his smile had returned and his eyes were clear. "I'll call you later."

She managed a bewildered nod. After taking a few steps, she glanced over her shoulder. He waved. She waved back. A moment later she'd disappeared into the crowd.

Larkin watched until the top of her curly head had been completely swallowed up by a surge of youngsters swarming through the center's front door, then he leaned against the doorjamb and whispered, "Sorry, Tommy. I didn't think she'd understand."

He paused for a moment, as if awaiting an answer, then shook off the odd sensation that he'd actually gotten one.

As he turned to reenter his office, he spotted Mannie out of the corner of his eye and quickly ascertained that Letitia's assessment of her son's sexual interest had probably been right on target. The blond girl had apparently left, but Mannie had stayed behind, strutting and smirking to entertain an entourage of leering youngsters with the bragging ritual that had been a masculine right of passage since the days of caves and campfires.

Such behavior was normal, of course, if not particularly attractive. Larkin had noticed that the more insecure youngsters were inclined toward even more boasting and bravado, particularly those challenged by physical weakness. Boys like Mannie.

Boys like Tommy Murdock.

The thought shouldn't have been startling, but it was. Of course Larkin was aware of the similarities between Mannie and his childhood friend. He'd frequently noted that both boys had been driven to push and prove themselves, and to ignore their limitations without consideration of consequence.

But now as he studied Letitia's son, the boy's animated face seemed suddenly thinner, and his white, even smile melted into a crooked, gap-toothed grin. The bustling gymnasium dimmed; the din of voices became blurred, distant, like the constant hiss of steam in a dank and dreary basement.

In his mind, Larkin was surrounded by damp cinder blocks, watching a small group of youngsters clustered around the light of a single flashlight. It was a meeting of the Brotherhood.

As always, Devon was in charge. He called the meeting to order by banging a make-believe gavel, then turned to Tommy, who sat cross-legged on the cold concrete wearing institutional pajamas and a smug grin. "Okay, we've got two hours till the 3:00 a.m. bed check. Tommy called the meeting, so I'm gonna turn the floor over to him."

Roberto yawned. "This better be good, man. My butt is freezing."

More out of habit than necessity, Larkin defended his pal. "Hey, give him a chance. It's prob'ly something real important, right, Tommy?"

Tommy's grin widened to display that dumb, tweaked-out tooth. "I got somethin' for our treasure box."

Devon and Roberto both sat a bit straighter. Even Larkin's interest was piqued. After all, Tommy wouldn't have called the Brotherhood together in the middle of the night unless he had something special, maybe even better than that squished quarter Dev found in the parking lot.

"Well, hell," Devon finally growled. "Are you gonna show us or what?"

Milking the moment, Tommy gave his ponytail a flip, took a wheezing breath and reached under his pajama top. His hand froze. He tossed Roberto a wary look. "I dunno. Maybe Bobby should close his eyes or something."

Roberto's jaw drooped. "How come?"

"You're kinda young," Tommy noted. "This is for older guys."

Rigid with indignation, the skinny ten-year-old shook a fist at his eleven-year-old tormenter. "I ain't too young to punch that ugly nose all over your face."

Devon uttered a series of loud bops to simulate a banging gavel. Three faces turned dutifully in his direction. With order restored, Dev carefully laid down the imaginary mallet and took charge of the situation. "Nobody's gonna punch any noses," he told Roberto, who folded his arms and sulked while the Brotherhood's self-appointed chairman's attention turned to Tommy. "Bobby's got just as much right as any of us to see what you've got."

Tommy heaved a long-suffering sigh, but his eyes sparkled with mischief. "Okay, you asked for it." With that, he retrieved a magazine from under his pajama top, waved it over his head, then flopped it down on the floor in the middle of the circle so the flashlight beam illuminated the shocking cover.

"Geez," Larkin whispered, gulping.

Devon's eyes were as big as fishbowls. "Wow."

Roberto just sat there with his mouth open, ogling the glossy, full-color photograph of a bosomy nude cover model.

"So," Tommy gloated, smoothing the curled edges of the girlie magazine. "Is this, like, great or what?"

Devon nodded without lifting his eyes. "Where'd you find it?"

"In the administrator's lounge. I was delivering a box of stuff from the office and there it was, just laying on a chair." Frowning, Tommy noticed a brown coffee ring encircling the woman's face. He gave the stain a futile rub, then shrugged. "At least it ain't messing up nothing important," he said, eyeing the model's rosy breasts. "Besides, there's lots more pictures inside."

As Tommy opened the magazine, four heads lurched forward for a closer look. For the next hour, they silently examined page after page of the most incredibly beautiful women their young eyes had ever beheld.

When the final page had been turned, they heaved a collective sigh and sat back with expressions that ranged from wistful to slightly flushed. Behind them, the boiler belched and gurgled, breaking the dreamy silence.

Devon coughed, slapped his knees and took a shuddering breath. "It's getting late. We'd, uh, better put this away."

Larkin dried his palms on his pj's. "Tommy should do it."

"Yeah," Roberto mumbled, fidgeting with a hole in the thigh of his pajamas. "It's Tommy's find. He should put it in the box."

With a brisk nod, Devon made it unanimous, so Tommy went to retrieve the treasure box from its hiding place, wedged behind a maze of drippy pipes. The metal container, a discarded check file scrounged from a trash bin outside the administrative building, was laid reverently inside the circle. The lid was lifted to reveal the Brotherhood's treasure, the sum total of shared wealth that was their legacy—a broken yo-yo, a Saint Christopher medal on a tarnished chain, several glass marbles, a cat-shaped charm Roberto insisted was made of real gold and, of course, the flattened quarter.

Tommy solemnly laid the magazine inside, then all four boys raised their joined hands in a circle of unity. "One heart, one spirit, one mind," they murmured. "To the Brotherhood."

"To the Brotherhood," Larkin whispered. "To the Brotherhood."

"Huh? Whatsa matter, Doc? You feelin' okay?"

Blinking, Larkin glanced up at the buzz-headed adolescent who was eyeing him warily. "I, ah—" Larkin coughed into his hand, glancing around the bustling youth center. "I'm fine, Jackson, I'm just fine."

"Yeah? That's good, man. For a while there, I thought you was a few shots short of a clip, know what I mean?"

Larkin managed a pained smile.

"Well, gotta bounce. Later, Doc." Jackson raised a two-fingered fist and melted into the crowd.

Dazed and slightly disoriented, Larkin felt a familiar prickling sensation at the nape of his neck. It was time to go. The Brotherhood was waiting.

"It's about time," Devon said, swinging open the front door to Roberto's ranch-style home. "I can't tie this man down all by myself."

Larkin shifted the brown grocery bag he carried and stepped over a sleeping ball of prickly gray fur snoring in the entry. He grinned at their reluctant host, who was sitting on the sofa, arms folded, eyeing them suspiciously. "Hey, Bobby. Happy last day as a bachelor."

Roberto gave him a slitty-eyed stare. "I'm supposed to have a date with Erica tonight."

"A ruse," Devon said cheerfully. "Your soon-to-be wife is a coconspirator. Say, are those T-bones?" he asked, peering inside the grocery bag. Larkin allowed that they were, at which point Devon licked his lips and mumbled, "I don't care what anyone says, Lark. A man who treats his friends to a good steak can't be all bad."

"Your half of the bill is in the bag."

"Hey, I've already done my share," Devon protested, following Larkin into the neat kitchen. "Sixty-eight cents worth of Idaho's finest are baking in the oven as we speak."

Larkin set the bag on the counter. "Well hell, Dev, I'm impressed. Did you remember the sour cream?"

He blinked, then hollered over his shoulder. "Hey, Bobby, you got any sour cream?"

Roberto appeared in the doorway. "If you guys are planning to tie me to a damned palm tree, I'm obligated to warn you that my vicious attack dog has been trained to kill." As he spoke, a medium-size terrier-mix waddled into the doorway and yawned.

"Hi, Buddy," Larkin said to the dog. "How's it going?"

Buddy whined, yawned again, then ambled back into the living room.

Roberto glared at the animal's retreating back. "Okay, fine, but the next time you're in the mood for doggy treats, don't come begging to me."

Buddy glanced up with a "yeah, sure" look on his face, then flopped beside the sofa, laid his prickly chin on his paws, and went back to sleep.

"I think Buddy's 'kill' command needs a little work," Devon said, peering into Roberto's refrigerator. "There's nothing in here. No wonder you're so damned skinny."

"Now, now," Larkin mumbled, unloading the steaks and a plastic bowl of salad from his bag. "We mustn't insult poor Bobby. He can't help his shortcomings. By the way, Dev, did you at least remember to bring the rope?"

Devon closed the fridge. "Oh, yeah. After what you guys did to me, I've been waiting for retribution."

Roberto's eyes widened. "Hey, that was all Larkin's idea. He made me do it."

"As I recall, you didn't have a gun to your head. In fact, if memory serves, weren't you the one who stole my clothes and left me tied to that damned tree in my skivvies?"

"We're more mature now," Roberto argued in his best attorney style. "I'd like to think we've grown beyond such childish pranks."

When Devon pointed out that the incident in question took place less than six months ago, Roberto leaned against the doorjamb and stared glumly at the floor.

Larkin took pity on him. "Cheer up, Bobby. We're not going to tie you to a tree."

He glanced hopefully up. "You're not?"

"Nah. That's already been done. Besides, we *have* matured, right, Dev?"

Somehow Devon managed a serious expression. "Right."

Unconvinced, Roberto looked from Devon to Larkin and back again. "So, what are you guys doing here?"

"Celebrating, of course." Larkin pulled out a bottle of wine, dumped a couple of brightly wrapped presents on the counter and tossed the empty bag aside. "You don't think the Brotherhood would let you enter the solemn state of matrimony without wishing you well, do you?"

A narrowed expression indicated that Roberto had been hoping they would. "No tree?"

"Nope."

"You're not going to drive me into the desert and make me hitchhike back?"

Larkin chuckled at the memory of how his own Brotherhood bachelor party had nearly caused him to miss his own wedding. By the time he'd stumbled across a grizzled miner with a sputtering pickup truck, the church had been filling and Larkin had been plotting revenge. He'd gotten partial satisfaction from seeing Devon tethered to that damned tree; now it was Roberto's turn.

With final retribution close at hand, Larkin could barely contain his glee. "Like I said, Bobby, we've grown beyond such childish pranks."

Roberto seemed relieved, if slightly skeptical. "Well, good."

"So, let's get this show on the road," Devon mumbled, rooting through a utensil drawer until he located a corkscrew. "Since the potatoes won't be done for an hour, we might as well have a drink."

"Hmm? Oh, sure." Roberto retrieved four wineglasses from the cupboard.

While Devon popped the cork, Larkin swallowed a smug grin. "Speaking of potatoes, Bobby, do you remember KP duty at the Hall?"

Flinching, Roberto set the glasses on the kitchen table, which had four place settings already laid out. "Are you kidding? I must have peeled two tons of the damned things. I still can't stand the sight of a raw potato."

Larkin smiled. "We know."

"The thing that always ticked me off," Roberto said, "Was that the rest of you never spent a day on KP duty. I always wondered who you guys bought off."

"They weren't going to waste our talents in the kitchen. We were bigger and stronger." Devon poured a dollop of wine into each glass and offered one to Roberto. "Not to mention, better looking."

Roberto rolled his eyes, but took the glass without comment.

"Of course, the fact that Tommy worked in the office didn't hurt," Larkin added, helping himself to a glass of wine. "He switched a copy of the roster and changed our job assignments."

That bit of news seemed particularly distressing to Roberto. "Why didn't he change mine?"

Devon blinked. "Did you ask him to?"

"Well, no... but nobody ever told me he could do that."

"Ignorance is no excuse, counselor." Devon held up the two remaining glasses, his own and Tommy's. "A toast," he announced. "To Bobby's new family. May you and Erica and her little girls find the happiness you all deserve."

Larkin's glass joined the clinking rims. "Hear, hear."

They chatted amiably for a few minutes, then moved to the living room for the gift ceremony. Devon's presents were opened first, and although Roberto seemed pleased with the book on raising children, he didn't appear particularly enamored with a pair of silk boxer shorts adorned with tiny red hearts.

Devon grinned. "Romantic, huh? Erica will love 'em."

Grumbling, Roberto laid the gaudy underwear aside and picked up a foil-wrapped box from Larkin. He gave it a wary shake. "This isn't going to blow up, is it?"

Larkin adjusted his glasses and peeked over the wire rims. "I suppose they could be blown up, although I could personally think of a better use."

"*They?*" Roberto rattled the gift again, then ripped it open and pulled out a bag of loose condoms. He shook his head, grinning. "Well, thanks, Lark. I appreciate the thought but Erica and I are planning on having more kids."

"Of course you are," Larkin replied with feigned indignation. "That's why I poked holes in them."

Devon let out a hoot of laughter. "Good one, Lark. Wish I'd thought of it."

Larkin stood to take a bow.

"You guys are a bundle of yuks," Roberto grumbled, snatching up the last package, a tiny oblong box with a hand-curled bow. "This is probably a pair of glow-in-the-dark suspenders to hold up that ugly underwear."

"Hey," Devon protested, taking umbrage. "I'll have you know ugly underwear is very expensive nowadays. Set me back almost three bucks."

Larkin refilled his wineglass. ''A whole week's allowance, hmm? Jessica must have read you the riot act for being such a spendthrift.''

Meanwhile Roberto had dispensed with the wrapping paper. He opened the slender box, looked inside and gagged.

''No thanks necessary, bro','' Larkin said as Roberto held up the chrome-handled potato peeler. ''I knew you'd love it.''

''You're a real chum.'' He tossed the peeler aside and pointed to the coffee table. ''Hand me the last one and let's get this misery over with.''

Following the gesture, Larkin noticed yet another present lying in the midst of torn paper and wadded ribbon. ''Is that one from you, Dev?''

Devon frowned. ''No. I thought it was from you.''

''Not me.'' Larkin picked the tube-shaped gift up, turning it in his hand. ''No name tag.'' He slanted a knowing grin at Devon. ''Anonymous, huh?''

Devon's face was dead serious. ''Honest to God, Lark, it's not from me.''

Impatient now, Roberto snatched the present out of Larkin's hands. ''Give it up, *mi hermanos*. I've known you both long enough to recognize a con when I see one.'' As Devon and Larkin exchanged a puzzled look, Roberto ripped off the paper, unrolled the contents and sucked in a quick breath.

Larkin frowned. ''What's wrong, Bobby? You're white as a sheet.''

Taking a shuddering breath, Roberto laid the gift on the coffee table. Devon muttered a stunned oath; Larkin steadied himself on a nearby chair. All three men stared in amazement at the twenty-year-old girlie magazine with a coffee ring stain on the cover.

Larkin swallowed hard. ''I guess Tommy figured you were finally old enough to read it.''

Roberto nodded, then followed Devon's hand gesture to the glass of wine that had been set aside for their absent comrade. The glass, which had been half full, was now only a quarter full.

There could have been a rational explanation, of course, but none of the men bothered to search for one, nor did they conjure theories to justify the mysterious appearance of a magazine last seen two decades earlier when it had been placed inside the Brotherhood's treasure box. Over the years, each of them had been repeatedly touched by Tommy's presence. Now they simply accepted that he was sharing this Brotherhood moment as, in one way or another, he'd shared all the others.

Over the next few hours, the men enjoyed their evening together. They laughed, reminisced, exchanged jokes and enjoyed a fine meal, although Larkin groused continually about the lack of sour cream. Tommy's wineglass was set by his place at the table, although Larkin refused to cook him a steak, insisting that spirits didn't eat T-bones. Later, after putting out a grease fire in a cold and empty broiler, Larkin cast his eyes upward and promised that next time, he'd bring an extra steak.

The party broke up around midnight. As Larkin slid into his car, a dump truck rumbled up and deposited two tons of raw potatoes on the bridegroom's driveway.

Larkin drove away, whistling.

Chapter Nine

The chapel was gorgeous, with waterfalls of white roses cascading from huge ivory baskets and dripping from the delicate hands of the most incredibly beautiful bride Letitia had ever seen. In a swirl of Chantilly lace and seed pearls, Erica Franklin had floated into the arms of her attractive groom, oblivious to the teary smiles of her proud parents and the enthralled gasp of a beguiled congregation.

Standing beside his friend, Larkin had been the epitome of solemn dignity, so strikingly handsome that the sight of him took Letitia's breath away. The entire ceremony was permeated with an aura of profound love and enduring friendship, like an enchanted dream from which she never wanted to awaken.

And then, with the throbbing pulse of the organist's chord, Mr. and Mrs. Roberto Arroya had turned to greet their well-wishers.

Larkin had followed the radiant couple down the aisle escorting the matron of honor, who was apparently a business partner of Erica's. As he passed Letitia's pew, his gaze had sought her out. She'd returned his wink with a smile, which evolved into a tickled laugh as the bride's two little girls, ages three and six, finally tromped out clutching their flower baskets and grinning at the appreciative crowd.

Afterward, Devon Monroe, in his capacity as official wedding photographer, had lined up the bridal party for pictures. He'd been assisted by his wife, Jessica, an exquisitely lovely woman with whom Letitia felt an instant rapport. During the lengthy photo shoot, the two women had chatted, labeled film rolls, exchanged lens filters and otherwise made themselves useful during the all-important process of capturing magic moments for posterity.

But it had been later, at the reception, when the night had blossomed into something magical. Letitia had felt like Cinderella, introduced to and surrounded by a veritable Who's Who of Los Angeles politics. Larkin had whispered that the bride's father was, or rather had been, one of the county's better known politicos until his forced retirement a few months earlier. Letitia got the impression there had been some kind of scandal, although Larkin offered no details and she requested none. It had been apparent from the turnout of notables that Mr. Mallory was still highly regarded in the community.

The moments Letitia most cherished—besides those spent at Larkin's side—had taken place from afar, as she'd watched the amiable interaction of the three men who seemed closer than brothers. They'd spoken without words, exuding an almost telepathic empathy of thought and emotion. To Letitia, who'd been an only child, their closeness had been particularly moving.

But as she'd studied Roberto Arroya and Devon Monroe, Letitia had become intrigued by the same pensiveness and contemplative, disconnected gaze that Larkin had so frequently displayed. And she'd overheard a whispered word, one she couldn't quite place, but which struck a chord of vague familiarity.

The word had been Blackthorn.

Now, gazing out the car window into midnight darkness, the word again brushed Letitia's mind. Beside her, Larkin took one hand from the steering wheel and touched her knee. She looked up, smiling, and captured his strong fingers between her own palms.

"Did you have fun tonight?" he asked.

"You know I did." She sighed in contentment. "I can't ever remember having such an enjoyable time while surrounded by total strangers. The odd thing is that your friends didn't feel like strangers. After the first five minutes, I felt as if I'd known them for years. Everyone was so kind to me, and so accepting."

Larkin squeezed her hand. "Everyone liked you."

"I liked them too. They're all wonderful people. A little twisted, perhaps, but lots of fun." Laughing, she glanced into the rearview mirror at the massive pile of raw potatoes filling the entire back seat. The spud heap had mysteriously appeared sometime during the reception, rendering Larkin's back seat and most of Devon Monroe's minivan totally useless.

At first, Letitia had been horrified by what she'd considered a senseless act of vandalism, but when both Larkin and Devon had burst into gales of laughter, she'd learned about last night's bachelor bash prank, which had effectively blocked Roberto's garage and driveway with tons of the lumpy brown vegetables. Taken in that context, she'd finally decided that the groom's vengeance had been appropriate.

"What are you going to do with that mess?" Letitia asked, gesturing toward the back.

"The same thing Bobby will do," Larkin replied, smiling. "Only in my case, I can just drive into the downtown food bank and open the back door. Bobby will have to hire a front-loader and a dump truck.''

''That really was a pretty mean prank. The poor guy had to call a cab to his own wedding.''

''At least he didn't have to hitchhike.''

Since Larkin had filled her in on his own desert escape, compliments of yet another of the Brotherhood's infamous prenuptial antics, she allowed that the potato gag didn't seem so bad after all.

Larkin released Letitia's hand, then turned into the parking lot of his apartment building. After driving down a ramp into the underground garage, he pulled into his assigned space and flipped off the ignition.

They sat there for a moment, neither speaking nor looking at each other. Letitia, feeling awkward about having invited herself back to Larkin's place, finally broke the eerie silence. ''If you're too tired for company, I hope you'll say so.''

''I'm never too tired for your company.''

She fidgeted with her beaded evening bag. ''It's just that I've had such a lovely evening, I guess I don't want it to end.''

''Neither do I.'' Amber security lights illuminated deepening laugh lines at the corners of his eyes. ''I'm glad you're here.''

Taking as deep a breath as her fitted bodice would allow, she managed a nervous smile. ''Me, too.''

He gazed at her for another moment, then exited the car. Opening the passenger door, he helped her step out, his eyes still smoldering. ''Have I told you how beautiful you look tonight?''

''Several times,'' she said, laughing. ''But don't let that stop you. I never tire of hearing it.''

His fingertip brushed her cheek, lingering at the corner of her mouth. ''I never tire of saying it.''

They gazed at each other, unhurried, drinking in the sight, the scent, the aura of the moment. Heady perfume from the white rose pinned to Larkin's lapel mingled with musky cologne, an exotic blend more dizzying than the champagne punch that already had Letitia's head spinning. At least, she'd thought it was the punch, although she'd had only one glass. Now she wondered if the giddy sensation was caused by something—or someone—else.

Larkin stroked her throat, tracing her exposed collarbone across her bare skin. He hesitated, took a shuddering breath, then slid his hand to her elbow and escorted her toward the garage elevator. "You were right about that dress. At this very moment, my socks are bunched in the toes of my shoes."

"I'm glad you like it," she murmured, proud that she'd refrained from giggling aloud. She hadn't spent so much time and effort on her appearance since her own wedding; then, however, she'd appeared delicate and virginal. Now she looked like a femme fatale, an effect that was both surprising and, for Letitia, a bit nerve-racking. It wasn't exactly the image she was used to seeing in the mirror.

When she'd first viewed her reflection in the boutique fitting room, she'd been startled speechless. On the hanger, the dress had appeared to be rather simple, although the color, a vivid jewel-toned aqua with an elegant satin sheen, had intrigued her. On her body, however, the off-the-shoulder cap sleeves made the bodice appear more daring than it really was, and the fitted, drop waist style hugged her torso like a second skin before flaring into a soft drape swirling just above her knees.

To formalize her new look, Letitia had twisted her dark hair into a dramatic upsweep accentuated with delicate springs of tiny white blossoms from Mama Rose's garden. Then she'd stood back, chewing her lip, and wondered if Larkin would approve the result.

Apparently, he had. Throughout the evening, he'd watched her constantly, his eyes glowing with appreciation and something else that Letitia couldn't quite identify. And he'd continually touched her. Not in an overtly sexual manner, of course, but he was always either holding her hand, or stroking her wrist, or caressing a curled tendril of her hair with his fingertips.

Even now, as they stepped off the elevator into the apartment building's corridor, Larkin's palm was still cupped gently at her elbow holding her so close that his biceps pressed against her shoulder.

"It's right here," he said, guiding her toward the first door.

As Larkin dug the key from his pocket, Letitia glanced around the carpeted hallway, which was clean and well maintained, but not particularly special. The walls were a nondescript off-white, devoid of decoration. Illumination was provided by soft ceiling lights. She noticed three other doors before the hall veered left where, presumably, similar apartments were located.

Larkin opened the door to his own apartment but instead of entering the dark interior, he stood in the doorway looking oddly tense as he fumbled with something on the inside wall. In a moment, the apartment erupted with light. He relaxed visibly, then stepped back, clicked his heels together and gestured inside with a generous sweep of his hand. "Welcome to my humble abode."

Smiling, Letitia acknowledged him with a royal nod and stepped into the blinding room. She blinked. "I'd hate to pay your electric bill."

"I'm a big fan of Thomas Edison," Larkin replied, flipping off one of the six or more lamps that were blazing in the living room alone. "The lightbulb is a real miracle of science, don't you think?"

"I suppose so." She shaded her eyes until he'd turned off two more lamps and the apartment was emitting slightly less candlepower than the average airport runway. Beside the living area, a galley kitchen's fluorescent ceiling was glowing brightly, and if the emanating glare from beyond the living room was any clue, she suspected that connecting rooms were similarly illuminated. "I take it you're not big on mood lighting."

"It depends on the mood." He closed the hall door, although the fact that he'd left the lights on in there didn't escape her notice. "Actually, it's a known fact that light is the world's most effective antidepressant."

"Are you depressed?"

"Not at the moment."

"I'm serious, Larkin. You of all people should realize that clinical depression is nothing to fool with."

"Yes, I do know that. Fortunately, it's not one of my problems." His teasing smile turned pensive. "The truth is that I've never much cared for dark places. Besides, the kids used to leave every light in the house on. I guess I got used to it."

The sadness in his eyes touched Letitia to the core. Her gaze was drawn past the sparse furnishings to a wall of photographs portraying his children at varying stages of their young lives. "I know how much you miss them."

"Would you like some wine?"

"Larkin—" she began, then simply sighed as he strode around the open counter separating the kitchen from the living room. Since the subject of his children was too painful to discuss, Letitia respected his wishes. "Yes, thank you. A glass of wine would be nice."

"Red or white?" he asked, searching an overhead cupboard.

"You choose." As she wandered toward the kitchen, she noticed that the counter tile was clean to the point of glistening and held none of the knickknacks or kitchen gadgets one would expect from the workstation of a gourmet chief. There was, in fact, nothing on the counter except a shot glass and bottle of whiskey, the collar of which was coated by a thin layer of dust. Both items seemed oddly out of place in the otherwise immaculate kitchen.

"This is a sweet muscat," Larkin said, holding out a wineglass of rich, golden liquid. "It's kind of a dessert wine. I hope you like it."

Letitia took the glass, inhaling the wine's rich bouquet. Because he was watching anxiously, she took a delicate sip. "Hmm, it's lovely. Thank you."

They went into the living room, settling onto a well-used sofa that was entirely different in pattern and style from the overstuffed lounge chair that, except for a few mismatched lamp tables and a sleek rack stereo system, was the only other furniture in the room. Larkin sat awkwardly, balancing his wineglass on his knee as he tugged the starched collar of his rented tux shirt.

Letitia smiled. Courtesy dictated that she at least offer him the opportunity of changing into something more comfortable, but he looked so handsome, she couldn't bring herself to do it. Besides, such a suggestion hinted at an intimacy that the bashful side of her personality wasn't quite ready to broach. There was, however, a sensual seductress so long suppressed that Letitia barely recognized that part of herself. Recognized or not, that femme fatale was struggling to the surface, overwhelming her shyness.

An image flashed through her mind, a mental glimpse of seeking hands on bare skin, of faces blurred by passion, of bodies slick with desire.

She took a quick breath, closed her eyes and was swept away by the power of her imagination. The wineglass was lifted from her hand, although she was barely aware of the sensation. A warmth encircled her, a familiar strength of masculine arms combined with the distinctive scent of rose and cologne. She felt Larkin's lips tease the corner of her mouth, then slide provocatively down her throat, lingering to moisten the sensitive pulse point before gliding lower, and lower still.

"You're so beautiful," he whispered against her skin. "You take my breath away."

A shiver of anticipation slid down her spine. His mouth cherished her, blazing an erotic path along the edge of her bodice, over her bare shoulders and around the nape of her neck. Every inch of exposed skin was touched and tasted, stroked into a frenzy of pulsing sensation. She was alive with pleasure, and a passion so intense it pounded in the pit of her, a painful throb in her belly that silently begged for liberation. It fascinated her; it frightened her. It consumed her with a fervor beyond her experience.

When his lips returned to claim her mouth, she melted bonelessly into his embrace, surrendering to the sweetness of his deepening kiss. Her palms pressed against the stiff pleats of his formal shirt, sliding beneath his jacket. Something sharp scratched the back of her hand. Startled, she pulled away, retrieved her hand and inspected the stinging knuckle.

"What's wrong?" Larkin asked between short, rasping breaths. "Are you hurt?"

Letitia wasn't breathing too easily, either. "It's just a scratch. I can't even see it."

Reaching into the inside breast pocket of his tux jacket, Larkin retrieved a half dozen, sharp-cornered Polaroid photographs taken by one of the reception guests and passed out as mementos to members of the wedding party. "I forgot all about these," he said, tossing the pictures aside. He lifted her hand to his lips. "Does it hurt terribly?"

"Hmm, terribly," she murmured. "It hurts higher, too."

He kissed the sensitive flesh inside her elbow. "Here?"

A tingling sensation spread up her arm and down her belly. "Uh-huh."

"And maybe here, too?"

She shivered as his lips traced a moist path along her throat. "Oh, yes." The words slid out like a breath of contentment. Before she could contemplate the consequence, she heard herself saying, "Just in case there are more land mines in your jacket, maybe you should take it off."

Straightening, he gazed into her eyes for a moment, then shrugged off the garment and laid it over the lounge chair. "Is that better?"

Letitia's only response was to undo his bow tie, which then draped around his neck like a limp white snake. Larkin stiffened slightly, but otherwise made no protest. She licked her lips, staring straight into the center of his starched and pleated shirt. Trembling fingers that looked oddly like her own suddenly appeared in front of her face and began fumbling with a tiny pearl button at his collar. The buttonhole was tight; the button, slippery. Nonetheless, she somehow succeeded in that small quest, then focused on the next button, and the next, until an enticing glimpse of golden hair peeked through the open shirt and her fingers touched the folded edge of his satin cummerbund.

She stared at the obstruction, bewildered as to what should be done to remove it. Larkin, bless him, resolved the dilemma by reaching behind his back and unfastening it himself.

After the formal sash had joined the tux jacket on the lounge chair, Letitia completed the unbuttoning until she was stopped again, this time by the waistband of his trousers. A vibration beneath the gray fabric was evidence that despite her clumsiness, the desired result had been at least partially achieved.

Now what? Should she brazenly attack his fly, or should she opt for trying to tug his shirttail out of a fastened waistband? And what about those weird suspenders? Should she slip them over his shoulders and let them dangle, or was she expected to try to unclip the darn things and remove them completely?

Frustrated, confused, and more than a little embarrassed, she tossed up her hands and confessed, "I don't know what to do next. I've never undressed a man wearing rented clothes."

Larkin's laugh betrayed his own nervousness. "I guess we're even, because I've never undressed a woman wearing such a beautiful gown."

Her cheeks felt as if they'd been hit with a blowtorch. "Mine's easy. It falls right off if you just undo the zipper."

"I can hardly wait," he murmured, brushing a sweet kiss along her burning forehead. "Let's check that out."

"You first."

The corners of his eyes crinkled. "Are we feeling a bit timid?"

"I don't know about you, but I certainly am." She avoided his gaze. "This is all pretty new to me."

"I know." His gaze grew somber. "If you're not ready—"

She touched a fingertip to his lips, silencing him. "I am."

"Me, too." A subtle shiver trembled through his shoulders. He stood, hooked his thumbs under the suspenders and slipped them off, letting them dangle along his hips.

Letitia made a mental note of that. She tried to avert her eyes as he shrugged out of his shirt, but the sheer magnificence of his golden chest kept her gaze riveted in place. He was incredibly beautiful with deep, sculpted muscles and a belly so flat, it was almost nonexistent. Before she could take a breath, he'd kicked off his shoes, stepped out of his trousers, and was standing there like a mythical god. Except, of course, that few gods wore cotton briefs, ankle socks and an expression hovering between anticipation and stark terror.

"Your turn." He appeared to have difficulty deciding what to do with his hands and finally used one of them to help Letitia stand, an excellent idea since her knees felt like warm gelatin. Bracing her gently, Larkin reached around between her shoulder blades. "Let's see if this works."

A cool draft brushed her skin as he drew the zipper down past her waist. Letitia took a deep breath, shrugged her shoulders and the gown fell forward. Larkin caught it and knelt down so she could brace herself on his shoulders and step easily out of the garment.

After smoothing the sleek fabric and carefully spreading it over the sofa, he gave her a nervous smile. "Would you be more comfortable in the bedroom?"

Nodding, she reached out and took his hand, then angled a glance at the blinding light streaming out from under the hall door. "Will we need sunglasses?"

He laughed. "I'll turn off some of the lamps."

"Some?"

His laughter died. "All of them?"

"Not all," she purred, stroking the soft mat on his chest. "I want to see what I'm doing."

His grip convulsed, and his Adam's apple dipped low in his throat. Then, with a deep, shuddering breath, he led her to the bedroom.

Nerves disappeared in a burst of passion, of seeking lips and searching hands, of intimate caresses and tiny gasps of pleasure. He cherished her body, worshiping her breasts with his mouth, thrilling her with each throbbing stroke of his fingers. Tears sprang to her eyes, tears of wonder, and of the most incredible joy. Larkin's lovemaking penetrated beyond her body, touching the most secret places deep in her soul.

And just when she thought she'd reached the very apex of ecstasy, he moved tenderly over her and filled her with his love.

Letitia was nearly swallowed alive by the massive terry cloth robe, which she wrapped twice around her body before knotting the matching belt. A quick finger comb of her hair was interrupted by a tangle of curls and hairpins that had partially slipped loose so that her fancy upsweep was now a twisted mass drooping around her shoulders. She extracted the fasteners, bent forward to shake her hair into shape and finished the chore with her fingers.

After gathering her bra and panties from the foot of the bed, she smiled at Larkin, who was sprawled across the mattress in a tangle of bedclothes. He'd dozed off a few moments ago. Letitia didn't have the heart to wake him. After all, he'd had a strenuous evening. It was past 1:00 a.m. now, and the poor guy was certainly entitled to some well-deserved rest.

Letitia, on the other hand, was wide awake and feeling more refreshed than she had in years. She felt utterly alive, glowing and vibrant, as if she'd been buffed head to toe with a giant loofah sponge.

After draping her undergarments over her shoulder, she raised her arms to indulge in a luxurious stretch, then tiptoed through the hall, across the living room and into the kitchen, where she poured herself a cooling glass of water. She took a sip, then carried the glass into the living room, where her pretty satin dress was still neatly spread over the sofa.

Sighing, she fingered the slick fabric, not wanting to get dressed again but knowing that she'd have to call a cab soon. It was late and Mama Rose would be worried. She glanced back toward the bedroom where Larkin was blissfully asleep. When he awoke in the morning, he'd find a sexy note and an invitation to Sunday dinner tomorrow.

And hopefully, every Sunday thereafter.

Setting her water glass on the lamp table, she picked up the Polaroid photographs of the reception, shuffling through the stack then repeating the process slowly to relive each detail of the evening. There was a beautiful shot of the bride and groom cutting the wedding cake, and several photos of the crowded dance floor. She spotted Larkin in the group, along with the top of her own head and was disappointed that her pretty dress hadn't been included in the shot.

Laying that photo aside, she concentrated on a picture of Larkin, Devon and Roberto toasting each other beside the wedding party's banquet table. There was an extra place setting at the table, complete with a full glass of champagne and an untouched slice of wedding cake. She'd noticed that at the reception, and had assumed that a member of the wedding party had apparently canceled at the last minute.

"Letitia!"

Startled, Letitia spun toward the hall just as Larkin emerged looking pale and panicked. The moment he saw her, he blew out a breath and his shoulders relaxed. "Thank God," he murmured. "For a minute there, I was afraid the entire evening had been a dream."

"It was wonderfully real," she assured him. "And by the way, your underwear is on backward."

He glanced down, muttered something, then looked back up with a sheepish shrug. "Guess I'm not quite awake yet."

"There's no reason why you should be. Why don't you go back to bed? I can take a cab."

"Absolutely not!" From his horrified expression, one would think she'd planned to hitchhike nude. "I picked you up at your front door and that's exactly where I'm going to return you, safe and sound." His gaze fell on the photograph in her hand. "Are those pictures from the reception?" When she nodded, he crossed the room and looked over her shoulder. "I haven't had a chance to look at them yet. Some guy just shoved them in my hand as we were walking out the door."

Letitia held them up, one at a time. "Some bash, huh?"

Larkin chuckled. "Is this the top of your head?"

"It better be. I don't recall you dancing with anyone else…except the bride, of course." She picked up the photo of the toast with the question, "Did a member of the wedding party miss the reception?"

"Not that I know of. Why?"

She pointed at the unused place setting. "Who was supposed to sit there?" When he didn't answer immediately, she glanced up and saw that familiar, pensive expression. "Larkin? Is something wrong?"

He wasn't looking at the picture anymore. Instead, he was gazing across the room as if contemplating a response. After a moment, his jaw firmed as if he'd made some kind of decision. "That was Tommy's place," he said finally. "Sit down, Letitia. You have a right to know what kind of man I really am."

The tone of his voice scared her half to death. She perched on the sofa, waiting while Larkin moved her gown to the lounge chair. When he settled beside her, he stared across the room, refusing to meet her frightened gaze. "It started twenty years ago," he whispered. "In a place called Blackthorn Hall."

Except for Letitia's quiet sobs, the room was silent. Larkin was staring into space, his jaw rigid, his fist balled in his lap.

For the past forty minutes, he'd relayed the events of those terrible, long-ago days in a voice that sometimes broke, sometimes was barely audible. The story was too terrible to be believed, but Larkin's anguish was too real to dismiss. Letitia had no doubt it had happened. She just couldn't comprehend how anyone could have lived so long with that kind of pain. Or that kind of crushing guilt.

Wiping her eyes one last time, she balled the damp tissue in her hand. "It wasn't your fault."

Several seconds passed. "It was my idea," he said finally.

"It was a desperate act by group of kids who felt betrayed by the entire adult world. You couldn't have predicted what would happen. Dear God, you were only children.''

''I should have known. Tommy and I were closer than brothers. I knew his asthma was serious, and I also knew that Tommy would rather—'' Larkin took a sharp breath. He bowed his head, massaging his temples. When composed, his hand dropped away and he spoke with great effort. ''I knew Tommy would rather die than acknowledge his physical limitations.''

''You weren't responsible for that. Going along with the group was his choice and he made it.''

Larkin shook his head. ''No, he had no choice, no choice at all. We were the Brotherhood...one heart, one spirit, one mind. What one did, we all did. Don't you understand that the moment I put the fatal plan in motion, Tommy's fate was sealed?''

''How can I understand something that's not true? What happened to Tommy was tragic, but it was an accident. If there's blame to be laid, put it where it belongs, with an uncaring system that treats sick, abandoned children like hardcore felons.'' Letitia struggled for words that would alleviate Larkin's suffering, words that simply didn't exist. The only person who could heal Larkin's emotional wounds was Larkin himself. ''You've devoted your life to kids like Tommy. You've guided them, cared about them, understood them and forgiven them. You've touched so many lives, helped so many desperate children, and yet there's one child, one broken little boy who needs you more than all the rest. He lives in here,'' she murmured, laying her palm on his chest. ''Can't you find it in your heart to love and forgive him, too?''

Larkin removed her hand, cradling it between his palms. ''One of the things I learned at Blackthorn Hall was that not everyone is entitled to forgiveness, or even love, for that matter. I learned that life is cruel and people can be crueler. The old saying that 'there's no such thing as a bad boy' is bull. There *are* bad boys, and bad girls, too. In my line of work, I see them every day. I can't save those kids. No one can. So I concentrate on the ones who are worth saving and try to keep them out of places that will destroy their innocence and turn them into stone-cold criminals."

"Places like Blackthorn Hall?"

"Yes." As Larkin bit off the word, his eyes grew cold.

Letitia hesitated, unnerved by the glimpse of his raw fury lurking just below the surface. "Because of you, hundreds of kids have had the opportunity for a better, more productive life. I am surprised, however, that you didn't choose to direct your efforts toward the real problem."

He looked around, startled. "What do you mean?"

"From what you've told me, the system that violated you and countless other innocent children hasn't been changed in twenty years. Please don't get me wrong," she added quickly. "But for every child you're able to help, there are hundreds you can't get to, desperate kids sucked into the same nightmare that you and your friends endured. Who's there for them, Larkin? Who was there for you?"

He didn't answer; she hadn't expected him to. Her heart ached for the lost child he'd once been, and for the wounded man he'd become. Still, she understood him now, understood the paradox of his soul. Larkin McKay stifled his feelings out of fear, and with good reason. He craved a family, a sense of belonging. He craved love. Yet each time he'd risked his heart, he'd suffered incalculable loss—his parents, his best friend, even his wife and children.

Letitia touched his face, caressing the stoic jaw, the sweet, vulnerable lips that she knew so very well. "I'm here for you," she whispered. "You're not alone anymore."

Then she led him into the bedroom and proved it.

Chapter Ten

Letitia staggered out of the bedroom, yawning, and nearly ran into her mother-in-law, who eyed her with overt disapproval. "You missed church," Rose said.

Raking her disheveled tangle of hair, Letitia squinted at a shaft of brilliant sunlight streaming down the hall. "I got home late. What time is it?"

"Nearly noon."

"You must be joking." She looked at her naked wrist before remembering that her watch was still on her nightstand. "Oh, good grief. I'm sorry, Mama. I must have forgotten to set my alarm. Why didn't you wake me?"

The woman shrugged. "You didn't get in until four. You needed rest."

Letitia tightened her robe belt. "I told you not to wait up."

"I didn't. I heard you come in, that's all." Rose followed her daughter-in-law into the kitchen, fidgeting around the stove while she poured herself a cup of strong coffee. When

Letitia had settled at the table, the older woman cleared her throat. ''The wedding was nice?''

''Very nice.'' Taking a packet of sweetener from the container, Letitia tapped it on the tabletop before tearing the top open and pouring the contents into her cup. ''The bride was lovely, the groom was handsome. It was a picture-perfect ceremony.''

''And afterward?''

Letitia stirred slowly, hoping the warmth she felt on her cheeks was nothing more revealing than a touch of sunlight streaming through the window. She'd hoped to avoid a discussion of everything that had happened last night, and why it had been nearly dawn before she'd returned home.

Unfortunately, ignoring the question would not only be rude, it would validate the suspicion already lurking in the woman's reproachful dark eyes.

Laying down the spoon, Letitia lifted the mug and chose her words carefully. ''There was a reception afterward. Dinner, dancing, the whole nine yards. Where's Mannie?''

Rose gave a discouraged snort. ''It's Sunday. Where do you think he is?''

Letitia straightened, setting the mug down hard enough to slosh coffee over the rim. She stared at Rose, then spun in her chair, parted the curtains and looked out the window just as Mannie lobbed a football halfway down the block. Larkin caught it.

''Oh, Lord. He's here.'' Pushing the chair back, Letitia jumped to her feet, frantically patting her wild mop of sleep-tangled hair. Looking down at her robe, she uttered a cry of dismay and dashed down the hall, muttering madly.

Remaining in the kitchen, Rose watched her daughter-in-law's frantic exit with sad and knowing eyes. What she'd feared most had happened. Only God could help them now.

Larkin drew his forearm across his damp brow, angling yet another glance at the quiet house. A moment ago, he'd thought he'd seen Letitia at the kitchen window. The window was empty now. Perhaps it had been a mirage.

He felt rather than saw Mannie lope toward him. "Yo, Doc, are we gonna play or what?"

"Let me catch my breath." Stifling a yawn, Larkin sat on the curb, tossing a final, hopeful glance toward the house. "Do you think your mom is up yet?"

"I dunno," Mannie replied, squatting awkwardly with the football in his lap. "Nana said she was real tired. What did you guys do last night, anyway?"

After a minor fit of coughing, Larkin cleared his throat and managed to croak out, "Wedding."

The boy nodded sagely. "Well, I ain't never gonna get married."

"Why not?" Larkin asked, wiping his eyes. "You like girls, don't you?"

"Sure! I mean, they're okay. I'm not gay or nothing."

Larkin nearly choked again. When he'd composed himself, he donned his psychologist persona, deciding this was as good a time as any for the dreaded man-to-boy talk Letitia had requested of him. "So, Mannie, exactly what is it about marriage that worries you?"

The youngster rolled his eyes. "It's boring. I mean, with hundreds of babes out there, why should a guy have to stick with only one?" He gave Larkin a just-between-us-guys wink. "Like, if God hadn't wanted men to do a lot of fishing, he wouldn't have given 'em reusable poles."

Thankful that Letitia hadn't over heard that crass philosophy, Larkin managed to maintain a bland expression. "Who told you that, Mannie?"

"Jason. He's got lotsa babes. Says girls appreciate a guy who knows what he's doing."

"Jason," Larkin repeated, searching his memory. "Isn't that Will Doherty's brother, the boy who hangs out with Todd Minger?"

Staring at his knees, Mannie replied with a nonchalant shrug.

"I thought your mom asked you to avoid the Doherty boys."

The youngster, suddenly fascinated by a tiny rip in his jeans, concentrated on tracing the tear with his finger. "They live 'round the corner. I see 'em sometimes, you know, hangin' in the 'hood."

Larkin picked a twig off the grass, twirling it between his thumb and index finger to buy a moment of time. Despite Mannie's understandable caution in admitting a relationship with the Doherty boys, there was a troubling gleam of admiration in his young eyes whenever their names were mentioned. The fact that those boys were also members of a gang infamous for criminal activity made that doubly disturbing.

Although reluctant to criticize the Dohertys for fear Mannie would become defensive, he knew that ignoring the outrageous attitude he'd parroted would be tantamount to agreement.

Finally, Larkin settled on casual contradiction, hoping to exercise at least a modicum of influence and defuse the youngster's sexist conviction. "I don't believe that sexual conquest is a reasonable measure of manhood," he said carefully. "Women are entitled to respect and courtesy. They are not objects to be lusted after and scored upon."

Mannie's eyes narrowed skeptically. "You gonna give me that 'sex is for marriage' stuff?"

"Well..." Squirming, Larkin blinked away the image of Letitia's hair splayed across his pillow. "It certainly should be."

The boy considered that for a moment. "Didn't you ever do it...you know...before?"

Puffing his cheeks, Larkin blew out a breath and wished to hell he'd insisted Letitia simply sign the kid up for a sex education class. But no. He'd wanted to impress her with his communication skills, and his ability to effectively relate with young people.

Well, they were relating all right. Mannie was digging through Larkin's least favorite closet, rattling old skeletons he'd just as soon leave buried. But the boy had asked an honest question and like it or not, Larkin was honor-bound to provide an honest reply. "Yes, I experimented with sex, although I was considerably older than you."

"How old?"

"Ah . . . high school. Late in high school."

"I'm in junior high," Mannie pointed out. "That's pretty close."

Larkin flinched. This wasn't going well at all. "I don't think age should be the issue. No person, male or female, should pursue physical gratification at someone else's emotional expense. That's wrong."

"Yeah, but—" Ducking his head, Mannie's attention returned to his ripped jeans. "Isn't it okay to practice a little?"

"Sex isn't a game, Mannie. There are consequences."

The boy waved that away as irrelevant. "I know about babies and stuff. Smart guys don't get caught." He glanced toward the house, assuring himself that his mother wasn't watching, then dug through his pocket and pulled out a packaged condom. "See? I figure if somethin' comes up, I'm gonna be ready."

Larkin simply shook his head, torn between outrage that an eleven-year-old felt pressured to carry a condom, and relief that the hormone-filled little fool had enough sense to protect himself. His first instinct was to take the damn thing away and command the boy to remain celibate until he was thirty. Of course, any adult edict, particularly on this subject, would be at best ineffective and at worst, would completely cut off whatever communication had already been established.

As Mannie tucked the flat package back into his pocket, Larkin took a deep breath. "I'm glad to see that you take your responsibility as a man seriously."

The boy nodded with a solemn expression that under other circumstances would have been laughable.

But Larkin wasn't laughing. "Do me a favor, will you?"

"Sure."

"When the time comes, just ask yourself one question— 'Is this the person I want to spend the rest of my life with?' If the answer is no, put that condom back in your pocket and walk away."

"Aw, man... that's so bogus. Everybody does it. It's no big deal."

"It's a very big deal," Larkin told him firmly. "Sex is a beautiful gift for two people who are deeply in love and committed to each other." Images of Letitia flashed through his mind again, images of her sated smile and dark eyes glowing beneath passion-drugged lids. "Anything else is a cheap imitation—"

Hypocrite, cried a voice in his mind.

"—of something sacred—"

Fraud.

"—and precious."

Larkin wiped a shaky hand across his forehead. Commitment, he'd said, between two people deeply in love.

Love, as in the nurturing warmth he felt when he looked into Letitia's eyes.

Commitment, as in permanence, marriage, forever.

Only marriage didn't mean forever anymore. It meant for a while, until things get tough, until something—or someone—better comes along. It meant eventual loss.

It meant heartbreak.

After squeezing a dollop of liquid detergent into the dishwasher, Letitia closed the door and dried her hands on a tea towel. She glanced over her shoulder at Larkin, who sat at the kitchen table staring out the window. "A penny for your thoughts," she said.

"Hmm?" He turned around, adjusting his glasses.

Smiling, she tossed the towel aside and joined him at the table. "You seemed a million miles away."

He returned her smile, a bit weakly, she thought. "Just tired, I guess. I'm too old to stay up all night."

"A thirty-one-year-old codger? I think not. After last night, I certainly can't accuse you of lacking stamina." If she'd hoped to bring a sparkle to his eyes and a quip to his lips, she was disappointed. What she did see, or thought she saw, was a flash of chagrin. "Is something wrong, Larkin? You seem preoccupied."

"Do I?" Sighing, he wiped his palms across his face, then leaned back, raking his fingers through his hair. "Sorry. A lack of sleep makes me grumpy."

"You haven't been grumpy. Just quiet." She draped her elbow over the back of her chair, regarding him thoughtfully. "I noticed you and Mannie had quite a long chat this morning, out by the curb. Has the, ah, eagle landed by any chance?"

Larkin's lips flattened into a thin line. "Oh, yeah."

"Sounds ominous," she murmured, feeling terrible for having pushed him into what had apparently been an unpleasant conversation. "Was it awful?"

"Not really." Pushing back his chair, he rotated his shoulders as if working out kinks. "It's just that I got to him a little late." When Letitia bolted upright, he hastened to assure her. "Not *that* late. I just meant that he's already learned about the, ah, physical mechanics from other sources."

"Probably from a diagram in the school bathroom," she muttered with a sigh. "I keep forgetting that today's kids are light-years ahead of where I was at the same age. Thank you for trying, even though it wasn't fair of me to ask."

His smile was so stiff it seemed ready to crack. "You can ask me anything. That's what friends are for."

Something in his voice gave her pause. "We're more than friends, aren't we?"

"You shouldn't even have to ask that question." Larkin pushed back his chair, avoiding her eyes. "Where's Rose?"

The fact that he'd switched subjects with the same ploy she'd used with her mother-in-law did little to calm nerves that were growing increasingly raw. "She's out back, working in the garden. Why?"

He stood. "I want to thank her for the wonderful meal. She really outdid herself this time."

Letitia, too, stood, although her legs felt a bit rubbery. "You're leaving?"

"I think I should. You could probably use some extra rest, too."

"But I was going to rent a video tonight. There's this movie about a hijacked airplane that Mannie's been dying to see . . ." The words trailed away as the stubborn set of his jaw certified the argument was falling on deaf ears. "I'm sorry. You've already said that you were tired."

He reached out, stroking her cheek with a feathery caress that sent tingles down her spine. His brow furrowed below the rim of his glasses, as if he wanted to say something, then thought better of it. After a moment, his features relaxed in fatigued resignation. "I'll call you tomorrow," he murmured. Then he brushed a chaste kiss across her forehead and left.

Letitia stood there, staring at his empty chair, feeling more frightened and alone than she had since her husband had died. She loved Larkin deeply, with every ounce of her heart and her soul. It was precisely because she loved him that she knew something was terribly wrong. She didn't know what; she didn't know why, but it felt as if she were losing him. And that scared her half to death.

* * *

The apartment was ablaze with lights. Larkin flipped on yet another lamp, as if a few more watts could alleviate the darkness in his soul. Picking up a magazine, he sat on the sofa, flipped through a couple of pages, then tossed it aside.

Love. Commitment. Marriage.

The words circled his mind like hungry vultures.

After the divorce, he'd sworn that he'd never allow himself to be that vulnerable again. He'd loved his wife and he'd lost her. The failure had been shattering. Now, despite the fervent promises he'd made to himself, he was falling in love all over again. This time, the feelings were deeper, even more profound.

The transition had been so smooth, so natural that Larkin hadn't even realized what was happening. For years, he'd settled into a holding pattern, filling the lonely void in his life with work and friends and more work. Suddenly, the clouds shrouding his heart had lifted and for the first time since the early years of his marriage, he'd been truly happy. Letitia was everything he'd ever dreamed of in a friend, a lover, a lifetime companion; yet it was that last designation that was most unnerving, because it was the most important to him.

Throughout his life, all relationships that had been important to him had repeated the same heartbreaking cycle: a few happy years, followed by restlessness, emotional distance, anger and inevitably, moving on. He couldn't go through it again. Loneliness wasn't a pleasant way to live but it was predictable. It was safe.

Sighing, Larkin scrubbed his face with his palms. He stood quickly, rounded the couch and headed toward the kitchen, flipping on the last two lamps as he went. His eye was drawn to the whiskey bottle on the counter. He picked it up, absently perusing the label, as he realized that he hadn't taken a drink since the day he'd met Letitia. But he wanted one now. He wanted to stop thinking. He wanted to stop feeling. He wanted to stop the fear.

The fear.

Startled by the thought, Larkin set the bottle back on the counter, wondering when he'd turned into such a coward. When had his own emotional safety taken precedence over that which made life worth living?

Perhaps he hadn't been looking for love, but he'd undeniably found it. Every night he dreamed of a future with Letitia and Mannie and, yes, even with Rose. He'd become a part of their family. He'd belonged. Those dreams had given him the hope that his fear was trying to destroy.

Larkin stood there for a while, fingering the bottle, then spun on his heel and walked away. He'd allow himself to hope for a while longer.

"I hate him!" Justin screamed into the phone. "He's mean and he's always bossing us around and he makes Mom take his side all the time! I wish he'd just curl up 'n die!"

Larkin pushed away from his desk, swiveling the chair so his back was to the open door. "Calm down, son. Tell me what happened."

"He won't let me play Little League," the eight-year-old sobbed. "I'm the best pitcher in the whole, entire school and John won't even let me play."

Confused, Larkin glanced at his desk calendar. "Little League doesn't start for months. How do you know that you won't be able to play?"

"'Cause sign-ups are this week and he won't let me go! I hate him!"

"Shh, son, I know you're upset but I can't help you unless you calm down enough to answer my questions." Larkin waited, massaging his aching temples, until the boy's sobs had subsided. "Now, what reason did your stepfather give you for saying you couldn't go to sign-ups?"

A loud sniff filtered through the line. "He said I wasn't doin' enough work, only I can't do *everything!* I'm just a kid. Make 'em let me play, Dad. Please? Tell 'em if they don't, I'm gonna come live with you."

Larkin felt as if a giant hand had been thrust into his chest, grabbing his heart and squeezing the life out of him. "I—" His voice broke. He tried again. "You know nothing would please me more than having you and your sister live with me, but it's not that simple, Justin."

"Please, Dad—"

"Besides, I can't believe your mother would allow anyone to treat you unfairly. Let me talk to her, son. Maybe we can straighten this out."

The boy was silent for several seconds. "She's not here."

Larkin swallowed hard, deliberately uncurling his fist. "All right, then. Let me talk to John."

"H-He's outside."

"Please call him in."

"I...I can't. He's in the fields. It won't do no good anyway," Justin said in a rush. "He's just gonna tell you stuff, but it isn't true!"

Larkin lifted his head. "What isn't true?"

"He's always ordering me around," the boy replied, ignoring the question. "He pretends like he's my father and everything, only he's not my dad and he's never gonna be my dad and I hate him!"

As the invisible fist gave another cruel twist to his heart, Larkin winced at his son's venomous words. The boy was barely nine, yet his voice resonated with frightening fury. Justin had always been a sweet, easygoing child, never prone to temper tantrums or uncontrollable bursts of anger. All that had changed when his mother remarried, a turn of events that uncomfortably mirrored Larkin's own childhood situation. He, too, had resented his stepfather and not without cause. The man had been cold and hostile, considering young Larkin as unwanted baggage and not the least bit shy about announcing that to anyone who'd listen.

Larkin wouldn't let his own son go through that. "Justin, listen to me. I'm going to take care of this, all right?"

Sniff, sniff. "Promise?"

"Yes, I promise. Tell your mother that I'll call her tonight."

"Okay," he replied brightly. "Bye."

"And son?"

"Yeah?"

Larkin moistened his dry lips. "I love you."

"I love you, too, Dad."

The next sound Larkin heard was the dial tone. It took two tries to cradle the receiver, because his hands were shaking.

Propping his elbows on the desk, he pressed his bowed head into his hands, swallowing a surge of emotion that rushed up his throat. God, he missed them so. Larkin could deal with his own pain as long as his children were happy. But they weren't happy and the worst part was knowing that they might never be happy again.

Even if Larkin went back to court and won physical custody of his kids, they'd miss their mother so much that they'd be just as miserable—perhaps even more so. For children of divorce, it seemed that grief was a constant companion. One way or another, they were always forced to choose between the two people they loved most in the world. Shattered little hearts, forever scarred. Just like his own.

"Dr. McKay?"

Startled, Larkin looked up and saw a visibly shaken Jack Peterson leaning through the doorway. "Hi, Jack. Is something wrong?"

"Looks like we've got problems out back," Jack said. "There's a couple of carloads of gang members parked in the alley, behind the basketball courts. The rumor is that there are drug deals going on."

Before Jack had finished speaking, Larkin was on his feet. "Are they on the center's property?"

"I don't think so. From what I hear, they're outside the fence calling our kids out into the alley."

Larkin brushed past the portly volunteer, crossing the gymnasium with long, fast strides. "Did any of them go?"

"Yeah," Jack said, puffing to keep up. "A few."

Bursting through the double door at the rear of the gym, Larkin exploded onto the outdoor courts, pushed through a group of adolescents and headed toward the fence. The cars in question were parked just outside the gate. A group of youngsters was clustered around the vehicles, most wearing gang colors.

Inside the fenced area, Larkin spotted Mick and Big'un leaning against one of the hoop braces. He whistled, gesturing them over. The wiry redhead arrived first, looking somber. "Yo, Doc. Gonna bench the bangers for jaw jacking homies?" Larkin's mind quickly translated, *Are you going to reprimand the gang members for talking to members of the youth center?*

"That depends on what they're talking about," Larkin murmured without taking his eyes off the activity outside the gate. "Have you seen any drugs change hands?"

Mick shook his shaggy head, adding, "Them hoopties came in cruising and clocking, then the bangers spilled to crest the home squad, giving fives to track 'em over." *The cars drove by to survey the area before the gang members exited the vehicles, smiling at the youth center kids and waving them over.*

"Saw some dimes," Big'un announced as he swaggered into range.

That got Larkin's attention, since *dime* was slang for a ten-dollar bag of illegal narcotics, usually heroine or crack cocaine. "Who had them?"

"B-boy in the 'chief," Big'un replied, nodding toward an older youth in a paisley blue bandanna.

Larkin's gaze narrowed. All he could see of the youth in question was the top of his head and the back of another, slightly shorter boy with whom he was speaking. When the conversation ended, the bandanna-clad head raised, as did the hair on Larkin's nape. "Todd Minger," he muttered. "Damn."

Big'un nodded. "JoDog's one tripping jacker. Word's down that he's the dude what hearsed that Double K on the boulevard." *Todd Minger is an irrational hoodlum, rumored to have killed a rival gang member in a drive-by shooting.*

At that moment, Minger glanced up to meet Larkin's gaze with gloating eyes and an infuriating smirk. He held up a two-fingered fist announcing his gang affiliation and extending an irrefutable challenge that clearly dared Larkin, or anyone else, to interfere.

Intimidation was the key here. Larkin knew that Minger was trying to lure him off center property, where he'd be outnumbered and surrounded. Although he saw no weapons, he didn't doubt that a variety of firearms were concealed beneath floppy plaid shirttails and tucked in the oversize pockets of baggy cholos.

Larkin had no intention of obliging. Ego wasn't a priority when the safety of his kids was threatened. To confront Minger on his own terms could escalate and draw the center members into the resulting violence, a situation Larkin was determined to avoid.

Without breaking the visual stalemate, Larkin spoke to Jack Peterson, who was standing slightly behind his left shoulder. "Call the police. Explain the situation and tell them we need enough officers to control a dozen, possibly armed."

"Sure...will do."

A breeze brushed Larkin's shoulder, signaling that Jack had hurried off to complete his task. "Mick, you and Big'un clear the courts."

Mick, apparently pleased by the assignment, elbowed his huge friend. "Hey, man, we're large and in charge. Let's break 'em out."

As the youths plunged exuberantly into their task of funneling the curious crowd back into the building, Minger reached out to toss a chummy arm around the boy who'd originally been blocking Larkin's view. That boy turned, staring at Larkin with huge, frightened eyes. It was Mannie.

Larkin's heart nearly stopped. Before he gave himself a moment to think, he was halfway across the court, heading toward the gate. Behind him, he heard Mick holler, "Yo, Doc, hold up!"

Ignoring the words and the warning that came with them, Larkin crashed through the gate, elbowing through the taunting group until he was eyeball to eyeball with the main man himself.

Minger greeted him with a contemptuous grin. "Welcome to the party, Doc. Got a special order, or are you just browsing?"

Without acknowledging either the question or the one who'd issued it, Larkin grabbed Mannie's wrist, yanking him out from under the gangster's draped arm. "Get into the gym," he told the startled youngster.

Mannie shot a wary look at the gang leader. "But I was just—"

"Now!" Larkin growled.

Before Mannie had a chance to comply, Larkin tightened his grip on the boy's wrist, spun on his heel and hauled the stumbling youngster back through the cluster of toughs who were jeering, sneering and hurling a variety of colorfully creative insults.

Paying no attention to the ridicule, Larkin removed one grinning obstacle with an elbow to the belly and muscled another aside with a crude, but effective, shoulder block.

By the time he reached the gate, Mannie was clawing the fingers encircling his wrist. "Let go!" he shouted. "Everyone's laughing at me!"

Larkin wasn't listening. Shaken to the core by a fury born of pure terror, he dragged Mannie, struggling, across the courts and into the building, parting the crowd of curious youngsters still gathered by the back door. Only when they'd reached the safety of the gymnasium did Larkin release his grip, then he whirled on the boy. "What's the matter with you? Your mother has told you time and time again to stay away from those thugs. Don't you know they have drugs out there? The police are going to bust everyone within spitting distance of those cars. Do you think going to jail is cool? Is that what you want? *Is it?*"

Mannie simply stood there, staring up with an expression of disbelief and horror. Silence hung like a shroud, broken only by incredulous whispers scattered throughout the surrounding crowd.

Blinking, Larkin looked around and realized what he'd done. He'd committed the cardinal sin of public reprimand, of humiliating Mannie in front of his friends.

Nearly moaning aloud, Larkin's anger turned inward. He knew better. Dear God, he knew better, but when he'd seen the boy he loved like his own son trapped in what could have become a life-and-death situation, something inside him had snapped.

Breathing deeply, he extended a hand. "Mannie, I'm sorry—"

The conciliatory gesture was slapped aside. "Get away from me!" Mannie shouted, fighting tears. "You can't tell me what to do. You're not my father!"

"Mannie—"

The boy ducked under Larkin's arm and ran through the crowd, sobbing.

An icy pit opened deep in Larkin's belly. Coldness spread from the inside out, freezing him in place. He couldn't move. He couldn't speak. He could barely breathe.

You're not my father!

Larkin had once said those words, as had Justin and now Mannie. Voices, past and present, blended in his mind. Mannie's eyes had been filled with the familiar hopelessness of being unable to control one's own destiny. Larkin remembered that feeling, and the pain that went with it.

Mannie had been right. Larkin wasn't now and never could be a father to him. Believing otherwise had been nothing more than wishful thinking, an absurd and impossible dream. But he'd just received one hell of a wake-up call, and that dream had become his worst nightmare.

Chapter Eleven

"He won't come out of his room," Letitia told Larkin. "Perhaps if you tried talking directly to him—"

"No." Looking strained and tired, Larkin removed his glasses to massage the bridge of his nose. "I've said enough already. I don't blame him for not wanting to hear any more."

Letitia clasped her hands, struggling to think of something, anything that would magically ease the tension between the two most important males in her life.

A few hours earlier, Mannie had slammed into the house and barricaded himself in his bedroom without providing his bewildered mother with so much as a hint about the cause of his angst. Fortunately Rose, who'd been at the center during the incident, had relayed the gist of what had happened. Even so, Letitia didn't understand how an obvious misunderstanding had escalated into what now seemed a complete breakdown in communications. The few sketchy details gleaned from her sullen son had confirmed only that

Mannie considered the episode as a complete betrayal by the man who had once been his hero.

Letitia was caught in the middle. Certainly she empathized with her son's embarrassment, but she could also see the situation from Larkin's point of view. Her explanation of how Larkin might have been misled, however, had fallen on deaf ears. Mannie had even accused her of taking Larkin's side, a shocking allegation that made it seem as if her son were, on some level, in competition with the man she loved.

Obviously, she'd misunderstood.

Mannie adored Larkin, admiring him even more than the sports superstars represented by the immense posters adorning his bedroom walls. Why, only a few days ago Mannie had expressed a wistful prediction that Larkin McKay would soon become a permanent part of their family. It was a wish his mother shared, so fervently, in fact, that she refused to believe that their future dreams could be jeopardized by a minor dispute.

"Mannie's feelings are hurt," Letitia finally said. "He told me that the only reason he went into the alley was to tell the boys they had to leave. Of course, you couldn't know that, and he didn't understand how serious the consequences would have been if the police arrived and found him with those hoodlums."

Larkin sighed. "I should have given him a chance to explain. Instead, I dragged him off as if he were a child and chewed him out in front of his friends. There's no excuse for that."

Reaching out to touch his arm, Letitia flinched when he turned away. Her hand dropped to her side. "Mannie *is* a child, Larkin. I realize there were probably better ways to handle the situation, but you did what you thought best at the time. I understand that. Eventually, Mannie will too."

Facing away from her, Larkin bowed his head. He shuddered, a movement so sudden and violent that his entire body shook as if buffeted by a powerful wind. After a moment, he straightened and spoke softly. "I wish it was that easy."

A tremor of quiet determination in his voice made her skin prickle. "Of course it is," she insisted, a bit too strongly to be believed. "It *is* that easy. Mannie will be angry for a day or so, then you two will talk things out, and everything will be back to normal."

From the corner of her eye, she noticed Rose hovering in the kitchen door, but the focus of Letitia's attention was riveted on the rigid man who was completely unmoved by her ardent plea.

"What happened today was inevitable," Larkin said. "I should have known that... in fact, I probably did know it, only I wanted something so much, so very, very much that I was willing to ignore reality just to keep the dream alive for a few more days, a few more hours. Over the past few weeks, I've thought only about myself without considering how my actions would hurt those I cared about most. I can't let that happen again."

Nausea born of fear swept up to crowd into her throat, weaken her knees. Letitia steadied herself against the lounge chair. "You're tired," she said, beginning to feel oddly desperate. "And you must be starved. A hot meal will make everything look brighter. After dinner we'll—"

"Letitia—" Spinning around to face her, Larkin fell silent when he saw Rose standing in the kitchen doorway. She quickly wiped her palms on the front of her skirt, ducked her head and hurried down the hall to her bedroom. When the door clicked shut, Larkin returned his gaze to the trembling woman who had a death grip on the chair. "Sit down, Letitia. We have to talk."

She was too sick to move. "We can talk later, after dinner."

"I won't be staying," he said gently. Slipping an arm around her waist, he loosened her clenched fingers and guided her to the sofa. He sat down, urging her to join him.

She perched stiffly on the edge of the cushion, searching his bleak eyes. "You're scaring me, Larkin. I don't understand what's happening."

His gaze slid away, settling on the exposed strip of sofa cushion stretching between them like an upholstered canyon. "I'm sorry. I'd rather cut off my arm than upset you, but the longer we avoid facing this, the more difficult it's going to be."

Somehow, she managed to lift her chin and respond in a voice that was thankfully solid. "Exactly what, pray tell, are we avoiding?"

Larkin reached out to stroke the back of her hand with his thumb. The gesture, which she recognized as a delaying tactic, did little to calm her mounting fear. After what seemed a small eternity, he finally spoke. "I've been asking myself how I could be a father to your child after having failed so miserably with my own. The answer, articulated quite clearly by Mannie himself, is that I can't."

She regarded him warily. "Mannie loves you, Larkin... and so do I."

A tremor moved up his arm. He closed his eyes with a peculiar expression that flickered between anguish and joy, yet portrayed neither with any sense of certainty. "You'll never know how desperately I've wanted to hear those words, or how much I cherish them now. It's selfish of me, despicable, really, to think only of my own needs without considering the consequences to you and Mannie."

Opening his eyes, he held her gaze with a grimness that took her breath away. "You are everything I've ever hoped for, Letitia, and so much more. My love for you is more profound than anything I could have ever imagined. You are the best thing that's ever happened to me, but I'm not worthy. The truth is that I've led you to believe I can be someone I'm not. My life is littered with failed relationships, as a husband, as a father, even as a son and a friend. In one way or another, I've damaged or destroyed everyone I've ever loved. I promised myself I'd never let it happen again."

Letitia heard the words. Perhaps she even understood them, although her heart refused to acknowledge the warning issued by her mind. Instead, she concentrated on one sentence that made her want to weep with joy. *My love for you is more profound than anything I could have ever imagined,* he'd said.

Dear God, he *did* love her. Nothing else mattered.

"I love you, Larkin McKay, and unless my ears have deceived me, you've just confessed that you love me, too." Pausing to moisten her lips, she took a calming breath. "What I don't understand is why we aren't celebrating. Isn't that what people in love usually do?"

Larkin looked away. His Adam's apple bounced once, and when he again met her gaze, the rims of his eyes had reddened. "In my dreams of this moment, we were both happy. But in reality, every decision we make affects the lives of others, particularly our children."

A troubling chill swept down her spine. "Mannie adores you," she insisted.

"Mannie adores the man he thought I was, but I've disappointed him. It's bound to happen again unless—" The words stuck in his throat, quivering when he forced them out. "Unless I stop it now."

Letitia sat there, staring at him, listening to the cry of her heart. "Are you saying that we shouldn't see each other again?"

Larkin flinched as if struck. "Yes."

The numbness started in the pit of her stomach and spread outward, until even her lungs felt paralyzed. Staring straight ahead, Letitia was vaguely aware that her body continued the act of breathing, and if she could breathe, she could speak. "What about Mannie? How do you think this is going to make him feel?"

Larkin considered that. "I think he'll be relieved. Mannie is confused right now, and conflicted. The boy is torn between needing someone to reconstruct the role his dad played in his life, and knowing to a moral certainty that nobody ever can."

Releasing Letitia's hand, Larkin broke their final physical contact, widening an emotional gulf that already stretched between them with an enormity she could barely comprehend.

"What Mannie can have," Larkin said, staring vacantly across the room, "and what he so desperately needs is a man who can establish a separate and distinct relationship to fulfill his needs without challenging his father's memory. I can't provide that, and Mannie doesn't want me to. If I forced myself into his life, his anger would escalate. Eventually, I'd become his enemy, a hated villain vying for his mother's attention. In the end, you'd feel pressured to choose between us. That would rip your heart out and I can't... I won't let that happen."

Letitia studied the back of her own knuckles. Odd, she thought, that she could sit here so calmly while her heart was being methodically hammered into a thousand bleeding shards. "That's a very creative scenario, Larkin," she said, barely recognizing the firm, steady voice as her own. "Did it come out of a psychology book or did you think it up all by yourself?"

She felt, rather than saw his startled expression. Still inspecting the back of her own hands, she caught sight of a dishy brown eye peeking around the coffee table. Poor Rasputin. Even the dog had grown to love Larkin. Another broken little heart added to the list.

A twinge of pain broke through the numbness. She swallowed it. "I should be grateful, of course, that you've taken it upon yourself to protect me and my son from future disappointment. The problem is that I don't believe it's us that you're protecting.'' A half turn of her head brought his grim face into view. ''I know you've been hurt in the past, and I'm sorry for that, I truly am. But it's not fair to assume that every relationship is doomed to a similar fate... unless, of course, that's simply an excuse to justify a lack of courage on your part. Commitment requires a certain amount of intestinal fortitude, along with the grit and determination to tough out adversity. I thought you had that kind of resolve. Apparently, I was mistaken.''

With each quiet word, Larkin seemed to shrink before her eyes. She wanted to comfort him, to take him in her arms and beg him to give their love a chance. But she couldn't force him to stay, and loved him too much to try.

Mama Rose had been right about Larkin's demons. They were devouring him alive. Letitia would have given anything, even her life, to free him from that torment; but the healing sword was in Larkin's own hands. Only he could slay the dragons of his soul. Letitia could only watch and pray.

Beside her, Larkin heaved a shudder so violent that his body cracked. He stood, cupping the back of his neck with one hand while the other clung to his hip. ''I'm sorry,'' he whispered.

Unable to move, Letitia remained seated. ''I know.''

A pitiful whine emanated from beneath the coffee table. Glancing down, Larkin dug into his pocket and laid a small rawhide bone on the table's edge. By the time Rasputin scurried off with his new toy, Larkin was gone.

From a distance, Letitia heard a familiar engine sputter to life. The spark plugs still needed to be replaced. Since Larkin didn't own a plug wrench, she'd promised to help—

''We don't need him!''

Startled, Letitia spun around and saw Mannie in the hall, his face contorted with anger, his cheeks wet with tears. She bolted to her feet. ''How much of that did you hear?''

Sobbing, the boy wiped his face with the back of his hand. "I don't care if he doesn't want us. I don't want him, either."

Letitia took a step forward. "Mannie . . . sweetie . . . listen to me—"

"We don't need him!" Mannie shouted again. "We don't need anybody!"

Before Letitia could do more than extend a helpless hand, the youngster had whirled and darted into his room, slamming the door.

"Mannie, wait!" Quickly rounding the sofa, Letitia hurried into the hallway and nearly collided with her mother-in-law.

Rose lifted an arm, blocking her path. "Give him time, *nuera*. He doesn't want you to see his tears."

"But I have to talk to him," Letitia insisted, torn by the choking sobs emanating from behind her son's closed bedroom door. "I have to tell him that despite anything he may have heard, he's not responsible for what happened here tonight."

"Later is soon enough." The older woman's hand moved forward to rest on Letitia's shoulder. "The responsibility isn't yours, either. A man who fears love is an enemy to himself."

A sharp pain sliced through her chest. An enemy to himself. How could anyone endure such loneliness, such utter sorrow? "I don't know what to do, Mama. It kills me to see how much Larkin is suffering, but I don't know how to help him."

"You can't help him, Letitia."

"But I love him."

Clucking softly, Rose slipped a motherly arm around Letitia's shoulders, guiding her toward the kitchen. "Contrary to popular opinion, love does not and cannot conquer all. That is a cruel myth initiated by those without the courage to accept hardship as an inevitable part of life."

Letitia flinched, remembering her callous accusation. "I called Larkin a coward, Mama. I can't believe I did that."

"People in pain say things they regret." Reaching the kitchen table, Rose pulled out a chair for her daughter-in-law and one for herself. When they were both seated, she propped her clasped hands on the table and spoke carefully. "Dr. McKay is not a coward, *nuera*. He is simply a wounded man who, fearing his love exposes you to harm, is protecting you the only way he knows how."

"Protecting me," Letitia murmured, rubbing her stinging eyes. "Strangely enough, that's exactly what Larkin said. I didn't believe it. I still don't. It sounds like the kind of noble rationalization civilized men concoct when the words *I'm tired of you* are too crass."

"Oh, I think you are wrong, Letitia. Even an old woman like me can remember and recognize love in a man's eyes." Her palm massaged a soothing circle between her daughter-in-law's shoulders. "He is simply afraid."

"Of what, Mama? That's what I don't understand."

She shrugged. "Of himself, perhaps. Of becoming that which he despises. There are things in his past..." Sighing, Rose leaned back in her chair, shaking her head. "I only feel this, Letitia. No person knows what is in the mind of another, but my bones tell me that Dr. McKay is a man of strength and honor."

A frisson of hope skittered into her heart. "Do you think he'll come back to us?"

Rose looked quickly away. Too quickly. "*¿Quién sabe?*" she murmured. "Who can tell?"

The hope drained away as quickly as it had appeared. Although her mother-in-law had never claimed to be psychic, Letitia had great respect for her intuitive powers. The woman's instinct was nearly flawless, and her sad eyes clearly revealed her belief that Larkin McKay would not return. Ever.

Dropping her head onto her upraised hands, Letitia swallowed the sob that was creeping up her throat. She couldn't fall apart now. She'd cry later, in the privacy of her room, with a lonely pillow to absorb her tears.

And then, because there was no other choice, Letitia would go on with her life.

The whiskey bottle was nearly empty.

According to the blinking LED on his clock radio, it was 5:00 a.m. on Wednesday. It had been two days since Larkin had seen Letitia, two of the longest, most agonizing days—and nights—of his life. His brain, it seemed, had become immune to liquor's numbing effect. God knows, he'd tried. Since returning to his apartment Monday afternoon, Larkin had hunkered down with the bottle that had once been his closest friend.

But even the whiskey had betrayed him. It used to wrap his anguished mind in hazy stupor, allowing hours to speed by, unlived and unremembered. Now the process had been brutally reversed, slowing the passage of time to a virtual crawl. He'd lived a lifetime in two days.

No, not lived. Merely existed.

Rolling the glass between his palms, he stared into the amber liquid, mesmerized by the rhythmic ripple of golden swells gliding along the surface. He saw a distorted reflection, pale and unshaven. Himself, of course. Or was it?

The reflection reached deep into his mind, touching a vague memory and bringing it home. The man in the glass was staring out, cold and angry. There was a voice in the background. A child's voice.

You're not my father!

Larkin frowned. Was that Mannie's voice?

I hate you!

No, not Mannie's. Justin's, perhaps.

I don't hafta do what you say. You're not my father. You can't tell me what to do.

The hairs on his neck prickled. The voice in Larkin's mind didn't belong to Mannie, or to Justin. It was his own voice he heard, the voice of that tormented little boy that still lived in his heart.

As the memories flooded back, Larkin remembered every detail of that long-ago scene. He'd been eleven at the time, too young to handle his terror and too old to reveal it.

With his small hands bunched into fists and tears streaming down his face, he'd stood his ground against the man who'd stolen his family, stolen his childhood, stolen his life. "Why'd you hafta go and marry my mom? You went and ruined everything!"

The man towered above him, unmoved, unshakable, with frigid eyes that could freeze a small boy with a single icy stare. "This is my house and as long as you're in it, you'll do exactly what I say."

"You can't tell me what to do. You're not my father!"

The man's voice was low, deadly. "Thank God for that. I'd sooner castrate myself than sire a sniveling, ungrateful brat like you." Before Larkin could react, his stepfather had an iron grip on his arm and was hauling him off his feet. "Now you listen to me, you whiny little bastard, the only reason you're under my roof now is because I promised your mother to give you a home as long as you adhere to my rules...*my* rules, do you understand? I don't give a damn if you're happy. In fact, I don't give a damn about you at all. Mess with me and I'll kick you to the curb so fast you won't know what hit you."

With that, the man flung Larkin into a wall with enough force to knock the wind out of him. Larkin crumpled, sinking onto the bare floor and gasping for breath. When he could finally speak, he fought tears and glared up at his tormentor. "I'm gonna tell my dad. You're gonna be real sorry you were so mean to me."

A chilling chuckle slid from his stepfather's twisted mouth. "Yeah, you do that, kid. If you can find him. He left because he doesn't want you." He leaned over, sneering. "Nobody wants a loser, and you're a loser, kid. Always have been, always will be. Just like your old man."

And Larkin had thought about it. He'd thought about it that night, when he'd climbed out the window and run away for the third time. He'd thought about it the next night, as the policeman ushered him to a solitary holding cell. He'd thought about it during those grueling months in Blackthorn Hall; and he'd thought about it throughout the past twenty years, whenever he looked into the mirror and saw the blended image of his father and stepfather staring back at him.

For the first time, Larkin realized that although he'd despised the man his mother had married, the deepest, most private and intense anger had been held in reserve for the father who'd abandoned him. Recognizing that, he finally understood what he had to do.

Poking the cold, coagulated noodles, Letitia glanced anxiously at the kitchen wall clock, the hands of which had barely moved since her last observation. She covered the pan, fretting silently about the late hour and her son's absence. Mannie hadn't come home after school. Earlier, Rose had called the center to speak with Dr. Senagal, Larkin's professional stand-in, and had been told that Mannie wasn't there, either.

Now Rose was at her bingo game, it was well past suppertime and Letitia was beginning to panic. She was about to get into the car and cruise the neighborhood when she heard the front door open.

Letitia dashed into the living room as Mannie was shrugging out of his jacket. "Where have you been?"

"Around," he mumbled, tossing the jacket on the sofa. "Is supper done?"

"Done and dead," she snapped, as angry as she was relieved. "And I don't consider 'around' a proper answer to my question. Now, where have you been?"

He slipped her a sullen look and folded his arms. "I was just hanging with the guys, that's all."

"At the center?" Since she already knew Mannie hadn't been at the youth center, she held her breath, wondering if he would lie to her.

He didn't. "No."

Somehow, that didn't make her feel much better. "You know that's the only place you're allowed to go after school, and then only if you have permission to do so."

"Guess I forgot." Shifting, he sniffed the air and wrinkled his nose. "Bingo night, huh?"

Brushing by his stunned mother, Mannie limped into the kitchen. Letitia waited a moment to gather her composure before following. She found him spooning glued-together noodles out of the pan. "There's meat and gravy in the oven."

"Thanks." Mannie heaped his plate and carried his meal to the table.

Since Letitia had lost her appetite an hour ago, she propped a hip against the counter and watched her son eat. "I'm not willing to let this go, Mannie. I've been worried about you."

"Sorry." He spooned a huge bite into his mouth, washing it down with half a glass of milk.

"Sorry isn't good enough," Letitia said softly. "You're grounded for the rest of the week."

Mannie's head snapped up. "No way!"

"I don't enjoy punishing you, Mannie, but breaking family rules and ignoring your responsibilities isn't acceptable behavior. From now on, I expect you to be in this house within thirty minutes of your last class."

Shoving his plate away, Mannie leapt to his feet, eyes flashing. "That's not fair!"

"Fair or not, those are the rules."

Mannie stood there, seething, his furious gaze boring a hole through the very center of his mother's heart. Letitia stared back, unflinching, yet deeply troubled by the fierce anger in her son's eyes. There was something different about this anger, something explosive, almost violent. She wasn't afraid of her son; she was afraid for him.

He bolted from the table.

"Mannie!" Letitia spun and ran after him. The front door slammed in her face. She muscled it open and dashed into the front yard. The cul-de-sac was deserted. Letitia stood there, stunned and defeated, realizing that she'd actually lost control of her own son. Mannie had suddenly become a defiant stranger, disrespectful and disobedient, filled with destructive rage. Letitia couldn't reach him anymore, couldn't break through the angry shield he'd erected to keep her and everyone else away.

Returning to the house, Letitia closed the front door, then sagged against the wall, shaking and terrified. Mannie would be back when he was ready. The boy she knew as her son might already be lost.

Chapter Twelve

The school bus shuddered to a stop at the shoulder of a winding dirt drive. As the door hissed open, a din of childish giggles and shouts spilled out, along with two jubilant youngsters who bounced down the steps and hit the road running. Behind them, the bus emitted a massive whoosh, then headed on down the highway, belching and blowing smoke.

"Dad! Dad!"

Waving, Larkin watched his towheaded son sprint down the muddy drive without the slightest effort to avoid puddles left by last night's rain. Lagging a few yards back, Larkin's daughter picked her way around the goo, selecting a somewhat drier path along the raised edge of the driveway.

Justin, flushed and grinning, skidded to a sloppy stop in front of his father. "I was afraid you'd be gone already."

Larkin ruffled the boy's prickle-cut hair. "I told you last night that I'd be here through the weekend."

"Yeah, but I thought you mighta changed your mind or something."

"Not a chance, sport." Stroking his son's moist cheek, he glanced up to check on Susie's progress. She'd hoisted her lunch box over her head, tucked her books under an arm and was carefully tiptoeing around the gloppy puddle her brother had gleefully churned into mud pudding. Larkin chuckled at the way she wrinkled her stubby nose in a universal expression of feminine disgust. "How're you doing, princess?"

"I hate rain," she muttered, eyeing her splotched sneakers. "It makes everything all yucky."

Justin, oblivious to the fact that his own shoes were completely encrusted in a layer of thick brown gunk, disputed his sister's observation. "If we don't get rain, the crops will fail and there won't be enough feed for the livestock."

With a toss of her silky blond head, Susie gave her brother a withering stare. "John isn't even gonna plant till next week, only now the fields are too muddy to plow."

As the argument about the merits of unseasonal midwestern rain continued between the two little McKays, Larkin took his daughter's books—Justin insisted on carrying his own—and walked with his children toward the rambling farmhouse where his ex-wife lived with her new husband. It was strange listening to kids who'd once been well-versed only on in-line skates and the newest video games now discuss details of farm life with such casual expertise.

Larkin supposed it was almost as strange as being a guest in his ex-wife's home.

When Larkin had decided on this spur-of-the-moment trip, he'd planned to rent a motel room. Bonnie and John wouldn't hear of it, reasoning that he'd be able to spend much more time with the children if he stayed under the same roof. The logic was sound, of course, particularly since the primary motivation for this unscheduled visit was first-hand observation of the children's day-to-day home life.

Besides, he'd already heard Justin's version, unflattering as it was, so Larkin considered it only fair to see for himself how much, if any, of his son's complaint was justified. He'd expected a certain amount of resistance from their mother; so far, there'd been none. Quite the contrary. When he'd telephoned to inform Bonnie of his plans, she'd been openly enthusiastic and, he'd thought, oddly relieved.

Lingering tension over her new husband's reaction had dissolved the moment Larkin had pulled his rented car in front of the house in last night's blinding rain. John Haggarty had been waiting on the porch holding an umbrella and a wearing a smile of welcome.

Larkin and Haggarty had met before, of course, and the man had always come across as a pleasant, quiet fellow who seemed slow to anger and quick to praise. It was difficult to dislike him, although God knew Larkin had certainly tried. In the end, he couldn't muster even the slightest resentment for the soft-spoken bear of a man whose gaze reflected a certain gentleness each time he looked at his wife's children.

Larkin supposed that those affectionate glances could have been a ruse for his benefit, but he doubted it. Faking feelings would be exceptionally difficult for a man from whom a raised eyebrow constituted a virulent emotional display.

"Daddy," Susie said, tugging the hem of Larkin's sweatshirt. "After chores, can we play a game?"

"I don't see why not—"

Justin interrupted, visibly irritated by his sister's request. "He can't play no dumb games with you 'cause he's taking me to Little League sign-ups, right, Dad?"

"All I said was that I'd talk to your mother and John about that, and I did."

The boy scrunched up his mouth, looking worried. "Did you tell 'em they weren't being fair?"

"No, I didn't, son, because you haven't been honest with me about the reason they wouldn't let you play this season."

"It wasn't my fault," Justin insisted, his lip quivering. "My dumb teacher gives too much homework. Hardly anybody in the whole entire class gets it all done."

"But you didn't get any of it done, and what's worse, you lied about it to your mother."

Tears of defeat trickled down his freckled face. "John makes me do too many chores. There's no time left for homework."

"From what I understand, there was enough time after chores for you to play hockey with your friends." Having reached the porch, Susie scurried up the steps. "You go on in, princess," Larkin told her. "Let your mommy know that Justin and I will be there in a few minutes."

"Okay," she chirped, then pushed open the front door and disappeared into the cavernous house.

Larkin turned his attention to his disheartened son, who sniffed pitifully and wiped his nose with his sleeve. "It's not fair," the boy muttered, kicking a muddy rock. "I wanna live with you."

"All right," Larkin replied without hesitation.

Justin blinked. "You mean it's okay?"

"Of course. You're my son and I love you. I'd like nothing better than having you and your sister with me all the time . . . if that's what you really want."

"'Course it is," Justin mumbled without conviction.

A lump was forming in Larkin's throat, a lump of hope tempered by the suspicion that his son, like so many children of divorce, was simply using one parent to get what he wanted from the other. "Sit down, son. Let's talk."

Larkin settled on a wooden step, waiting as Justin sat down beside him, cradling his books and lunch pail in his lap. "First of all, your mother and I share joint custody, which means that we are equally responsible for both you and your sister. Right now, the arrangement is for you kids to spend the school year living here, and summers with me. What I hear you saying is that you want to reverse that, to live with me during the school year and spend summers on the farm. Is that right?''

Squirming, the boy issued a listless shrug. ''Yeah, I guess so, only Mom would never let us go.''

''Your mother is willing to allow each of you to make your own decision.''

Justin twitched once, then looked up, incredulous. ''She is?''

''Yes. Of course, there will be some ground rules.''

''What kinda—'' he gulped ''—rules?''

''For one thing, no changing schools in the middle of the year. That means you'll finish the term here, and begin the September school year in California. If you decide you don't like your new school either, you'll have to tough it out until the end of the term in June. Understood?'' An angled glance confirmed that the poor kid's eyes were bulging and his jaw drooped like a gate with a broken hinge. ''You'll still have chores, of course, and homework will be a priority. If you fall behind on your schoolwork, extracurricular activities will be subject to forfeiture.''

''Huh?''

Larkin swallowed a smile. ''That means keep your grades up or you can kiss off next year's Little League, too.''

''Aw, jeez…'' The poor kid looked as if he were about to throw up.

Sliding an arm around his son's thin shoulders, Larkin brushed a kiss across the boy's buzzed hair and gave him a comforting squeeze. ''What you need to understand is that taking responsibility is a fact of life. No matter where you are, certain things will always be expected of you, and that's as it should be. Whether you decide to stay here or move in with me, your mother and I both want what's best for you.'' He took a deep breath, adding, ''And so does John.''

Justin rolled his eyes but said nothing.

Larkin regarded him thoughtfully. "You don't really dislike John, do you?"

The boy fidgeted with the handle of his lunch pail. "He's okay, I guess."

"Hmm." Removing his arm, Larkin propped an elbow on his knee and rubbed his chin. "If John is 'okay,' why are you so rude to him?"

Appearing shocked by the question, Justin looked up then down again, studying the pail's plastic handle as if he'd never seen it before.

"I was outside the barn this morning when John asked you to shift fresh hay into the stalls." Larkin paused, awaiting a response. There wasn't one. "You were quite disrespectful, Justin. I was disappointed that you'd speak to anyone that way."

The boy's shoulders quivered in another limp shrug. "He's always telling me what to do."

"He's teaching you what to do, son. There's a difference. But even if there wasn't a difference, John is your stepfather and is entitled to be treated with respect and civility."

Apparently Justin disagreed, because his mouth flattened into a stubborn line and he glared down at the hapless lunch pail as if wishing it dead.

It was time, Larkin decided, to offer more than fatherly platitudes. It was time to dig deep into his own soul and reveal that he understood his son's plight because once he had shared it. Larkin knew what had to be said; the words, however, hung heavily in his throat. Few people knew of those bitter days because it hurt to discuss them. Except with Letitia. With her, the words had flowed like a river, purging him clean.

God, he missed her. She'd given him so much, and he'd repaid her with cowardice. He'd run away from her love.

He'd run away from the fear of being rejected by her son. He'd run away from his own feelings.

But he wouldn't run from his responsibility as a parent, and he wouldn't be a coward with his son. "I had a stepfather, too. Did you know that?"

The bowed blond head swiveled sideways. "Really?"

"My stepfather wasn't a very nice man—not like John— but the truth is that I never actually gave him a chance to be nice. The first time I met my mother's new husband, I started mouthing off with every mean thing I could think of. I called him names, tattled if he tried to correct me and generally acted like a first-class brat."

Justin squared his slumping shoulders and stared, awestruck. "You did? How come?"

"I resented him, blamed him for my parents' divorce even though I knew he and my mother hadn't met until months afterward." Leaning back against the stoop, Larkin cupped a bent knee with his palm and gazed out over the flat, unplowed fields. Strange, he thought, how this morning, as he'd listened to his son echo hateful words out of his own childhood, the dogging bitterness had begun seeping away. He'd suddenly seen his youth and his troubled relationship with the man his mother had married in a new and deeply disturbing light.

"I doubt my stepfather and I would ever have become friends," Larkin told his now attentive son. "He resented me as much as I resented him. Still, we might have eventually achieved a civilized relationship, if I'd allowed it. Instead, I was determined to drive him away in the vain hope that once he was out of the picture, my mom and dad would get back together so my family would be whole again."

Justin's eyes were as big as saucers. "Did that ever happen? Your mom and dad getting back together, I mean."

"No, son, and it's not going to happen with your mother and me, either."

A swell of tears brightened the boy's blue eyes. "You don't know. It might..."

Larkin embraced his son, hugging him fiercely. "It's not going to happen, Justin. You have to accept that. Your mother has a new husband now and someday—" Letitia's image flashed into his mind. "Someday I might have a new wife."

Apparently Justin found that concept startling, as did Larkin himself. "Uh-uh! You wouldn't really marry anybody else... would you?"

"Would that upset you?"

"Sure. I mean, it's kinda weird thinking about it, you know?"

Larkin managed a smile. "Yes, son. I know. It's kind of weird to me, too."

Particularly when he may have already lost the one woman he loved more than life itself. Fear, he thought sadly, is the most destructive emotion on earth. He'd been so afraid to fail that he hadn't even tried to succeed.

That had always been his major weakness, a weakness he was now determined to conquer.

"I guess that'd be sorta okay," Justin said.

"Hmm?"

"It's okay if you get a new wife, as long as she's nice."

"She's very nice," Larkin assured him. "And while we're on the subject, what would you think about having a big brother?"

"A brother! Wow, that'd be so cool." Justin slipped a covert glance toward the house, then screened his mouth with his hand. "Sisters are a pain," he confided. "They don't like to do nothing fun 'cause they're always worried about getting dirty and stuff."

"Ah... well, I see your point."

"Can he come visit me?"

"Who?"

"My new brother."

"I, uh—" Coughing into his closed fist, Larkin tried to climb out of the hole he'd just dug for himself. "This conversation is a little premature. I was just wondering how you'd feel about it, that's all."

"Oh." A flicker of disappointment dissipated quickly. "Dad?"

"Yes, son?"

"You wanna help me do my chores?"

Larkin laughed. "Sure, that sounds like fun."

As Justin leapt up to take his books and lunch pail into the house, Larkin's mind drifted back to Letitia and Mannie. There was, he knew, a very real possibility that they'd never forgive him, but he couldn't consider that now. If he did, the fear would grab him by the throat and squeeze the life out of him. No, he had to push away negative thoughts and find a way to convince them that he was worthy of their trust, that he *did* have grit and determination and the intestinal fortitude to tough out adversity.

But first he'd have to convince himself.

Reluctantly, Letitia turned off the shower. She could have stayed there all night, absorbing the steamy warmth. In her watery retreat, tension and troubles melted like magic and were symbolically swirled down the drain. Outside the frosted glass door, reality would pounce with icy fingers. And she'd be cold again.

She stepped out, shivering.

A moment later, she slipped on a robe, wrapped a towel around her wet head and emerged into the hallway. Rock music vibrated from Mannie's room, not loud but definitely audible. That wasn't unusual. The radio was always on when Mannie was in his room, but it was nearly 11:00 p.m. now and judging by the sliver of light emanating from beneath his door, he was still awake.

Letitia tapped lightly. "Bedtime, Mannie. You have school tomorrow."

Continuing down the hall, she went into the living room to check the front door lock and turn out the lights. The routine was repeated in the kitchen, after she'd paused for a glass of water and taped a note on the fridge reminding herself that tomorrow was trash day.

As she reentered the darkened hallway, light continued to spray beneath Mannie's door and she could still hear the music. She knocked more forcefully. "Turn the radio off and go to bed, Mannie. It's late."

This time, she waited for a reply. When she didn't get one, she twisted the knob and went inside. The room was empty.

A knot of pure terror wedged in her throat. "Mannie?" She yanked open the closet, praying he was playing a joke. Although she frantically pawed through his clothes and repeatedly shouted his name, Mannie was nowhere to be found.

She backed out of the closet as Rose appeared in the doorway. "What is it, Letitia?"

"Mannie's gone," she blurted.

"Gone?" Blinking, Rose repeated the word twice before gazing around the room. "No, he's hiding, that's all, like he used to do when he was a little boy."

Letitia dropped to her knees, lifting a corner of the coverlet to peer under the bed. Seeing nothing, she sat back on her heels, helplessly spreading her hands. "I don't understand. Except for a few minutes in the shower, I've been in the living room all evening. I would have seen him— Oh, God!"

Two pairs of horrified eyes focused on the window.

Leaping up, Letitia dashed over and saw instantly that it was unlocked. She raised the lower sash. The screen had been removed. Feeling as if she'd swallowed a brick, she leaned out and saw the screen propped neatly against the outside of the house next to an upended trash container that had apparently been used as a step stool.

Her eyelids fluttered shut. Oblivious to the frigid wind sweeping into the room, she clenched her fists, bowing her head and fighting tears. Anger at the deception was drowned in a sea of helplessness and fear. Since the trash container must have been positioned in advance, the escape hadn't been a last minute whim. It had been methodically planned.

Letitia felt sick. Wednesday's rebellious episode had ended within thirty minutes, after which time Mannie had returned, repentant and apologetic, spouting promises that he'd never disobey her again. That had been two days ago. Apparently Mannie's definition of *never* was less extensive than her own.

"Letitia...?"

The terror in Rose's voice stiffened her resolve. She couldn't panic. If she did, Rose would go to pieces and then both of them would be hysterical.

Wiping her eyes, she straightened and closed the window, deliberately leaving it unlocked. "It's all right, Mama. Mannie's things are all here, so I think it's safe to conclude that he hasn't run away. My guess is that he's still seething about having been put on restriction and this is his way of evening the score."

Looking hurt and bewildered, Rose raised both hands to her mouth. She shook her head once, then sagged against the doorjamb. "Manuel wouldn't do such a thing," she whispered into her palms. "He's a good boy."

Too numb to argue, Letitia flipped off the light and radio as a signal to her returning son that he'd been caught.

As she started to leave the room, Rose clutched at her arm. "What are you going to do, *nuera?*"

Letitia started to shake. "I don't know, Mama. Dear God, I just don't know."

The two women embraced, trembling and afraid, yet each mustering her own inner strength for the sake of the other. "I'll talk to him," Letitia murmured against her mother-in-law's warm shoulder. "We'll work something out . . . it'll be okay—"

The doorbell rang, shattering her words and what was left of her nerves. She spun around as if shot, with her palm pressed over her pounding heart.

"It's Manuel!" Rose exclaimed. Issuing a prayer of thanks, the relieved woman crossed herself and hurried after Letitia, who was sprinting through the living room.

Letitia yanked the door open expecting to see a contrite eleven-year-old. Instead, she was greeted by a parent's worst nightmare. A grim-faced policeman was standing on her porch, holding her son's wallet.

Chapter Thirteen

Letitia's car wasn't in the driveway when Larkin pulled in front of the house. Ordinarily she was home early on Monday, which she'd once mentioned was the slowest day of her workweek. He hesitated, glancing at his watch. It was barely past 5:00 p.m., so he decided that she'd probably stopped at the store.

That might work out even better, since it would give him the chance to speak with Mannie alone. After mentally rehearsing his words on the plane and having driven here directly from the airport, he was grateful for an opportunity to deliver at least one of his speeches before losing his nerve.

As expected, Rose answered the door, but her appearance was shocking. Wrapped in a limp cotton robe, she wore no makeup and her normally neat hair looked as if it hadn't seen a comb in days. "My God, Rose, are you ill?"

She stared up with benumbed eyes. "You're too late," she mumbled. "Too late."

Turning, she shuffled back into the living room and dropped heavily in the lounge chair. Larkin entered, closing the door behind him. "Too late for what?" he asked. When the dazed woman offered no reply, his gaze flickered toward the hallway. "Is Mannie home?"

Rose grimaced at the mention of her grandson's name and after a moment, she slowly shook her head.

A disturbing prickle slid down Larkin's spine. Squatting in front of the lounge chair, he cupped the woman's limp hands between his palms. Without resisting or sparing a glance in his direction, the woman continued to stare into space. Larkin gentled his tone. "Rose, do you know where Letitia is?" She reacted slowly, blinking her red eyes and focusing on the man who knelt before her. After a long moment, Larkin repeated the question. "Where is Letitia?"

A small shudder vibrated her thin shoulders. "She went to be with Manuel. I should have gone with her, but I... I didn't have the courage."

The disturbing prickle turned into an ominous chill. Larkin tightened his grip on her hands. "Where?" Fear made the word harsh, even to his own ears, but inside him, panic was mounting and gave a desperate edge to his voice. "Where are they, Rose? Where are Mannie and Letitia?"

She flinched as though struck. Moisture swelled in her dark eyes and her mouth opened, although the only sound she uttered was a hushed sob. In less than a heartbeat, tears streamed down her cheeks and her fragile body was racked by violent weeping.

It took several moments for Larkin to calm the distraught woman. Speaking in slow, soothing tones, he dried her face with a tissue and tried again. "Start from the beginning, please, and try to tell me what has happened."

Struggling for composure, she heaved a shuddering sigh and nodded. "Manuel... has not been himself since you left. Letitia and I, we didn't know what to do. He was so angry, you see." She paused, as if requesting confirmation that she was being understood.

Larkin squeezed her hands. "You're doing fine. Go on."

"Last Friday, Manuel sneaked out to be with his friends. He didn't know the car was stolen. H-He didn't know there was a gun—" A sob cut off her words.

Larkin's blood went cold. "What happened? You have to tell me what happened!"

She met his frightened gaze with one of incredible grief. "A boy died."

His lungs deflated as if he'd been kicked in the chest. "Who?" he croaked. "What was the boy's name?"

The front door slammed.

Startled, Larkin bolted to his feet, spun around and stared into Letitia's pale face. "Leave Mama alone," she said quietly. "She doesn't know anything else."

Larkin stood there, struck mute and feeling ill. Letitia, looking pinched and wan, avoided his gaze as she dropped her purse and keys on the table. Her dark eyes were drab, lifeless, shadowed with fatigue. Stress lines bracketed her mouth, which was clamped into a tight line. She raked her fingers through her thick hair and took a shallow breath. "What are you doing here, Larkin?"

"I...I wanted to see you and Mannie."

Bowing her head, she massaged her eyelids for a moment, then looked up. "Mannie can't have visitors."

Larkin clenched the fist at his side to keep from clutching at his churning stomach. A question teetered on his lips, only to be silenced by Rose's hushed gasp.

"I thought the judge would let Manuel come home now," the woman whispered. "He's just a child."

"They're all children, Mama."

"But how could the judge not understand that Manuel is innocent?"

"Today was an arraignment, not a trial. They didn't even let Mannie speak."

"Not let him speak?" Bewildered, Rose glanced bleakly around the room as if searching for divine guidance. "I don't understand...."

Letitia laid a comforting hand on her mother-in-law's shoulder. "I don't understand, either. I waited all day, but everything was over in less than a minute. I think what happened is that all the boys found in the car were formally charged and the judge scheduled a date for pleas to be entered. Then they—" Her voice broke. "T-They took Mannie away."

Larkin moistened his lips. "Do you know where they took him?"

Letitia looked up, her eyes filled with the most incredible fear. She didn't answer; she didn't have to. In that sickening moment, Larkin knew without doubt that Mannie was on his way to Blackthorn Hall.

Sitting at the kitchen table, Letitia felt dead inside. This was the worst nightmare she could imagine. Not once since her son's birth had they been separated for more than a few hours. Mannie had never even spent the night with a friend. Now he'd been gone for three days, three grueling days, and no one could tell her when—or if—he'd come home.

It was more than she could endure. Her mother-in-law was on the verge of emotional collapse and if not for Larkin's calming presence, Letitia would have been, too. Even so, every breath was a supreme effort, every coherent word a victory over terror.

Across the room, Larkin was on the phone with Roberto Arroya, who'd just returned from his honeymoon. To give her dazed mind a point of focus, Letitia forced herself to listen.

"...Mannie's going to need a lawyer, Bobby. With your contacts, you ought to be able to pull a string or two and find a decent one... Hmm? Yes, Letitia's talked to a couple of Yellow Page shysters, but the greedy bastards wanted the deed to her house before they'd even talk to her.'' Listening intently, Larkin shifted the phone and scrawled something on a scratch pad. ''That's right, four boys were in the car.... Mannie and another eleven-year-old, William Doherty, along with two sixteen-year-olds. No, Letitia wasn't allowed to see her son until Saturday night.... Yes, I know he's a juvenile, but from what I understand, he was interrogated without either a parent or lawyer present.

''Hmm? I'm not sure about the details, but apparently Mannie told his mother that a verbal altercation took place between the sixteen-year-old passenger, Todd Minger, and a group of youths in front of an apartment complex. Todd demanded that the driver, Jason Doherty, circle the block. When Doherty complied, Todd suddenly whipped out a pistol and shot into the group. The car sped off but was pulled over by police less than a mile away and the gun was located under the front passenger seat. What's that? Oh... Just a minute.'' Larkin lowered the receiver and spoke to Letitia. ''Are you certain the police didn't have your consent to interrogate Mannie?''

Confused, she massaged her temples trying to remember the details of those hellish hours at the police station. ''Of course I'm certain,'' she said. ''I was at the station from midnight Friday until late Saturday afternoon and no one spoke to me until a sergeant finally came over to say I could have five minutes with my son. That's when Mannie told me his version of what had happened that night and said that the police didn't believe him because they'd been asking the same questions over and over for hours.''

Tucking the phone under his chin, Larkin relayed that information to Roberto, then added, ''I know the shooter, Bobby. He's hard core, but from what I hear, they're keeping all four boys together.... Yeah, I know. It's an engraved invitation for Todd to intimidate the other kids into forgetting everything they saw. Do you know a sympathetic judge who could order Mannie's transfer to another facility?'' His shoulders slumped. He lowered his voice. "Twenty-four hours could be too late, Bobby. We've got to get him out of there now.... Yes, I've already called Dev. He's going to scope out his police sources to see what he can learn. Yeah. Okay.''

Hanging up the phone, Larkin pursed his lips and studied the floor.

"Can he help?'' Letitia asked anxiously.

Distracted, he nonetheless managed an encouraging smile. "You can count on Bobby. He knows a crackerjack defense lawyer with a ton of juvenile court experience and a spotless reputation.''

Buoyed by the first good news she'd heard in days, Letitia felt a smidgen of warmth seep into her icy veins. "Do you think he'll take our case?''

"Bobby seems to think so.'' Larkin pulled up a chair to join Letitia at the table. "Bobby and Devon both have your phone number. They'll call as soon as they know anything. Try not to worry,'' he said, laying his palm over her hand. "Now that the Brotherhood has been mobilized, Mannie has powerful advocates working on his behalf. We won't let him down.''

Larkin's comforting warmth seeped into Letitia's hand; his confidence soothed her. It was temporary, of course, she understood that. There would be no long-term relationship. On that subject, Larkin had made his feelings clear. But so much had happened since then that she'd pushed her grief aside; now, in his presence, her loss seemed more acute, the pain more debilitating.

Last week, she'd lost the man she loved. This week, she'd lost her son.

The only way to maintain sanity was to remind herself that she had nothing left to lose. All she could do now was to fight for her son's return. It was a fight she was determined to win.

Retrieving her hand, she forced a stoic pose, hoping Larkin wouldn't notice how deeply his presence affected her. "It wasn't easy for me to ask your help, and I know the decision to offer it must have been difficult, but I want you to know how deeply I appreciate what you've done."

As she spoke, a bewildered frown creased his forehead. "The decision wasn't difficult at all," he murmured, obviously puzzled. "If I'd known what was happening, I would have been here days ago."

"If you'd known—?" Letitia shook her head in confusion. "I've left messages for you at the center and on the answering machine at your apartment. When you didn't respond, I assumed that you were too busy." Actually, she'd assumed that Larkin simply hadn't cared, which was why his unexpected appearance this afternoon had been so startling.

Larkin's mystified expression melted into one of abject misery. "Oh, Lord," he moaned, rubbing the back of his neck. "I'm so sorry. This is all my fault." Sighing, he leaned over the table, his impassioned gaze drilling into her own. "I never got those messages, Letitia. I left town last Wednesday without telling anyone at the center where I could be reached, and I never gave a thought about calling in for messages. I just got back this afternoon and drove directly here from the airport."

At first, the significance of that statement eluded her. "You really didn't know?"

His gaze didn't waver. "If I had, nothing on earth could have kept me away."

Letitia didn't know whether to laugh or cry. As deeply as she'd been hurt by Larkin's confession that he wasn't ready for commitment, that pain had been softened by the belief that deep down, he honestly cared about her. When her repeated pleas for help had been ignored, she'd been utterly devastated and had come to the heartbreaking conclusion that Larkin's professed love had been a ploy, a graceful way of extricating himself from a relationship he'd apparently considered to be nothing more than a casual fling.

Despite relief at the discovery that Larkin hadn't deliberately disregarded her cries for help, Letitia was still leery of reading more into his motives than had been meant. She'd already been stung by her own false assumptions, and understood that a willingness to help her son wasn't evidence that Larkin suddenly wanted to be a permanent part of their lives.

Still, he was here now. And she was grateful.

"Letitia?"

As she looked into his melting blue eyes, her conviction faltered. She wanted to touch and to be touched. She wanted to be held, to be embraced by his comfort and his strength. She wanted him to convince her that Mannie would be home soon and everything would be wonderful.

But experience had taught her that life wasn't always wonderful. Good men die. Lovers part. Innocent boys go to prison.

Dabbing her moist cheek, she took a deep breath. "You went to see your children, didn't you?"

"Yes. How did you know?"

"Wild guess." She sighed. "Actually, it wasn't much of a stretch, considering how worried you've been about them. Are they all right?"

"They're fine. Great, in fact." His smile held none of the sadness she'd come to expect when he spoke about his kids. "Justin's sprouting like a weed, but eight-year-olds do tend to grow in spurts. Susie hasn't changed much, although her hair's long enough to wear in a ponytail now. She thinks it makes her look older, which is, of course, powerful incentive for a first grader."

"Of course," Letitia agreed. "Young ladies want to look old, and old ladies want to look young. It's a fact of nature."

"Apparently so." Larkin inspected the sweetener bowl, twirling it between his palms. "But I found out what I needed to know."

"What was that?"

"I found out that they're going to be okay," he said quietly. "And so are we."

Then, as Letitia sat in stunned silence, Larkin relayed the result of his soul-searching, and the conclusions he'd reached.

"You were right about me," he added. "All my life I've run away from anything I couldn't control. I've isolated myself emotionally, distanced myself from responsibility and refused to accept either blame or credit for my actions. That has changed, Letitia. I've changed. I don't expect you to believe that until you see it, so I'm going to make my intentions known, then plant myself on the edge of your life with the hope that someday you'll find room in your heart to forgive the foolish things I've done."

Letitia's heart pounded so loudly, she wondered if he could hear it. The softness of his eyes, the anxious intensity of his words had struck a chord deep inside her. Something momentous was happening here, something she dared not presume.

She moistened her lips, willing her voice to remain steady. "What exactly are your intentions, Larkin? I want to be absolutely certain that I understand."

Pushing away the sweetener bowl, he wiped his forehead, took a shuddering breath and looked straight at her. Just as he opened his mouth to speak, the telephone rang.

Letitia went rigid. Her gaze flickered from Larkin to the jangling wall phone and back again. "Would Roberto be calling back so soon?" she asked.

"There's only one way to find out." Kicking his lean leg over the chair back, Larkin took two great strides, snatched the receiver and issued a clipped greeting. As he stood there, listening, his eyes widened and his skin blanched. Still, he said nothing.

A giant lump was pushing into Letitia's throat. "What is it?"

Larkin responded by turning toward the wall, effectively concealing his expression. After a moment, he cupped a hand around his mouth and spoke too softly to be overheard. Then he cradled the receiver, pausing for a deep breath before facing the woman who was now on her feet. "What's happening?" she demanded, slamming a palm against the table. "I have a right to know!"

Before answering, Larkin crossed the room and would have embraced her had she not pushed away his hands. She stumbled back, terrified by the look on his face. "Please," she croaked. "Tell me."

His hands dropped to his side. "All right," he said calmly. "There was an escape attempt while the boys were being transferred from the transport van to Blackthorn Hall's lockup facility."

"A what? No...don't say it again." Shielding herself with an upraised palm, she turned away, trembling, unwilling to believe that such a thing could have happened. "It's not true. It can't be true."

"A guard's gun was taken," he said quietly.

Letitia shook her head. "Mannie didn't do that. He couldn't...."

"No, it was Todd Minger but Mannie and the Doherty boys are there, too." Larkin took her shoulders, gently rotating her until she faced him. "I won't lie to you, Letitia. The situation is serious. The authorities are gearing up for a riot."

Her hand flew to her face. She shook her head, unable to comprehend the magnitude of what she'd heard. "That's ridiculous. They're only children—"

"Letitia, honey, their ages don't matter now." He smoothed her hair, trying to calm her even as his own eyes filled with fear. "They've taken hostages."

And with those three words, Letitia's entire world collapsed.

Dozens of police cars and vans blanketed Blackthorn Hall's parking lot, parked haphazardly, strewn about as if in the aftermath of a flood. After adding his own vehicle to the clutter, Larkin took Letitia's arm, bracing her as they crossed the cracked asphalt toward the security gate.

Redbrick buildings loomed into view behind the open chain-link fence. A smothering heat exploded inside his chest.

Larkin faltered, slowing their pace, and finally stopped a hundred yards from the gate. Voices haunted his mind, lost memories of cries and whispers and the silence of fear. His lungs were paralyzed. He couldn't breathe.

Fingers pressed the flesh of his arm, slender fingers, convulsed by panic. Letitia's fingers.

Air shuddered into his lungs. He had to be strong, for Letitia. And for Mannie.

He licked his lips. "Letitia—"

Anticipating his request, she cut him off. "I'm going inside with you."

There was no sense in arguing. Letitia's face was as white as death, but Larkin knew that even the gates of hell couldn't keep her from her son. She wouldn't leave until Mannie was safe; neither would Larkin.

Letitia's petrified gaze settled a few feet from the gate. "There's Roberto."

"He's waiting for us," Larkin told her, using the sheer force of his will to propel his feet into motion. Beside him, Letitia moved with quick steps, two to his one, allowing Larkin to guide her through the maze of emergency vehicles.

"Devon's inside," Roberto said when they arrived. "Most of the press has been cordoned in the mess hall, but Dev knows the captain in charge, so he's trying to gain access to the command center."

Larkin issued a curt nod, his gaze riveted on the gate. And beyond. For twenty years, he'd dreaded this moment; yet in the deepest corner of his heart, he'd always known it would occur, that the Brotherhood would someday be reunited here, in the place where it had all begun.

A firm hand gripped his shoulder. Roberto's strained voice broke Larkin's paralysis. "Ogden Marlow isn't here. Rumor has it that when he learned what happened, he made an excuse about having an appointment and took off, leaving his staff to deal with the crisis."

"That sounds like Marlow," Larkin muttered, not bothering to hide his disgust. "Lousy coward."

"Yeah," Roberto said, gazing through the chain-link toward the administration building. He took a shuddering breath. "Are you ready to go inside?"

The answer was no. Larkin would never be ready to relive the past, to face the ghosts that had haunted his nightmares. But ready or not, he had no choice. "Let's do it."

All three of them moved toward the gate, where Roberto displayed his U.S. Attorney identification to a security guard wearing a tan uniform. The guard studied Roberto's I.D., then motioned them through the gate onto a campus crawling with uniformed officers and troops garbed in riot gear. Holding up his I.D. card, Roberto muscled a path through security patrols and plotted a direct course toward the administration building, where the command center was located.

Their final obstacle was a pair of determined officers stationed at the entrance. Letitia waited at the end of the building while Larkin and Roberto went into the command center.

Because her wobbling knees threatened to buckle, she braced herself against the rough brick, feeling sick and chilled to the bone. Her face felt like ice. Her hands were so cold she couldn't feel them anymore. And she was even colder inside.

So this was it, the notorious Blackthorn Hall. It wasn't what she'd expected. With winding green belts and expansive, manicured lawns, the grounds resembled an ordinary college campus. Brick buildings, some two-story, were arranged in organized patterns around a landscaped quad. At the farthest end of the compound was a line of two-story structures that she assumed to be dormitories. Silhouettes moved across each rooftop. Her heart sank. The shadowy contours belonged to marksmen, snipers preparing for the kill.

Letitia started to shake, her gaze darting around the campus which was now an armed camp. Men with weapons lurked behind every building, every wall. The focus of their attention was a long, rectangular structure at the eastern boundary of the detention facility. Constructed of drab gray concrete, the structure was surrounded by a second fence capped by coils of razor-wire, creating a small, secured enclosure within the walled perimeter of the first.

At the sound of footsteps, Letitia turned and saw Roberto hurrying toward her. She pointed to the gray building. "Is that the lockup? Is that where my son is?"

Cupping her elbow, he issued a grim nod. "You can't stay in this area," he told her, ushering her across the clipped lawn. "We managed to get permission for you to wait with the press corps."

Struggling to look back over her shoulder, Letitia was struck by another surge of panic. "Is Mannie all right?"

"There's no evidence that anyone has been hurt," he told her. "I'm sure your son is fine."

"But—" Twisting around, Letitia scanned the entrance to the administration building and saw only the uniformed guards posted at the door. "Where's Larkin?"

"He's inside, talking with the negotiators." Sliding a supportive arm around her shoulders, Roberto guided Letitia into a cavernous building filled with meal tables and reporters milling about. "This is the mess hall," he told Letitia, although it looked like a cafeteria to her. "You can see the lockup from the east windows."

She spun around, saw a cluster of people staring out a windowed wall and would have rushed over had Roberto not taken hold of her arm.

"Listen to me, Letitia. I know how difficult this is, but this is important." Roberto waited until he had her attention. "Under no circumstance are you to leave this building. No matter what you see, no matter what you hear…you must stay here."

She actually felt the blood drain from her face. "Why? What is going to happen?"

"I don't know."

"You *do* know!" Alien fingers reached out from her own hands to clutch at the man's expensive lapels. "Tell me, dammit! What's happening to my son?"

"Letitia, please…" Roberto gently cupped her wrists but made no attempt to loosen her grip on his suit coat. "The only way you can help Larkin and Mannie is to stay calm."

Although vaguely aware that a hushed silence had fallen over the room and eyes had turned in her direction, Letitia was focused on the perplexing essence of Roberto's words. "Help Larkin?" she repeated, both bewildered and terrified by the confusing concept that Larkin would require help. "But it's Mannie who's in danger. I don't understand."

The answer was in Roberto's bleak eyes; Letitia simply couldn't interpret what she saw there.

Her attention, and his, was diverted by a sudden commotion across the room. Reporters that had been milling around tables now dashed to join the human crush at the windows. Cameras were focused; shots were snapped excited shouts emanated from the crowd.

Letitia wrenched out of Roberto's grasp. A moment later, she was elbowing through the crowd, panting and pushing, sobbing with fear and frustration. She finally pressed her hands against the glass, desperately scanning the campus for the source of the excitement. In less than a heartbeat, she saw it.

A man was walking toward the gray building with his arms raised above his head. Stopping at the open gate, the man turned in a slow circle, as if displaying that he was unarmed. After a moment, the lockup door opened. A hand emerged from the doorway, aiming a pistol.

The crowd of reporters issued a simultaneous gasp, followed by a hushed sigh of relief as the gun was lowered and the man was motioned inside. Then the lockup door closed.

The mess hall erupted in a din of speculation as to what they had seen and what it all meant. Letitia stood motionless, barely able to breathe. She knew exactly what she'd seen.

Larkin McKay had just traded himself for her son.

Chapter Fourteen

Pressed against a mess hall window, Letitia watched in stunned disbelief as sharpshooters continued their rooftop vigil. Uniformed officers clumped behind buildings and walls. Antennae sprouted from every hand, with walkie-talkies and cellular telephones forming a communication link between scattered groups.

Grueling minutes had stretched into an hour; shock had dissolved into uncontrollable terror. Somewhere in the bowels of that gray bunker, Letitia's son and the man she loved were the hostages of a homicidal adolescent who'd already been accused of gunning down one person, and was rumored to be responsible for attacks on several others.

Throughout the ordeal, Roberto had been stoically protective, shooing away curious reporters who, bored by the protracted standoff, had attempted to personalize stories with an interview with a distraught mother. The poor man had also been busy on his own cellular phone, making call after call to people whose names Letitia didn't recognize, with the sole exception of Devon Monroe, who was still in the administration building monitoring command center activity.

One of Devon's updates confirmed what Letitia had already guessed—that Larkin had volunteered to change places with the younger boys in exchange for taking up an advocate sword for those who'd initiated the crisis in the first place.

On the surface, the plan seemed sound enough; Larkin was, after all, a trained negotiator. But Letitia instinctively understood that Larkin had been compelled by something deeper than mere logic. By saving the youngsters now trapped by violence, he was making amends for the past, confronting the crippling guilt that had haunted him for decades.

Larkin McKay was facing his demons.

But he was doing so at enormous risk. Letitia had overheard enough conversational tidbits at the youth center to realize that Todd Minger—alias JoDog—resented the center's influence on local youth and considered Larkin a threat to his own despotic street rule. Now that Minger had the perfect opportunity for retaliation, Letitia was terrified for Larkin's safety.

Roberto had tried to assuage her fears by pointing out that the perpetrators hunkered down in the processing lockup knew perfectly well that the building was surrounded, and that Larkin's negotiating skills represented their only hope of survival.

That was true, of course. Unfortunately, Roberto's encouraging words ignored the fact that logic wasn't Todd Minger's strong suit; vengeance was. Past behavior had proved him to be impulsive and vindictive, displaying no regard for the consequence of his actions.

He was also a stone-cold killer.

The thought was so horrifying, Letitia felt faint. A cornered killer with nothing to lose would have few qualms about increasing his body count. He may, in fact, relish the idea of enhancing his notoriety, believing a posthumous notation in history books preferable to life as just another anonymous inmate.

She turned away from the window, sagging against the wall.

Roberto lowered his cellular phone and hurried to her side. "Are you all right?"

Biting her lip, Letitia fought tears. No, she wasn't all right; she might never be all right again. But sniveling aloud wouldn't resolve anything, so she lifted her chin, sniffed and forced a firm nod. "I'm fine, thank you."

Apparently she sounded convincing enough, because Roberto returned his attention to the telephone, completing the conversation in low, clipped tones. "Once you've displayed the court order, the guard will let you through the gate. The mess hall is the first building on your left." Abruptly ending the discussion, Roberto folded the phone and shoved it into his breast pocket. With his hands free, he slipped a brotherly arm around Letitia, urging her toward an empty table. "Why don't you sit down for a few minutes? I'll get coffee—"

Shaking him off, Letitia turned away, stubbornly refusing to vacate her place beside the window. When an excited voice from the crowd hollered, "Look!", she spun around, pressing her hands against the glass, anxiously scrutinizing the grounds.

At first, she noticed nothing different, but after a moment she realized that the officers surrounding the gray building had geared up and were in motion, moving quickly toward the gate in the lockup's security fence. Once in position, they crouched, aiming their weapons at the processing center door.

The door that was opening.

Holding her breath, Letitia watched three figures emerge. They hesitated, fearfully watching the armed officers at the gate. The three boys raised their hands all at once, as if responding to a sharp command, then they stuttered across the fenced compound with stiff, jerky steps.

One of the boys was limping.

With a strangled sob, Letitia pivoted away from the window and shoved her way through the mesmerized throng of reporters. Roberto, caught in the crowd, shouted her name. She broke into a run, exploding through the mess hall door and sprinting across the campus without considering that the muzzle sights of a dozen weapons were tracking her every move.

"Mannie!" she screamed, waving frantically. *"Mannie!"*

At the security gate, the freed boys had been surrounded by officers and were now being hustled across the campus toward the administrative building.

Letitia continued to run and scream and wave until she saw Mannie pull away from his captor. "Mom! Stay back!" It was all he had a chance to say before a police officer in body armor grabbed Mannie's arm, herding him back into the group.

With her attention riveted on her son, Letitia stumbled over a rise in the lawn and would have fallen if someone hadn't caught her from behind. Roberto hauled her up, pinioning her back to his chest by wrapping a strong arm around her waist. "Mannie's...fine," he said between pants. "Let the police...do their...jobs."

"Let go!" Twisting madly, she pried at the constricting arm. "He's my son! Let me go!"

"It's not over yet," Roberto insisted, dragging her back toward the mess hall.

From the corner of her eye, Letitia was vaguely aware of a middle-aged, professional woman hurrying toward them, although the focus of her frantic gaze was her son, who'd managed to get an arm free and was gesturing wildly. "Mom!"

When the woman reached them, Roberto nodded toward Mannie, who was still waving. "There's your client, counselor."

Shifting her valise, the woman followed Roberto's gesture, visually identifying Mannie a moment before he was hauled into the administration building. She issued a curt nod before speaking. "Mrs. Cervantes?"

Tearing her gaze from the door behind which her son had disappeared, Letitia blinked at the unfamiliar lady whose pleasant smile and unruffled demeanor was, given the chaotic circumstance, somewhat surprising.

"This is Barbara George," Roberto said, loosening his grip when he realized that Letitia was no longer struggling. "She's the attorney I told you about."

Letitia took several shallow breaths before she could muster the strength to speak. "Can you h-help my son?"

"I'm certainly going to try," Ms. George replied in a matter-of-fact manner that was oddly comforting. "I have a court order demanding my client's immediate transfer to another holding facility, and I've scheduled an emergency hearing tomorrow morning. With any luck, Mannie will be remanded to your custody at that time."

"Oh..." A sudden surge of tears blurred her vision. She choked up, unable to speak. All she could do was grab the woman's hand, squeezing it with a silent plea.

Ms. George squeezed back. "It's settled, then." The attorney's smile faded into grim determination as she hoisted her valise and hurried toward the administration building.

Pressing her palm over her mouth, Letitia closed her eyes, allowing warm tears to stream down her face. A surge of relief weakened her knees. *Tomorrow... remanded to your custody.*

For the first time in days, she felt a glimmer of hope that everything would be all right. Mannie would be home and Larkin...

Her head snapped up. Larkin was still inside that building, and a swarm of uniformed officers were now pouring through the gate to take up position inside the lockup's fenced perimeter. Letitia clutched at Roberto's arm. "What are they doing?"

"I don't know," Roberto replied, shading his eyes. He looked from the lockup to the administration building, where Ms. George was displaying a sheath of legal documents to the guards. Suddenly, the administration door opened. Devon Monroe rushed out, along with several men in civilian clothes.

"Something's happening," Letitia whispered, her blood chilled by the distant wail of a siren. "Maybe someone's been shot...maybe someone is dead! Oh, God—" She spun around, seizing the lapels of Roberto's jacket. "What if it's Larkin?"

"It's not." A nervous jaw twitch belied the firm denial, but Roberto's gaze remained riveted on the activity around the lockup.

Letitia watched in horror as the troops stormed the building with weapons drawn. Devon and the other men, whom Letitia assumed to be from the command center, stayed outside the perimeter fence, staring at the open door as if expecting the devil himself to emerge.

Just as Letitia's legs were buckling with fear, several uniformed men emerged from the concrete building. It took a moment for her to realize that two of the men were wearing tan security uniforms rather than police blues.

"They've released the guards," Roberto murmured.

The siren, which had been growing louder by the minute, now seemed to be emanating from the outside parking lot. Then, with a final, high-pitched chirp, the incessant wail suddenly stopped.

Meanwhile, the liberated security guards were conferring with plainclothes detectives clustered around the gate. Devon Monroe hovered nearby, apparently eavesdropping on the guards' conversation, which was punctuated with glances toward the lockup's open door and an occasional grim nod.

During the discussion, one man gazed across the grassy quad as if awaiting an arrival. When the same man suddenly raised an arm, gesturing someone over, Letitia assumed he must be looking at her. She stumbled forward a few steps before realizing that he'd been signaling the EMS personnel who hurried past her carrying medical equipment and supply chests.

Letitia jerked to a stop, her heart pounding. The paramedics headed directly toward the processing center, pausing at the gate for brief instructions before rushing into the building.

Uttering a terrified cry, Letitia broke into a full run. This time, she didn't have to worry about Roberto stopping her. He'd already sprinted halfway to the gate.

Devon, hustling out to meet them, lifted a hand to stop Roberto and snagged Letitia's waist as she tried to dash by. Thwarted, she pummeled Devon's chest, babbling incoherently. Somewhere deep in her mind, she heard Devon's voice and understood that he was trying to soothe her. But she was inconsolable, unable to hear because her ears roared with terror, unable to blurt out a decipherable question because her throat was on the verge of collapse. Every ounce of Letitia's energy was focused on the lockup's open door, on getting to it and through it and finding the man she loved more than life itself.

Suddenly, there he was.

Larkin emerged into the fenced yard, raking his tousled hair. He looked tired; he looked tense; he looked wonderful.

Letitia's fists slid limply down the front of Devon's sweater. She tried to call Larkin's name, but could manage nothing more impressive than a quavering croak.

It didn't matter. Larkin glanced through the chain-link fence and saw her, and his eyes lit like sunshine. He took a step, then another, then erupted into a trot and finally a full run. He burst through the startled group gathered at the gate and a moment later, swept Letitia into his arms.

She clung to him, sobbing, laughing, uttering nonsense and hugging him fiercely. Larkin was whispering in a voice too broken to be understood, but that didn't matter, either. She could touch him, feel the warmth of his body, the pulsation of his life force permeating every fiber of her being. He was alive. He was safe. He was home.

Loosening her grasp, Letitia pulled just far enough away to anxiously inspect Larkin's face with her fingertips, grazing his eyelids and lips, exploring the contour of his jaw and examining the stress lines bracketing his mouth. Only then was she convinced that he was real and not the hallucinogenic creation of her hysterical heart.

"I've been so frightened," she murmured, still probing his dear face with her hands. "When the paramedics went in, I was afraid you'd been shot."

Larkin caressed her cheek, first with his fingertips, then with the back of his knuckles. "One of the boys hit his head during the original altercation with the security guards," he told her. "The injury isn't serious, but it needs a few stitches, and the boy will probably be held in the infirmary overnight to make sure he doesn't have a concussion."

Letitia began to tremble all over again. "No one else was hurt?"

"No, thank God. Apparently Todd and a couple of other boys on the county's transport bus concocted a plan to overpower the guards in Blackthorn's exterior parking lot. When they realized that the bus had passed through that lot into the lockup's security perimeter, Todd's cohorts assumed the plan was off. They were as surprised as anyone when Todd went into action. From there on, everything pretty much dissolved into chaos."

The question Letitia most feared tumbled off her quaking tongue. "This escape attempt... Was Mannie involved?"

Larkin smiled. "No. He was pretty brave, though. There wasn't anything he could do to help the guards, of course—Todd had a gun trained on them—but by the time I got here, Mannie had herded the younger boys into one of the open cells and kept them there, out of harm's way."

She closed her eyes, trying not to imagine the fear her beloved son must have endured crouching in a dank corner watching an armed fanatic threatening to shoot people. "I shudder to think what would have happened if you hadn't been there."

"It's over now."

"Why did you do it?" Letitia knew why, of course—to chase demons and slay dragons—but her mouth, it seemed, had a mind of its own. Every time she opened it, pure panic spilled out. "You could have been killed!"

"Someone had to be on the inside, doling information to the authorities."

"But it didn't have to be you. It could have been—" Her eyes darted frantically, settled on a bespectacled man in a tweed sport jacket. "Him!" she sputtered, wiggling her finger. "Why didn't he do it?"

Larkin sighed. "I think he's one of the staff accountants."

"Then someone else should have gone in there," she insisted stubbornly. "It didn't have to be you."

"Yes, it did."

"Why? Todd considers you an enemy. He might have killed you just for the hell of it—"

"But he didn't." Larkin pressed her hands against his chest, calming her. "Do you remember when I first told you about this place?"

She did, of course. It had been the night they'd made love, and she remembered every detail, every whispered word.

"We were talking about why I'd started the youth center and you made a comment about being surprised that I hadn't directed my efforts toward the real problem. You talked about the kids that had already been sucked into the system, and asked who was there for them. That question has haunted me, Letitia, because the answer is that no one, including me, has ever been there for them."

Letitia's heart seemed to sink into the pit of her soul at the thought that her own careless words had compelled Larkin to put himself at risk. "You should never listen to me. I don't know what I'm talking about."

"You're the wisest, most loving person I know," he said, curling a strand of her hand around his index finger. "Everything you said was right on track, but it was only part of my decision to go inside. The main reason was that when I learned Mannie was in danger, something inside me cracked. I love him, Letitia, as much as I love my own children . . . and almost as much as I love you. For a very long time, a part of me had been lost. You found it, Letitia, you and Mannie. I'm whole again. You're a part of that, too, and you always will be." He filled his lungs, then exhaled slowly. "Mannie and I have talked. He's forgiven me. Maybe someday, you will, too."

Letitia laid a fingertip against his lips, silencing him. "Someday is here, Dr. McKay. It has always been here."

Stroking her wrist, Larkin kissed her fingertip, then pressed his lips against the palm of her hand. He closed his eyes with a shuddering breath, and when he opened them again, they were shining with tears. "Then let's go see our boy."

True to her word, Ms. George had Mannie transferred from Blackthorn Hall to a temporary detention facility across from the county courthouse. The following morning, a hearing was held and as predicted, Mannie was remanded into his mother's custody.

Afterward, when Letitia had expressed concern about her son's trial, Ms. George had been confident that the case would never get that far. The ever efficient attorney had already scheduled a meeting with juvenile prosecutors, at which time she planned to request dismissal, although she'd warned them—Rose included—that they should be prepared to accept a reduction of charges and a couple years of probation. Mannie, who'd learned a valuable lesson about behavioral consequence, could return to a normal life, and his juvenile record would eventually be sealed.

Considering the alternatives, they'd unanimously agreed.

The trip home from the courthouse had been one of silent relief, with everyone mulling his or her own thoughts. In the back seat, Rose had a death grip on her grandson, who'd allowed her constant fussing without protest. Letitia, slumped in the front passenger seat, hadn't opened her eyes during the short trip home. To the casual observer, she'd appeared to be asleep, although Larkin suspected she'd been issuing a prayer of gratitude that her son had been safely returned to the loving arms of his family.

Having returned to Letitia's home thirty minutes ago, Larkin was now in the backyard repeatedly tossing a rubber ball for the tireless little Rasputin. In the house, Letitia and Mannie were having a serious parent-child conversation; Larkin had wandered outside to give them privacy. It was, after all, a family matter, and as much as he wished otherwise, Larkin wasn't a member of the family. Not yet anyway. Someday, perhaps.

The memory of Letitia's soft voice comforted him. *Someday is here,* she'd told him. Larkin prayed that was true—

A frantic yipping interrupted his thoughts when Rasputin deposited the slimy ball he'd just retrieved and ran frantic circles around his human playmate's feet.

"Look at that thing," Larkin said, wrinkling his nose. "You've drooled all over it. I hope you don't expect me to touch it now."

Rasputin wagged his tail.

"Forget it."

The dog picked up the ball and dropped it on Larkin's shoe.

"No. It's disgusting." When the whining Chihuahua pawed at his ankle, Larkin sighed and carefully retrieved the ball by pinching it between his thumb and the very tip of his index finger. "The least you could do is dry it off on the grass," he muttered as the excited animal charged across the yard in anticipation.

The back door opened. Letitia emerged with a dog biscuit. Rasputin skidded to a stop, eyes bulging, his pointy nose sniffing the air. "Want a bony-bone?" she cooed, holding the delectable treat just inside the kitchen door.

Quivering with indecision, the dog eyed the drippy ball, then the biscuit. The biscuit won. When Rasputin zipped into the kitchen, Letitia tossed the treat on the floor and shut the door.

Larkin tossed the ball aside and sat on the stoop, wiping his hands on his slacks. "That was a dirty trick," he told Letitia as she settled beside him. "The poor little guy's probably in there crying his buggy eyes out."

She smiled sweetly. "Shall I open the door?"

"God forbid."

"That's what I thought."

Larkin nervously flicked a pebble off the concrete step. There was so much he wanted to say, so much he was afraid to say. He cleared his throat, then chickened out at the last minute. "Where's Mannie?"

"On the phone with his school guidance counselor, who's dictating a list of make-up assignments." She smoothed her skirt and propped her elbows on her knees. "Mannie wants to talk to you later, if you have time."

"I have all the time in the world."

She angled a hesitant smile, then refocused on her skirt, absently scratching a tiny flaw in the material. After a moment, she sighed and dropped one hand into her lap. "This is awkward."

Larkin went rigid. "Do you want me to leave?"

"No! I mean, not unless you want to."

"I don't."

Seeming relieved by the assurance, she chewed her lower lip and shrugged. "By awkward, I meant that there are so many things I want to ask you, but I don't exactly know how."

Larkin took her hand. "Just ask, Letitia. Say what's on your mind."

She licked her lips, avoiding his gaze. "I'm confused about...well, about us. A week ago, you didn't want to see me anymore. Then you show up talking about intentions—" She inched toward him, frowning prettily. "Speaking of which, you never actually specified what those intentions were."

Larkin traced the lines of her palm with his fingertips. This was it. All he could do now was be honest and brace himself for rejection. "I intend to marry you, if you'll have me." From the corner of his eye, he saw her stiffen and rushed on before she had a chance to stop him. "I know that I'm not a prize, Letitia. I'd bring a lot of baggage into the relationship, old scars that I haven't had the courage to deal with. All I can promise is that I'll do whatever it takes to deal with them now, and to keep my problems from affecting our family."

"Our family," she murmured. "I like the sound of that."

A flicker of joy flared deep inside him he contained it. There was more he had to say, more Letitia had a right to know before she made the decision that would alter the course of her life—of both their lives. "It's going to be difficult. My children will always be a priority. They spend several weeks a year with me now and in the future, they may decide to live here full-time. They're good kids, but like everyone else in the world, they come with their own set of unique problems, problems that will naturally affect you and Rose and Mannie. I can't guarantee you'll all love each other. I can't even guarantee that you'll like each other—"

"Shh." Letitia caressed the corner of his mouth, silencing him. "The only guarantee I ask is that you love me, and commit yourself to our future together. As for your children, I already love them because they're a part of you. If there are problems, we'll work them out. I know that sounds naive, but I believe we can do it. I feel it in here." The hand that had been stroking his face moved down to cover her heart. "The question now is, are you ready to make that commitment?"

His response was instantaneous. "Yes."

She smiled. "In that case, Dr. McKay, I think we're going to need a bigger house."

The joy Larkin had been restraining burst into a jubilant flame. He gathered Letitia into his arms, holding her so tightly he could feel her heart pounding against his chest. For the past twenty years, he'd never allowed himself to feel love or be vulnerable to the pain he'd suffered as a child.

Now the cycle had been broken. Larkin's heart swelled with love for this special woman who'd shattered his protective shield and made him part of a family that needed and loved him, a family so precious that he'd offered his own life to protect it.

For Larkin McKay, the Blackthorn legacy was over.

Epilogue

A spray of autumn sunshine illuminated blue flecks buried in pits and cavities of the porous redbrick. Three shadows fell across the wall to blend with ghostly silhouettes of the past. Long-ago whispers floated on the wind, paying homage to the three who had returned, and to the fourth who'd never left.

Devon Monroe reached out to touch the hidden hint of blue, barely visible after repeated scouring and twenty years of weather. A few feet away, Roberto Arroya posed at the corner where he'd once crouched as the Brotherhood's sentry. Larkin McKay moved to position halfway between the administration building and the concealing shrubs where three terrified youngsters had once viewed a horror that forever altered the course of their lives.

Lost in silent reflection, each man relived that moment.

Larkin gazed down, studying the grass at his feet. His mind conjured the image of a white inhaler, partially obscured by shaggy green blades. The vision was utterly real, a mental recreation of what he'd seen that day, and what he'd felt. A chill slid down his spine; his stomach tightened; an icy block of fear spread through his belly. He'd cried that day. He nearly cried now.

The vision undulated into transparency, then faded away. There was nothing left but grass and memories.

At the building's corner observation post, Roberto suddenly stepped back, flattening against the wall as he'd done once before. Beneath his expensive clothing, the executive suit and imported leather shoes, beat the heart of a skinny kid garbed in an oversize detention shirt and poor-fitting pants.

"Someone's coming," Roberto hissed, unaware that his anxious whisper mirrored that of the past.

Devon stiffened, automatically turning toward the shrubs at the far side of the lawn. He pulled his hand away from the brick wall, away from the past, and stood erect, with the raised chin and defiant eyes of that brave young leader he'd been a lifetime ago.

A pinch-faced man hurried around the corner, peering over the rims of his wire glasses and clutching a clipboard of papers. He stopped to glance from Roberto to Devon. When his questioning gaze settled on Larkin, it lit with relief. "Chancellor!" Ducking his bald head, the man scurried across the grass like a nervous rodent. "I need your signature on the processing forms," he blurted, thrusting out the clipboard. "And Judge Monahan wants a meeting to discuss the new admission policies. I took the liberty of checking your calendar. You're free Thursday morning."

Larkin took the clipboard, scanning and signing each document. "Thursday is fine. Go ahead and set it up, then call Monahan to confirm."

"Very well." The man retrieved his signed forms. "Oh, and your wife called. She asked me to tell you that she'll be home late this evening—apparently she and Dr. Senagal will be working on a rush-rush grant application for the youth center. Also, she wished to remind you that your daughter's birthday present is on the kitchen table, wrapped and ready for shipment and that, eh,..." He paused to study his notes. "Mail-Express is open until six and it's bingo night...whatever that means."

Larkin laughed. "It means that I'm to mail the parcel and pick up pizza."

The little man's Adam's apple bobbed. "I see. Well then, Chancellor, if there's nothing further..."

"No, thank you, Jonathan. I'll be back in the office shortly."

With a curt nod, Jonathan spun on his heel and hurried back the way he'd come.

"So, how's the new assistant?" Devon asked when the man had disappeared around the corner.

"Intense," Larkin replied, removing his glasses and blowing the dust off the lenses. "But very thorough. I haven't missed a meeting since I hired him."

Devon slipped his hands in his pockets and rocked back on his heels. "Say, you've been here a couple of months now. I don't suppose you've ever, well, checked out the boiler room."

"As a matter of fact I have." Larkin's smile was indulgent, and a little sad. "The treasure box is gone."

Roberto absently brushed his tailored lapel. "Maybe it fell down behind the pipes."

"I looked."

Devon glanced away to conceal his disappointment. "Of course it's gone. Hell, it's been twenty years."

"Maybe another group of kids found it," Roberto suggested. "Kids who needed the treasure box as much as we did."

"In that case," Larkin added, "It's a good thing Tommy rescued the magazine."

The three men smiled at each other. No one disputed the coffee-stained girlie magazine's mysterious appearance at

Roberto's bachelor party, although they were naturally careful about discussing such matters aloud. Others wouldn't understand.

After a moment of silent reminiscence, Devon slapped Larkin's shoulder. "We're proud of you, man," he told Larkin. "Who'd have ever thought a dirty-faced runaway would grow up to be the guy who actually kicked Ogden Marlow's butt out of the chancellor's chair."

"It's pretty amazing," Roberto agreed.

Larkin replaced his glasses. "I didn't kick anybody's butt anywhere. Marlow retired, remember?"

"As a matter of fact, I do remember," Roberto murmured. "An unexpected event, if I'm not mistaken, occurring immediately after Devon's front-page exposé of last spring's riot."

"And," Devon added, "after Bobby's office began an investigation of civil rights violations by Blackthorn's previous administration."

Larkin chuckled. "Since Marlow's in his sixties, the Board assured me that his retirement had already been scheduled and had nothing to do with—and I'm quoting here—'public unpleasantries.'"

"Sheer coincidence, huh?" Issuing a derisive snort, Devon shook his head. "And you believed that?"

"Nope, not a word," Larkin replied cheerfully. "But I don't believe that the board members were aware of Marlow's creative disciplinary procedures, either."

The three men exchanged a knowing glance. The vault in Ogden Marlow's office didn't exist anymore. Larkin had it torn out the day he'd arrived. Never again would a child suffer the claustrophobic terror of the Box, as his young bones bent beyond endurance; no little mind would be warped by the horror of frigid isolation. It was gone forever.

The lockup was gone, too. After canceling Blackthorn's contract as a county holding facility, Larkin had ordered the perimeter fence ripped down. The gray building had been gutted for conversion into a recreation room and library. Educational and counseling facilities were a priority now, and young residents were carefully screened to ascertain emotional needs. Violent offenders were now segregated from kids who, through no fault of their own, had been abandoned either by their families or by society as a whole.

In the past, those children had been relegated to a bureaucratic black hole, viewed as nothing more than another lucrative line item on a government funding form. Under Larkin's leadership, every youngster was considered to be special and unique, and he'd surrounded himself with a staff that shared his ideals.

Much had been accomplished; more needed to be done, but Larkin's goals had been propelled by the question Letitia had posed nearly eight months ago: Who was there for the children?

The Brotherhood was there for them, there for them now and there to provide a legacy of hope for the future.

Tommy, they decided, would be pleased.

* * * * *

SILHOUETTE®

SINS OF THE PAST

by

RACHEL LEE

❧ ❧ ❧

If you enjoyed reading our enormously popular miniseries from Sensation™, *Under Blue Wyoming Skies*, you'll love this compelling, emotional full-length novel by award-winning author Rachel Lee.

Police detective Abel Pierce comes to Conard County, Wyoming, to settle a score. He wants to find the three men responsible for his father's death. But the first person he meets is a beautiful pregnant woman—the unmarried daughter of one of his enemies. And suddenly, there is a very fine line between love and hate...

Available: September 1996   *Price:* £4.99

▼™ SILHOUETTE

> SPECIAL EDITION ®

COMING NEXT MONTH

A BRIDE FOR LUKE Trisha Alexander

Three Brides and a Baby

Wedding bells were in the air—but best man Luke Taylor refused to believe they were tolling for him! Sassy Clementine Bennelli soon had Luke hungering for some wild, unwedded bliss. But was Clem the woman who'd make Luke say 'I do'?

RENEGADE LOVER Barbara Bretton

That Special Woman!

When Megan McLean left her Australian hunk of a husband, she vowed two things: never to have regrets and never to tell him about the child they'd made. Megan thought it'd be easy—but she couldn't have been more wrong. For now Jake Lockwood was back. And he wanted her.

A FAMILY OF HER OWN Ellen Tanner Marsh

A sweet little girl had been entrusted to Jussy Waring's care, and she was determined to shelter her from any more heartache. Jussy hadn't counted on Sam Baker, who'd come to take away her home—and stayed to steal her heart…

EXPECTING: BABY Jennifer Mikels

An urgent knock at the door introduced Rick Sloan to his neighbour, Mara Vincetti, who was about to give birth. Rick was trying to keep a low profile, but the next thing he knew he was a father figure for the new single mum and her baby!

THE FALL OF SHANE MACKADE Nora Roberts

The MacKade Brothers

To Rebecca Knight, everything was explainable. Until she started having some very irrational thoughts about sexy Shane MacKade. She didn't know much about men, but she knew one thing for sure: loving Shane was dangerous—and Rebecca didn't like to take chances…

A WILL AND A WEDDING Judith Yates

Commitment and marriage were two words Amy Riordan never believed would apply to her. But after meeting like-minded and disturbingly handsome Paul Hanley, she began to think otherwise. Was this fairy-tale fantasy simply too good to be true?

SILHOUETTE Desire

COMING NEXT MONTH

SADDLE UP Mary Lynn Baxter

Man of the Month

Rugged rancher Jeremiah Davis joined a bachelor auction to find a willing wife. He found unsuspecting Bridget Martin, and roped her into marriage, but would his new bride be the perfect mum for his little girl?

FATHER OF THE BRAT Elizabeth Bevarly

Carver Venner got a double shock when he opened his door: a twelve-year-old child that he never knew he had—clutching the hand of the sexiest woman he had ever seen. Carver would have loved to concentrate on Maddy Garrett, but there was another problem at hand…his daughter!

INSTANT MUMMY Annette Broadrick

Daughters of Texas

For years, Mollie O'Brien had secretly loved widowed rancher Deke Crandall from afar. Now, suddenly, the man was asking her to marry him! The position of instant mummy was strictly no strings attached, but Mollie found herself hoping it wouldn't stay that way…

FORGOTTEN VOWS Modean Moon

The Wedding Night

Jennifer's amnesia meant she couldn't remember the man she'd married only months ago, or the circumstances that had separated them on their wedding night. Edward Carlton claimed they were legally wed, and when he held her in his arms she knew she would never have left *willingly*…

ETHAN Diana Palmer

Texan Lovers

Arabella Craig had been eighteen when Ethan Hardeman had opened passion's door, then slammed it just as fiercely. His subsequent marriage to another woman had left her devastated. Now, tragedy brought Ethan back into her life, rekindling the passion…and the pain. But Arabella was determined not to let him escape her again…

A STRANGER IN TEXAS Lass Small

The handsome stranger was Zachary Thomas, and one lust-filled night with the compelling man had left Jessica Channing one very pregnant woman! But Jessica wanted nothing to do with a reluctant groom, so she vowed to keep her baby a secret…

▼™ SILHOUETTE

Intrigue™

Intuition draws you to him...
but instinct keeps you away.
Is he really one of those...

Don't miss even one of the twelve sexy but secretive
men, coming to you one a month—within the Intrigue™
series—in 1996.

Dangerous Men promises to keep you on the edge of
your seat...and on the edge of desire.

In September '96 look out for:

Outlawed! by **B. J. Daniels**

SILHOUETTE

Sensation®

COMING NEXT MONTH

A WANTED MAN Kathleen Creighton

The sexy stranger who'd turned up out of the blue was obviously running from something. Lucy Brown was certain he'd given her a false name, but finding him a temporary job wasn't too much of a risk. Giving him her heart would be a serious mistake!

UNDERCOVER MAN Merline Lovelace

Code Name: Danger

David Jensen seemed great husband material—a very suitable man. But Paige Lawrence didn't want suitable; she wanted adventure—and she didn't think she'd get it from David. But the man Paige thought she knew had a secret life. And as for adventure—well, Paige learned to be careful what she wished for...

FOREVER, DAD Maggie Shayne

Torch Palamaro had finally found the mysterious Alexandra Holt— his only chance for revenge against the man who'd destroyed his family. Alexandra knew she was only a means to an end for Torch. But when she caught the dark and dangerous secret agent looking at his only photograph of his young sons with tears in his stony blue eyes, she knew what *she* wanted...

THE LONER Linda Turner

Heartbreakers

Dillon Cassidy was keeping a low profile. Burned out, fed up and with a bullet lodged in his back, the ex-DEA agent was through with work—and with women. Because despite the charms of investigative reporter Sydney O'Keefe, he knew he was a time bomb. But was Sydney about to find out what he had to hide?

GET 4 BOOKS AND A MYSTERY GIFT

Return this coupon and we'll send you 4 Silhouette Special Edition® novels and a mystery gift absolutely FREE! We'll even pay the postage and packing for you.

We're making you this offer to introduce you to the benefits of Reader Service: FREE home delivery of brand-new Silhouette® romances, at least a month before they are available in the shops, FREE gifts and a monthly Newsletter packed with information.

Accepting these FREE books and gift places you under no obligation to buy, you may cancel at any time, even after receiving just your free shipment. Simply complete the coupon below and send it to:
SILHOUETTE READER SERVICE, FREEPOST, CROYDON, CR9 3WZ.

No stamp needed

Yes, please send me 4 free Silhouette Special Edition novels and a mystery gift. I understand that unless you hear from me, I will receive 6 superb new titles every month for just £2.30* each postage and packing free. I am under no obligation to purchase any books and I may cancel or suspend my subscription at any time, but the free books and gifts will be mine to keep in any case. (I am over 18 years of age)

2EP6SE

Ms/Mrs/Miss/Mr _____

Address _____

_____

_____ Postcode _____

SILHOUETTE

Intrigue™

COMING NEXT MONTH

NOWHERE TO HIDE Jasmine Cresswell

When Alyssa woke up in hospital, she learned she'd been in a
plane crash and had total amnesia. She was engaged to a
charismatic politician…yet felt chilled by his touch. Only the
presence of Adam Stryker, her financial adviser, was oddly
reassuring. He warned her to be careful—but did anyone really
mean her any harm?

OUTLAWED! B.J. Daniels

Dangerous Men

Cooper McLeod arrived just when Delaney Lawson needed
help, right on the heels of a mysterious set of 'problems'. His
rock-hard body was enough to make her go weak at the knees,
and sin itself danced in this cowboy's indigo eyes. He was
looking to charm her—out of her senses *and* out of her ranch!

UNFORGETTABLE Molly Rice

Stacy Millman's search was supposed to lead to her family's
secrets—not to a romantic fantasy! But there was no avoiding
the rugged and seductive Derek Chancelor. His easy charm
quickly captured her big-city heart…but how would the sexy
sheriff react when he learned the *real* reason she'd come to
town?

BREAK THE NIGHT Anne Stuart

J.R. Damien was a prize-winning reporter with an obsession—
catching the murderer who stalked the streets of Los Angeles.
The police were getting nowhere, and if publishing the identity
of the link between the victims would help, then Damien
would do it. But Lizzie Stride felt that Damien had just pointed
her out as a likely target and left her vulnerable. After all, was
he going to be there to save her?